Hidden Destiny

A Redwood Pack Novel 6

By
CARRIE ANN RYAN

Hidden Destiny

North Jamenson has always held his wolf closer to the surface then others. He's the quiet one, the one no one really knows about yet he holds the darkest secret. He's watched his brothers find their mates and start families, and now it was his turn. He knows Lexi could be his and her son could be part of his family, but he doesn't know if he's ready to share the darkness that's entwined with his soul.

Lexi Anderson is a mother, a sister, a latent wolf, and a new member of the Redwood Pack. She's also holding secrets so close to her heart she's not even sure she knows the truth anymore. When North takes another step closer to wanting to cement their bond, Lexi must come to grips with her past and what it means for her future. The Centrals' war isn't over yet and Lexi's life is on the line as the paths they've chosen takes a drastic turn.

Dedication

To Michelle. Thank you for finding North.

Acknowledgements

As the Redwood Pack grows, as does the family that makes each book happen. Thank you Marie Harte for helping me plot a way to make North and Lexi's story grow within the world I love so much. Thank you Lia for holding my hand when I couldn't finish this book and not yelling at me when I told you what *needed* to happen. Thank you so much Michelle for coming with me on this journey and totally helping out. You and I aren't done yet, lady. Thank you Devin and Saya for taking North and Lexi into your hands and helping me figure out what the hell they needed!

Thank you so much readers for being with me each step of the way. I can't believe North's story is in your hands.

Redwood Pack Characters

With an ever growing list of characters in each book, I know that it might seem like there are too many to remember. Well don't worry; here is a list so you don't forget. Not all are seen in this exact book, but here are the ones you've met so far. As the series progresses, the list will as well.

Happy reading!

Adam Jamenson—Enforcer of the Redwood Pack, third son of the Alpha. Mate to Bay and father to Micah. Story told in *Enforcer's Redemption* and *Forgiveness*.

Anna Jamenson—late mate of Adam.

Bay Jamenson—new member of the Redwood Pack. Mate to Adam and mother to Micah. Story told in *Enforcer's Redemption* and *Forgiveness*.

Beth—member of the Redwood Pack. Aunt to Emily.

Brie Jamenson—daughter of Jasper and Willow.

Cailin Jamenson—Only daughter of Edward and Pat.

Camille—deceased former member of the Redwood Pack.

Caym—demon from Hell summoned by the Centrals. Lover of Corbin.

Charlotte Jamenson—half-sister of Ellie's. Will be raised as a daughter by Ellie and Maddox.

Conner Jamenson—son of Josh, Reed and Hannah. Twin to Kaylee.

Corbin Reyes—new Alpha of the Central Pack. Lover of Caym.

Cyrus Ferns—deceased former unit teammate of Josh's.

Donald—member of the Redwood Pack.

Edward Jamenson—Alpha of the Redwood Pack. Mate to Pat. Father to Kade, Jasper, Adam, Reed, Maddox, North and Cailin.

Ellie Jamenson—Daughter of the former Alpha of the Central Pack. Mate to Maddox and mother to Charlotte. Story told in *Shattered Emotions*.

Emily—young member of the Redwood Pack. Orphan and niece of Beth.

Emeline—elder of the Redwood Pack. Lost her mate in the first war with the Centrals.

Finn Jamenson—son of Kade and Melanie. Future Heir and Alpha of the Redwood Pack.

Franklin—deceased former member of the Redwood Pack. Camille's lover.

Gina Jamenson—newly adopted daughter of Kade and Melanie. Her birth parents, Larissa and Neil were killed during an attack.

Hannah—Healer of the Redwood Pack. Mate to Josh and Reed. Mother of Conner and Kaylee. Story told in *Trinity Bound* and *Blurred Expectations.*

Hector Reyes—deceased former Alpha of the Central Pack. Father to Corbin, Ellie, Charlotte and Ellie's twin.

Henry—Redwood Pack member and store owner for 60 years.

Isaac—deceased member of the Central Pack.

Jason—member of the Redwood Pack and one of the Alpha's enforcers.

Jasper—Beta of the Redwood Pack. Mate to Willow and father of Brie. Story told in *A Taste for a Mate.*

Jim—hot dog vendor and one of Josh's former friends.

Joseph Brentwood—deceased former Alpha of the Talon Pack.

Josh Jamenson—former human Navy Seal. A Finder and partial demon. Mated to Reed and Hannah. Father to Conner and Kaylee. Story told in *Trinity Bound* and *Blurred Expectations.*

Kade Jamenson—Heir and future Alpha of the Redwood Pack. Mate to Melanie. Father to Finn, Gina, and Mark. Story told in *An Alpha's Path* and *A Night Away*.

Kaylee Jamenson—daughter of Josh, Reed and Hannah. Twin to Conner.

Larissa—deceased member of the Redwood Pack. Witch and friend to Melanie. Mate to Neil and mother of Gina and Mark.

Lexi Anderson—former Talon Pack member and new Redwood Pack member. Mother to Parker and sister to Logan.

Logan Anderson—former Talon Pack member and new Redwood Pack member. Uncle to Parker and brother to Lexi.

Maddox Jamenson—Omega of the Redwood Pack. Mate to Ellie and father to Charlotte. Story told in *Shattered Emotions*.

Mark Jamenson—newly adopted son of Kade and Melanie. Her birth parents, Larissa and Neil were killed during an attack.

Melanie Jamenson—former human chemist and mate to Kade. Mother to Finn, Gina and Mark. Story told in *An Alpha's Path* and *A Night Away*.

Meryl—Redwood Pack Elder.

Micah Jamenson—son of Adam and Bay.

Mrs. Carnoski—elderly customer of Josh's when he was human.

Neil—deceased member of the Redwood Pack. Mate to Larissa and father of Gina and Mark.

Noah—member of the Redwood Pack and former lover of Cailin's.

North Jamenson—doctor in the Redwood Pack, son of the Alpha.

Parker Anderson—new member of the Redwood Pack and son of Lexi's.

Patricia (Pat) Jamenson—mate of the Alpha, Alpha female, and mother to Kade, Jasper, Adam, Reed, Maddox, North, and Cailin.

Patrick—disgruntled member of The Redwood Pack.

Reed Jamenson—artist and son of the Alpha of the Redwood Pack. Mate to Josh and Hannah. Story told in *Trinity Bound* and *Blurred Expectations*.

Reggie—deceased former member of the Central Pack.

Samuel—deceased former member of the Central Pack.

Willow Jamenson—former human baker and now mate to Jasper. Mother to Brie. Story told in *A Taste for a Mate*.

PROLOGUE

"You're going to get her back for me, right?" Caym closed his eyes at Corbin's repeated question. The pain behind his temples increased with each word, as if even his brain couldn't stand the man beside him anymore. With a flick of his wrist, he could kill the little wolf and be done with this game, but alas, it wasn't time.

Yet.

Corbin had only one thing on his mind...her. It seemed as if she was the only thing the bastard wolf talked about anymore.

No, not said, *demanded*, as if Corbin was the one really in control and pulling all the strings.

How little the big bad wolf knew.

Caym turned over on his side, the silky black sheet sliding down his hip to expose just enough to get what he wanted from the Alpha of the Central Pack. Corbin's eyes traced his body, yet Caym suppressed a dry quirk of his lips.

It never failed to amuse him that with just a little skin and light-to-heavy petting he could have this wolf eating out of the palm of his hand.

1

Well, maybe not amuse. Caym didn't feel amusement or any other form of real emotion. He might portray anger and other heightened feelings if the situation called for it and if it would help him in his conquest, but it was never real.

As a demon, he didn't *need* to feel anything. He could if he wanted to, but most days, he couldn't care less. The blood running through his veins had enough anger and betrayal flowing through it, he didn't need to add anything else to it.

If he wanted to feel emotions, though, at the moment, all he'd do was yawn with boredom.

First Corbin had wanted Caym to find Ellie, the wolf's sister, and bring her back.

Now the damn so-called Alpha wanted Caym to find this long-lost woman of his. How Corbin was consistently losing women boggled Caym's mind, but it wasn't his place to say anything about it.

Well, at least not yet.

Caym ran a hand down Corbin's naked chest and lifted a brow. "If you're awake enough to worry about a woman, then I must not have done my job." His hand slid lower, and Corbin groaned.

Sex meant nothing to Caym. He'd rather have the blood in the Alpha's veins or the heart beating in his chest. Fucking the wolf, though, let him have more control without having to show that he was the one actually in charge.

As long as Corbin took the blame for their actions against the Redwoods, Caym could sit back and wait for his chance to take it all.

The Redwoods and, of course, Corbin wouldn't know what hit them.

Corbin pulled away, but the heat didn't leave his eyes. "I want her, Caym. She left me, and I'll be damned if I let her get away with it."

That, at least, Caym could understand. He'd have killed the woman, but Corbin was a little sentimental with his...toys.

Caym thought back to the time when he'd let Corbin's previous toy, Ellie, leave the dungeon in the arms of her mate, Maddox. Caym had been weakened from using a large amount of power in a short period of time in order to save Corbin.

It hadn't been time for Corbin to die; Caym still needed him for his plans. As a result, he'd let the Omega of the Redwood Pack and his mate live.

That might have been a mistake, but Caym didn't feel Maddox would prove to be part of his plan as much as his twin, North, would.

Oh, yes, North, the doctor of the Pack was fated to be part of Caym's plans. He just needed to make sure certain key elements were put in place first. He already had a mole on the inside. Yes, his plans would work out perfectly.

He would accept nothing less.

"She's protected. We will find a way to get her though. We'll just have to be creative."

Yes, and when North found out exactly *what* those plans where, the next part of his destiny would be put in place.

After all, it was fated that North would kill Corbin.

That didn't mean, though, that Caym couldn't give the wolf a nudge.

CHAPTER ONE

H er wolf wanted to eat him up—one tasty
morsel at a time.

Lexi Anderson sighed.

No, that wouldn't be happening.

It didn't matter that she wanted to lick the man at
the party with many generous swipes of her tongue
because it just wouldn't happen.

It didn't matter that she wanted to bury her hands
in his hair while he pumped himself into her, their
sweat-slicked bodies sliding against one another as
they came together hard.

It still wouldn't be happening.

She took a deep breath, the outside air filling her
lungs and cooling her down—at least somewhat. As
she tried to relax, she took in her surroundings,
needing something far greater than her to function.
The trees stood around them, tall, ancient, almost
comforting. The sun warmed her skin in the cooling
air, though just from looking at the man across from
her, she was heated plenty already.

She took another breath, holding it in for as long as she could. The scent of forest and the coming rain would never be enough for her.

Lexi would never know the feeling of the land beneath her four paws, the brush of wind in her fur, nor the release of home and center when the moon's pull finally took her wolf.

No, she would never have any of that, yet she should have been used to it by now.

She'd been a latent wolf—a wolf trapped within her body, unable to shift, but still part of her in a sense—for all fifty years of her life, and wishing for something different was only making things harder for her. Since latent wolves couldn't shift into their wolf forms, they were forever bound to their human forms and cut off from the wolf part of their souls. They couldn't even hear their other half's thoughts. Oh, they could feel *something*, or at least feel the instincts and some of the urges that came with being a wolf, but they didn't feel the same connection that others did.

It had been a miracle in itself that she'd survived into adulthood, as most latent wolves died from the added stress to their bodies because of their inability to shift.

She was one of the lucky ones.

If one could call it that.

There were more important things in her world than the fact she would never be able to shift into a wolf.

Namely, the little boy playing in the front yard of the Alpha's home.

Parker, her eight-year-old son and love of her life, currently played in a pile of wolf babies. Well, only one baby was currently in wolf form, as the others were too young to change yet, but her Parker seemed to be in heaven.

Finn, the son of the Heir to the Redwood Pack, jumped on Parker's stomach. Luckily the three-year-old had learned enough control in wolf form that he didn't have his claws out. Wolf children didn't shift until they were at least two or three years old when they would have at least a semblance of control over their little bodies.

Even though Lexi had grown up in the Talon Pack and knew that children play-fought in both forms, she still winced. It had been awhile since she'd been around other wolves for long periods of time, and she didn't like the idea of her baby being hurt by Finn's little claws.

It was, after all, only the third time the other little boy had shifted into this form. He had remarkable control though, considering his age. Lexi wasn't sure if that had to do with the royal blood running through his veins, the fact that he would one day be the Heir and then eventually the Alpha, or that he was wise for his age. He'd already been through so much, almost being killed by the hands of their worst enemy. He'd been changed dramatically, even at a young age.

All of that together seemed to have made one strong little wolf.

The little fluff ball mock growled at Parker then rolled onto his back, leaving all four paws in the air. His cousins, Micah and Brie, who were both under two, gave up trying to tickle Parker and went to give Finn a belly rub.

Something oddly hollow echoed in Lexi's chest at the sight.

These babies were part of a family. A family that, while they had opened their home to her, Parker, and her brother, Logan, wasn't hers.

They would never be hers.

Not really.

She thought she had a family before with the Talons, and then that had been shattered. The Alpha had exiled her, cutting her off from the Pack because of something out of her control. Logan came with her because he was her brother. God, she hated that she'd caused him to be a lone wolf, shunned because of what had happened to her.

They spent over eight years on the run until finally coming into contact with the Redwoods. For some reason, they had opened their wards and let them into their Pack—blood bond and all.

She knew not everyone within the Pack was happy about it, but the Jamensons, the ruling family, wanted them.

Lexi still wasn't sure how she felt about that.

A man, Patrick, yes, that was his name, walked past her and glared. Not so odd considering most wolves who didn't really know her seemed to do that, but she didn't know this man or what his problem was.

She raised a brow, and he looked down on her as though she were five-day-old dog poo.

Great.

He walked away, and she looked off in the distance. It seemed making friends with people other than the Jamensons was going to be a lost cause. In Patrick's case, it didn't seem as though she was missing anything.

"Still on the outside looking in?" Cailin Jamenson, the Alpha's only daughter, asked as she walked up to Lexi's side.

Lexi gave the gorgeous woman a weak smile, feeling positively frumpy and old in her tattered jeans and shirt. It wasn't as if Lexi had a closet full of clothes after being on the run for so long. In fact, most of what she was wearing and possessed was borrowed.

Damn, she'd have to change that soon. It didn't sit well with her that she didn't have much to her name. She left most of her belongings when she left the Talons and hadn't been able to add to her wardrobe and personal things over time. That whole experience left Lexi feeling less than attractive.

Cailin, however, looked like God's gift to man with her long blue-black hair flowing down her back and her piercing green eyes that seemed to see more than Lexi wanted. The woman would make fashion models feel inferior with her sharp cheekbones, curves like a goddess, painted-on jeans, and a tight tank that only emphasized the woman's way-too-perky breasts.

Lexi had a decent body because of the healthy metabolism and genetics of being a wolf, but there must have been something special in the water the day Cailin Jamenson was conceived.

Logan didn't stand a chance.

Lexi snorted at that thought, and Cailin raised her brow. It was plain to see that Logan and Cailin were potential mates. Because fate was a fickle bitch, each wolf had many—or sometimes not so many—potential mates that they could meet throughout their long lifetimes. Just because the mating urge rode hard and a connection could click into place at any moment didn't mean that the two parties had to act on it.

From where Lexi stood, it seemed the lone Jamenson daughter wanted to be as far from Logan as possible.

There had to be a story there, but considering Lexi had even more secrets of her own, she wasn't about to start prying.

Much.

"Lexi?"

She blinked as Cailin moved closer, her eyebrows lowered.

"Sorry. I'm just thinking." Well, it was the truth, though Lexi wasn't about to tell Cailin what she was actually thinking about.

"Do I want to know what about?" Cailin asked, tucking a strand of hair behind her ear.

It was May and summer was already starting its angry burn across the rest of the country, but in the Northwest, it was still a bit cool with the cloud cover. Plus, the Pack's den was situated between two cliff faces and surrounded by tall trees. Though not actually Redwoods, they were close. It was a running joke—like a thousand years running—that the Pack was named after trees that didn't actually exist in their chosen area.

Lexi didn't quite get it, but it wasn't a big deal. She was just happy this Pack seemed to have opened their arms to her and her family.

At least the Jamensons had.

The rest of the Pack...yeah, not so much. An image of Patrick filled her mind, and she blinked it away.

That was a thought for another time. Right now, she had a little boy's birthday to celebrate, a certain wolf to avoid, and a pretense to show another wolf that everything was okay while she herself avoided that certain wolf.

It was confusing enough that Lexi didn't need to add another set of worries to her already full plate.

"Lexi, hon? What the heck is going on in that head of yours?" Cailin moved to block Lexi's view of the tangle of children and stared right at her face.

Lexi might have been a couple inches taller than the other woman, but Cailin had a presence that couldn't be ignored. She only had to ask her brother.

She shook her head then smiled. At least she thought she smiled. It might as well have been a grimace considering the way Cailin's eyebrow rose.

Again.

"I'm fine. Really. I think I'm just tired. That's all."

"Not sleeping?" Cailin asked.

"Not really." That wasn't a change though. Lexi rarely slept through the night. She never really had considering she was latent. Her body was a little more wired than most because she couldn't expel energy the way the other wolves could. Not to mention the whole on-the-run thing didn't exactly soothe one's nerves.

"Do you need to talk to Hannah about getting something to help you sleep?" Hannah was the Pack Healer, the one person connected to the Pack through bonds that enabled her to use the overall energy and her own powers to Heal others. "If you don't want to go to her, I can probably help. I used to grow the Pack herbs until Hannah took over."

Wolves' metabolisms were such that they couldn't take the usual human drugs or even get drunk on alcohol. It was great for the wolves, considering their genetics helped with maintaining their bodies for centuries and sometimes even longer, but sucked for things like the common cold. Wolves didn't actually die of old age like humans did. Those that reached a certain age became elders and usually shut themselves off from the world because of all their memories. Cailin had once grown the herbs and harvested other plants used as natural remedies to help the wolves. Now that Hannah had come into the Pack when she'd mated Cailin's brother, Reed—as well as another man named Josh—and become the Healer, Cailin had been out of a job.

From the tone Cailin used just then, Lexi had a feeling the woman didn't quite know what to do with herself now. Sure, Cailin babysat her numerous nieces and nephews—increasing in number daily it seemed—but the young woman didn't really seem to have a place in the Pack beyond the blood in her veins.

Cailin was only in her early twenties though and over eighty years younger than her brothers, who were all within a year or two in age.

No wonder the woman looked lost.

Oh great. Now Lexi was worrying about another's problems rather than her own. It made her forget the lingering doubts, fears, worries, and scariness in her own life at least a little while.

"I'm fine, Cailin, really," Lexi finally answered. "I don't need to take anything to sleep. Logan and I take turns freaking out around the house when we have long nights and can't sleep."

Cailin stiffened at the mention of Logan's name, and Lexi inwardly cursed. Great going. It wasn't as if Lexi didn't know the other woman was pointedly avoiding Logan.

An unwritten rule existed between the two of them.

Lexi didn't mention her brother.

Cailin didn't mention hers.

Ever.

Damn it.

"Thank you for offering though," Lexi added lamely. "It's nice that your family is still holding a birthday party, despite all that's going on."

Oh, holy hell. Her attempt at changing the subject had failed. This topic was just as bad as the original subject. Mentioning everything that was "going on"—war, death, and torture—wasn't the best way to cool the tension rising between the two women. No, it was the exact opposite of what she'd hoped to do.

Though, really, there didn't seem to be a safe topic. It wasn't as if Lexi knew the Jamensons that well since she'd just become a Redwood, and with the war with the Centrals—the main focal point and reason *why* Lexi, Logan, and Parker were there in the first place—there wasn't much else to talk about.

Honestly though...

Cailin grinned, despite the mood. "We're family. Finn's the first grandbaby, the first of them to shift. It's a big deal. Plus, he'll be Alpha one day."

"So he gets special treatment?"

Cailin shook her head. "Oh no. Not at all. Each of those babies, and the ones to come, will get parties, love, and everything else they need. If we didn't do that, then what the hell are we fighting for?"

"I guess that makes sense." It did. Though since she'd been shunned from her own Pack because of the actions of others, she still didn't quite believe it. Oh, she desperately wanted to, but she couldn't.

Not anymore.

"It damn well should," Cailin grumbled. "My Pack is in pain because of those assholes, and I'll be fucking pissed if we win and lose ourselves. We're Pack and family first, warriors second. That's what we need to be in order to stay who we are. I was wrong once when I asked my dad if we could go dark to win. Fucking wrong. I'm not going to do that again. We're going to beat those fucking bastards, and we're going to do it all the while blowing out candles on birthday cakes and making babies."

Lexi blinked at Cailin's impassioned speech.

Well then.

A blush crept over Cailin's cheeks, and she ducked her head. The look suited her and made her look her age, rather than the image of the sex goddess she usually presented without trying.

"Sorry. I get a little worked up thinking about all the shit my family has been through."

"And the fact that you haven't been able to help," Lexi whispered, knowing they had begun to attract the attention of the others. A few Jamensons glanced their way, but it was mostly the others not of the family that looked out of the corner of their eye or blatantly stared at them. Those had their normal sneer on their faces whenever they were near.

Lucky her.

Cailin's head shot up, and she blinked. "I *hate* it." She looked over her shoulder at her family, who had no doubt quieted to hear her words. Werewolves, after all, had exceptional hearing. "We can talk about it later."

Lexi nodded then watched the young woman, who looked so sure of herself but clearly wasn't, walk toward the pile of pups and start to play.

"I'm glad she talks to you when she won't talk to anyone else," a voice said from behind her, and she froze.

Hell, he was freaking quiet when he wanted to be.

North slid to her side but didn't look at her. Not that she was looking at him—oh no, she couldn't do that and breathe nowadays—but she could see him out of the corner of her eye.

Lexi swallowed hard and tried to regain the cool, collected composure she used when she had no earthly idea what else to do.

"She doesn't talk to the rest of you?" She found that hard to believe, considering Cailin had wonderful parents, six big brothers, a brother-in-law, and five sisters-in-law.

North shrugged. She felt the touch of his overheated skin against her arm, and she held back a shiver.

She would *not* show the man how he affected her. Ever.

"She's so much younger than the rest of us. Yes, she's the same age as a few of my brothers' mates, but it's different. They're family now but still new. Cailin's never felt comfortable about showing who she is to outsiders, and it's even worse really within the family. She's great with that façade of hers—the bitchy, twenty-something power attitude—but she doesn't break down with us. Not since she was a little girl."

Lexi's heart ached for Cailin and even more so for the man she felt a connection to, despite all the reasons she shouldn't. It wasn't as though Cailin was any different than the rest of them, but she was so much younger than her brothers, and there were things the woman might not even *want* to share.

"I'll do what I can. I like her." Lexi had no idea why she'd said that first part. She couldn't even take care of her own crap, let alone another person's. Okay, she could take care of Parker and Logan, but they were...hers.

North moved so he blocked her view of the pups again, and she sucked in a breath.

Gods, he was beautiful. Tanned skin created by genetics and touched by the sun covered a hard body that she'd seen naked only because of his shifts, not for anything more. And damn, she wanted to have that be for something more. He had those Jamenson jade-green eyes, framed by light lashes, that Lexi knew she could fall into if she didn't watch herself. Unlike most of his brothers, he and his twin Maddox had inherited their mother's hair, a dark blond, unruly mass that looked damn good on him.

She *really* needed to stop looking at him that way.

"Thank you for taking care of my sister," he whispered, tucking a lock of hair behind her ear.

She didn't dare breathe. She knew once she caught a whiff of that spicy scent, latent or not, her wolf—or what she thought of as her wolf—would want to hunt.

That wouldn't be happening.

Ever.

His fingers lingered on her cheek, and her body shuddered.

Traitor.

She pulled back, the loss of his touch like a deep abyss she knew she'd never be able to cross.

"I need to go."

She didn't even bother to lie. Not this time. She turned tail and ran back to her home. No, not her home, the place where her family slept.

Her name carried across the wind as North called her back, but she ignored it.

Ignored him.

She kicked the door closed, then turned, bracing her back against it. Her legs gave out, and she slid to the floor, the sobs wracking through her body as memories flooded and attacked her.

The darkness of his eyes tearing into her.

The feel of those callous fingers digging into her when she screamed.

She shut her eyes against the nightmares and banged her fists against her temples.

"Get out! Stop!" she screamed into the empty room, tears rolling down her cheeks.

She had to get it under control. The others couldn't know what had happened, or her baby boy's life would be forfeit.

It was a dangerous game living with the Redwoods as it was. It would be even more dangerous to get close to the one man who could break her.

Even though her body told her, just as his was no doubt doing to him, that they could be mates, she knew that would never happen.

The wolf in her dreams begged for the man—at least that was what she thought since she couldn't actually hear her wolf—she could feel the man's touch on her cheek and knew it was useless to dream.

To hope.

There would be no future with North Jamenson.

She was already mated.

CHAPTER TWO

"You seem to be doing okay with the prosthesis," North Jamenson said, his words on one thing, his mind on another.

His brother, Adam, sat on the exam table, his one leg touching the floor, his other leg—amputated at the knee—resting while North finished up the examination. Adam shrugged, tension still clearly riding him, though North knew the leg was completely healed.

"I don't really feel like it's on anymore, you know? It's just...there."

North gripped Adam's shoulder and squeezed. Adam had come a long way since the demon Caym had taken his leg in battle, but North knew his brother still had days where he missed his leg. It was only natural. Thankfully, Adam had his mate, Bay, and baby boy, Micah, to make things better.

Seriously, Adam had come a long way.

"You're good to go then," North said as he stepped back so Adam could put his prosthesis back on. In the past, North might have stepped in to help, but his older brother knew what he was doing by now and put it on with a practised ease.

Adam walked out of the clinic, leaving North to his thoughts, which frankly, he didn't need. He didn't want to think about the fear and shame that had hit him like a train when Lexi ran away from him. He didn't want to see the sorrow in her gaze when she looked at him with those wide hazel eyes.

He didn't want to picture the look of confusion on Parker's face when he watched his mom run away. Or the way the little boy had shied away from him when Lexi ran—as if Parker knew it was North's fault his mom had fled.

North sucked in a breath at a sharp, lancing pain arching across his palm and cursed. He'd clenched his fist and forgotten he'd been holding a fountain pen. Out of control, and with his werewolf strength, he'd smashed the damn thing and had even stabbed himself with the pointed edge.

Great.

Just fucking great.

He threw the pen in the trash and washed his hands. Sure, wolves couldn't get normal diseases like humans, but getting ink in a wound didn't seem like the best idea.

He didn't bother bandaging it because it was healing on its own, and in within the next twenty minutes, he'd be good as new again.

Fuck. He couldn't believe he'd lost control like that.

Again.

North was considered the calm one, the brother who was there to help the others but never on the front lines, never making waves. And he was good at it.

He *had* to be that person.

If he wasn't, the others might find out exactly what he was.

He'd hidden it from them for so long he knew he had to keep it buried.

If his family found out exactly what he was and what he could do, they'd... Well, he didn't know what they'd do.

He didn't want to know.

He put away the equipment he'd been using on Adam, then cleaned up his exam room. His clinic was three rooms—an exam room, an operating room, and his office—attached to his home. It used to be that he spent more time in his clinic than his home. However, since Hannah, one of his brother Reed's mates, had joined the Pack, he'd been relegated to glorified nurse.

Hannah was the Healer, the one who Healed the Pack and took care of their physical hurts. His twin Maddox, the Omega, took care of the Pack's emotional needs.

North, on the other hand, was on standby with a cold compress and bandage.

He let out a sigh.

Okay, it wasn't that bad. He still had to deal with things that Hannah couldn't deal with because of her energy levels. She relied on the Pack's bonds to Heal her patients. Sometimes, especially when she'd been pregnant, it was better for North to administer first aid or preform a procedure after Hannah had done all she could.

It still made him inferior.

He'd been a doctor for decades, learning new techniques and brushing up on modern medicine under false aliases within the human schools.

Now he figured he might need something else to focus on.

He'd *thought* that would be Lexi and Parker, but considering the woman refused to be alone with North for any extended period of time, North wasn't sure anymore.

He *knew* he and Lexi were potential mates. His wolf knew it and rode him hard to complete the mating, or at least initiate the mating dance.

All wolves had certain people out in the world they could mate with over time. Fate had decreed it, and usually, the human halves involved jumped in headfirst. To find one's mate was an amazing experience—or so North had heard.

North also knew that Lexi had been mated before. After all, she had Parker. Wolves couldn't have children without the mating bond in place. There was no doubt, considering the little boy looked just like his Uncle Logan with a little Lexi thrown in, that he was a product of Lexi and her late mate.

And that's how it had to be according to fate and what he'd known for so long. Lexi's previous mate must have died. Once a wolf completed the mating bond, no matter how many other potential mates a wolf met in the future, neither party would feel that new pull. It would be a cruel twist of fate to allow a wolf to bond their mate only to find out they had another half elsewhere.

There was no way fate was that sadistic.

He figured she'd lost her mate when she'd been kicked out of the Talons.

North growled and fisted his hands again at that thought. That fucking Pack was next on his list after the Centrals. Those bastards had hurt his mate and would have to pay. Though it hurt to think that Lexi had loved someone before him and had completed that mating, he'd take her as she was.

Not that there was anything wrong with her.

Far from it.

He loved her strength, the way she protected her family though she was much smaller than her brother. He loved those fierce eyes, that athletic body, and that silky blonde hair of hers.

He knew it was silky because he'd felt it when he'd tucked it behind her ear.

And the day he'd almost died.

That, though, wasn't something he wanted to dwell on at the moment.

If ever.

Someone made a rustling sound at the door, and he turned to find Patrick there—a lower-ranked wolf who pissed him off to no end. The wolf thought he was more badass than he was and had once tried to kill Ellie's mate because of circumstantial evidence.

The idiot was lucky North didn't tear his throat out right there.

"What can I do for you, Patrick?"

The other man lifted his chin. "Need to restock my first aid kit," he grunted.

North could almost taste the lie but showed the other man where he could get the things anyway. As the only doctor in the Pack, he routinely helped stock those things since wolves were always getting in scrapes. Though if North didn't know any better, it was almost as if the other man was casing the joint or just trying to get in his space.

Okay, North admitted he might be getting a little paranoid.

"Is that all?" North asked as he packed up Patrick's things.

"Yep. Thanks. Good to know you take care of all of us, not just your family."

North growled but held his wolf in check.

"You're done. Get the fuck out."

"Gladly."

Patrick stomped out, and North was left there confused. Okay, so the bastard was either going crazy, or North's family would have to deal with a wolf on the edge at some point. There was something else going on with Patrick, something North might not have seen today, but North couldn't shake the uneasy feeling. He'd have to talk to his father about it soon.

He ran his hand over his face and hoped there wouldn't be any more surprises for the night.

North scented the pup before he heard him and smiled.

He loved that little-boy smell—the bare hint of wolf and forest mixed with spice.

The acidic smell of fear and pain that slid under that little-boy smell caused North's hackles to rise. He turned toward Parker, who stood in the doorway, tear tracks running down his cheeks, but his lips were in a firm line as if the boy didn't want others to know how much pain he was in.

There was no hiding that pain to a fellow wolf, but North wouldn't clue Parker in on that fact.

At least not until he set Parker's bone.

"Parker," North rasped, holding back the growl that threatened to come. He didn't want to scare him anymore than he already was.

Parker held his arm to his chest at an odd angle, and North cursed under his breath.

"I'm fine," Parker bit out. "Really."

North shook his head then walked toward the boy slowly so as not to startle him. The two of them still weren't sure of how to act around each other. Parker was very observant, so North had a feeling the kid knew something was going on between him and Lexi.

"Let me see your arm, buddy."

Parker blinked but didn't move. "I...I didn't want to go to Hannah and make her deal with it. You know? She has Conner and Kaylee and is really busy. I figured you could just help me out a bit."

North grinned despite himself. The boy really was mature for his age if he'd noticed how tired Hannah had been lately. It didn't matter that she had two dominant mates at home to help her; taking care of twins at any age was tough. He should know considering he was a twin himself.

North thought back to all the crap he and Maddox had put his mother through.

He'd have to get his mother a present later.

He didn't even know how the little boy had been hurt. For all he knew it he'd fallen out of a tree but it didn't stop his wolf from wanting to react. Though his wolf was clawing at him, wanting to taste flesh and blood because Parker was hurt, North held himself in check.

Barely.

The wolf already thought of Parker as his own. It didn't matter that he didn't have the same blood running through his veins. Parker was family.

North felt the same, but he wasn't about to tell Parker and Lexi that.

At least not yet.

Some things had to be handled delicately.

"Buddy, your arm is broken." North's wolf could sense the break and by the odd angle Parker was holding his arm, it was obvious. "I can splint it for you, but we should get Hannah to see it anyway." He knelt down in front of Parker and took a look.

Yep. It was broken for sure, but at least it wasn't a compound fracture. Parker should be able to heal fully after his next shift.

Hannah would see to that.

North really wasn't needed.

Not that it was a bad feeling when Parker came to him and not Hannah.

"But I wanted to come to you," Parker whispered and warmth filled North's chest.

This boy. This little boy.

Fuck, he wanted Parker to be his son.

There was no way he'd let Lexi walk away. There had to be a reason she was shying away, and North would get to the bottom of it.

North ran a hand through Parker's dark brown hair and gave a reassuring smile. "I'm glad you did. No matter what happens, Park, I'll be here for you. You got that?"

Parker bit his lip and nodded. "I get it."

"Good," North said then stood. "Now, let's get you to the triad's house so Hannah can Heal that arm of yours."

"You mean I can't just shift to heal it better later?" Parker asked, an odd note of fear underlying his words.

North furrowed his brows. "That'll really hurt, Park. I wouldn't think you'd want to do that. Even the adult wolves would rather not deal with that kind of pain if they can help it. That's why Packs have Healers."

"But I've never had a Healer before," Parker whispered, and North finally got it.

"Hannah won't hurt you, Park. The Healing? It's like this warmth that soothes you. It's not gonna hurt. In fact, it feels kind of good."

"But what about Hannah? Won't it hurt her if she has to Heal me?"

Oh, this boy. Yep, North loved him.

"It might make her tired if she does it too quickly," North said honestly. He didn't see any reason to lie to the kid since Parker seemed to see too much as it was. "In fact, she had to learn how to use her powers when she came here. She's much better now than when she first started. She loves what she does, Park. Believe me," he muttered then shook it off. He needed to quit being so melancholy over the fact he wasn't needed in the same way anymore.

"You sure she'll be okay?"

"I'm sure. Now let's get moving. You've got to be in pain."

"I'm tough," Parker replied, though he winced when he said it.

North picked up his cell and called Lexi as they walked toward the triad's home. Most of the den was sprawled out enough that people drove if they needed. The Jameson clan, however, all lived really close to one another near the Alpha —his father's home.

"Hello?" Lexi answered, and North held back a groan at the sound of her voice.

His wolf clawed at him, needing his mate as much as the human did.

"Hey, Lex, it's North. I have Parker here, and I'm taking him to Hannah's. He seems to have broken his arm. He'll be okay, but I want Hannah to Heal him so he won't have to shift to Heal."

Lexi sucked in a breath, and North wanted to find a way to get through the phone line and pull her close. His wolf nudged him, but he ignored the tug. "I'm on my way," she said, her voice calm but with an edge of panic. "Tell him I'll be right there." She hung up, and pride filled him at how together she was and the fact that she was dropping everything to be with her son.

"She's on her way, bud," North said, pocketing his phone. "Let's get you to Hannah."

Parker held his arm to his chest, pain in his eyes, though North knew the kid was trying to hide it. "Was she mad?"

As they walked toward Hannah's, North frowned. "No, why would she be mad? You hurt yourself and went to an adult to get help."

"But I was supposed to be playing with the other boys." Parker's eyes widened, and he quickly shut his mouth.

What the hell?

"What's going on, bud?"

"Nothing," he mumbled.

They were at Hannah's front door, so North let the subject drop.

For now.

The door opened, and a curvy redhead stepped out onto the porch. "Parker," Hannah Jamenson whispered and held out her hand.

As if she were the moon goddess herself, she drew the little boy to her side, and she wrapped an arm around his shoulders carefully.

"Let's get you taken care of," she said quietly then looked at North. "I felt the break through the Pack but couldn't tell who it was. He's still a little new to the bonds."

North nodded. While other Healers might have been able to feel the exact person and feeling through the bonds, Hannah was still relatively new herself. Plus Parker hadn't been part of the Pack long enough for Hannah to fully connect to the boy beyond the initial bond.

That wouldn't be a problem anymore.

"I called Lexi," North explained as he walked into the triad's home. "She's on her way."

"I figured as much," Hannah said as she sat next to Parker on the couch.

North raised his chin at Josh, who stood in the entrance to the hallway with a sleeping Kaylee on his chest. For some reason, the sight of the ex-Navy SEAL holding his baby girl made North smile.

Josh quirked a smile then rubbed Kaylee's little back. "Reed's in the nursery with Conner changing him."

North smiled again. While most people in today's world thought true triads were odd, he thought the three of them worked perfectly together. Each loved the others with the fullest of their emotions—something not even some couples could say.

"Where is he?" Lexi said from behind him, and he spun around on his heel.

It looked as if she'd run straight to the triad's home. She wasn't breathless because she was a wolf and could run farther than she probably had if necessary, but the slight panicked look in her eyes made North want to bring her into his arms.

Fuck it.

He stalked toward her and gripped her chin, forcing her gaze to his. She let out a little gasp, and her eyes darkened. The pressure of his hand wasn't gentle, but neither was it too hard. His wolf liked the fact that Lexi seemed to almost get off on the touch.

He shelved that thought for a later time.

"He's fine," he said, his voice gruff. "Hannah is Healing him now. Calm." He'd lowered his face to hers and whispered that last part so not even the wolves in the room with the exceptional hearing could hear him.

Lexi stiffened for just a moment at his order then relaxed into him as if her body needed his words to calm.

At least that's what he'd like to think.

He honestly didn't know her well enough to figure out what her actions meant.

At least not yet.

"You can let go now," she said, her voice carefully devoid of emotion.

He let go slowly, running his thumb over the place he'd held her before stepping back.

Lexi moved around him and walked toward the couch. North's gaze landed on that rounded ass of hers, and he held back a groan.

Her son was in the room. His *family* was in the room.

Hell, he needed to get a grip.

North risked a glance at Josh, who merely raised a brow.

Fuck, he'd just deal with that later.

North made his way to the couch, where Lexi was now holding Parker to her side. Hannah was sitting on the other side, her hands in her lap, her body slightly damp with perspiration. He knew Healing took a lot of energy, and his sister-in-law was still getting a hold of her powers since she'd had the babies, so he was a bit worried at her physical reaction.

"I'm fine," Hannah said, a smile in her voice and on her face. "I seem to tire out a bit easier now, but I think it will all return to normal once I finish nursing."

"You need to take of yourself, baby," Reed said as he walked into the room, Conner in one arm, a glass of water and an orange in the other. He set the water and orange down and kissed Hannah's brow. "Drink that whole glass then eat that entire orange."

She rolled her eyes but took a bite.

"I'm sorry you're hurting because of me," Parker said, and North fisted his hands so he wouldn't reach out and soothe the boy.

"I'm okay, Parker. I promise. I just get a little tired, but that's nothing compared to breaking a bone."

"If it hurt her, she wouldn't be doing it," Josh said, his tone holding no argument.

North held back a snort. Sure, big and gruff Josh might think he could tell Hannah what to do, but that wouldn't go over well for long.

Hannah rolled her eyes then reached out for Conner. Reed handed over her son and went back to Josh's side.

"Tell me what happened, honey," Lexi said, and North moved to sit on the coffee table in front of them.

Lexi stiffened for only a moment before she looked as though she'd forced herself to relax, letting her shoulders fall a bit and her fists become unclenched. He reached out and gripped Parker's hand then did the same to Lexi. She didn't pull away, but from the glare in her eyes, North knew she wanted to.

It was past time to deal with what they were feeling. He wasn't going to tiptoe around anymore. If she didn't want to mate with him, then she'd have to flat-out tell him. No more hiding.

With that decision also came the knowledge he needed to know more about Parker. That meant that North needed to know why Parker seemed so afraid. He hadn't been able to sense it as much before, only slightly when Parker had mentioned the other kids, but now it was full-out fear.

"Parker? Honey? What happened?" Lexi asked again.

"Nothing," Parker mumbled, and North squeezed his hand.

"Don't lie, bud," North said. "If you were doing something stupid and broke your arm, that's fine, but if someone did this to you, we need to know. We don't hurt each other here, Park." He reached out and gripped Parker's chin like he had Lexi's, only this time softer. "Tell us."

Parker's gaze met his and held it before he let out a shaky breath. "I was with the other boys after class. They said they wanted to play with me." He turned to his mom. "They *never* want to play with me."

Lexi narrowed her eyes, and North held back a growl. Parker continued, "So I went to play with them. I should have known they were lying. They told me that they were going to play cat-shifters and climb trees. They wanted me to go first. So I did."

"Did they push you?" North growled.

Parker started to shake his head then stopped. "No. I don't think so. I think I just fell because I don't think there were others in the tree with me. I don't know," he mumbled.

Lexi squeezed North's hand hard, and he squeezed back.

"They called me tainted and ran away laughing." Parker let out a shaky breath, a tear falling down his cheek.

North couldn't hold back his wolf's need to protect anymore and moved fast, pulling Parker into his arms and sitting down on the couch next to Lexi. He still held her hand so she was, in essence, in his arms too. Parker stiffened only for a moment in his arms then sank into him, the little boy's wolf reaching for his own. Lexi froze as well before relaxing again and running a hand through Parker's hair.

"Tell me who they were, and I will take care of it. You are *not* tainted, Parker. You are Pack. If those boys don't understand that, then they need to be taught."

"And what if their parents don't care?" Lexi asked.

North's gaze rocked to hers. "What?"

She shook her head. "Never mind."

North narrowed his eyes then moved his gaze to the triad and their children in the room. "I'm taking Parker and Lexi home."

All three adults nodded, knowing there was something going on that Lexi wasn't saying.

They left and made their way to Lexi's. "You want to tell me what that was about?"

Lexi shook her head then looked down at Parker, who stood between them. North nodded, but he wasn't fucking happy about it.

They made their way to the door, and Parker stopped to look up at North. "Thank you," he whispered then threw his arms around North's waist.

North sucked in a breath and hugged Parker back, his wolf howling in happiness. "Get some sleep, Park. We can talk tomorrow."

"Okay," he said then looked between North and his mom before going inside.

Lexi tried to follow him, but North held her back. He pulled her hard to his chest, and she gasped.

"Tomorrow we talk, Lexi," he said, his voice low, promising—though to any other it would have sounded like a threat, she took it differently.. Sadness flashed over her eyes before she blinked it away. He had no idea what that meant, but he was going to find out.

"Tomorrow, North. You might not like what you hear though."

"I don't care. Tomorrow, Lexi." He traced her cheek with his finger, her breath catching, before he pulled back. "Tomorrow."

He left her standing there, her brother Logan darkening the doorway.

Tomorrow North would take the next steps. He just hoped to hell that Lexi wanted to take them with him.

CHAPTER THREE

"Just leave, Logan," Lexi said, exasperated. "You are *not* going to be here when North gets here, so stop even thinking about it."

"I don't want to leave you home with him. He's not good for you, Lex."

Lexi closed her eyes, that pain arcing across her chest at just how true Logan's words were. "Go, Logan. I can't...I can't do this with you here. Don't you understand that? I don't even want to have this conversation with North to begin with, but I can't hide it anymore."

"Do you understand what you're doing, Lex? They could kick us out of the Pack."

"I know that! Don't you think I know that? I can't lie to them anymore. I can't watch the way he looks at me, the way I can almost feel his wolf beg for me, and then turn around and lie to him. If they kick us out of the Pack, we will deal with it. We've dealt with it before."

Logan frowned then pushed his dark hair away from his face. "Lexi, it could be worse than that, and you know it."

"That's why you can't be here. Go with Parker. If something happens..." She took a deep breath. "If something happens, then you go. You take Parker, and I will catch up."

Logan framed her face, and she almost lost it. God, her brother had done *everything* for her, and here she was, ready to fuck it all up because the wolf she couldn't feel wanted a man she couldn't have. Though she couldn't feel her wolf she could still feel the connection to North that told her he was her mate.

Being latent was an odd thing that didn't make any sense to most people but she knew that her own urges and desires were not merely her one, but of another entity that she couldn't quite feel, but knew was there as well.

Fuck, she was worthless.

Totally fucking worthless.

"Get that look out of your eyes," Logan growled. "I don't care what the fuck you are thinking, but if you're about to sacrifice yourself or some shit, then forget it. I'm not leaving you alone with a Jamenson wolf where you could be hurt."

North wouldn't hurt her physically. Well, at least not too much. Her body heated at the reminder of the feel of his grip on his chin as he'd told her what to do.

It figured that the one time she actually found a wolf that would see to her needs she would never be able to be with him.

No, the only part he would hurt would be her soul. Really, though, she would be the one doing the hurting.

It wouldn't be his fault.

"Don't call him that," she mumbled, knowing she was ignoring the important parts of Logan's statement. It wasn't as if she didn't know what he was saying. She just didn't want to deal with it.

"A Jamenson wolf?" Logan asked, a smile in his words—*thank God*. "That's what he is, love. That's what they all are."

"Don't say it like that then. It's not like they're what we left behind, Logan. They're good people. You know that."

Logan raised a brow. "You can say that and believe it, knowing that you might take your last breath when you tell that Jamenson wolf what happened?"

Lexi raised her chin. "He won't kill me."

She hoped.

"And stop calling him 'that Jamenson wolf,'" she spat then forced herself to smile. "Come to think of it, isn't there a certain *Jamenson wolf* you should be talking to right now? Hmm, who could that be? Dark hair, piercing green eyes, an attitude that could melt most men..."

Logan moved toward her until he towered over her, a glower on his face. "Shut up, Lexi Anderson. You're playing a dangerous game."

She tilted her head, the wolf hiding within her close to the surface. "Which game is that? The one where I have to be honest or I'll never forgive myself? Or the one where I say straight out what you're thinking...and what you're missing?"

Annoyance and a touch of hurt passed over his face before he narrowed his eyes. "I see what you're doing, and I know you're doing it because you're scared to death, I will let that go. Know this though, sister, leave the latter of your thoughts alone. Do you understand me?"

She let out a breath and rested her head on his chest. He stayed unyielding for only a moment before melting slightly and wrapping his arms around her.

"I'm sorry, Logan. You're right. I'm being a bitch and lashing out because I'm scared. I'll stay out of what you and Cailin have."

For now.

He ran his hand down her back, and she calmed like she always did. Her big brother knew exactly what to do to help her—even if it was something he hated.

"I knew what you were doing. You just happened to hit a topic my wolf doesn't like at the moment."

She frowned at his tone and looked up. "What's going on, Logan?"

He shook his head then kissed her brow. "Nothing, honey. Deal with what you have to deal with. I will stay out of hearing distance only because of Parker. If you need me though, you scream. I can hear that. Got me?"

She nodded, praying she wouldn't have to scream.

He left her standing in the middle of her living room, the borrowed furniture seeming to mock her predicament.

"Lexi?"

Lexi started at North's voice. "I'm in here," she croaked unnecessarily. He was a wolf; of course he knew where she was.

He strode into the room, the power of his wolf seeming to fill the space even more than Logan had. She forced herself not to lean toward him and bare her throat.

"I scented Logan, so I waited out of earshot until I sensed he'd gone."

He walked toward her and reached out. She took a deep breath as he traced her cheek, the callousness of fingers sending shivers down her body.

"You don't need to fear me, Lexi. I wouldn't hurt you."

She had a feeling that might not be the case once he learned the truth. Once he learned the secrets she'd buried for so long.

Lexi backed up, creating a necessary distance between the two of them. As much as she wanted to throw herself into his arms and ride him like a cowgirl, she knew this wasn't the best time for that.

"You said we were going to talk today," she said, her voice thankfully even. "Well, go ahead. Talk."

North raised a brow and looked as though he was holding back a smile. "Okay, Lex, if that's how you want to play it. Talking, though, takes two people. I'm not going to stand here and lecture you, considering I need answers."

"You're lecturing right now, North."

He snorted and moved closer.

She took a step back and cursed herself for the movement.

He froze. "You're actually scared of me," he said, his voice hollow.

"No. No I'm not."

At least not yet.

"Prove it," he whispered then took that step again.

This time she stood where she was.

His lips slammed against hers, taking them without mercy. She opened up for him, eager, ready. His tongue slid against hers, and she wrapped her arms around his neck, her fingers tangling in his hair. He pulled her close, her breasts against his chest, his cock hard, full, against her belly. She rocked into him, and he deepened the kiss, his taste, his sweet, sweet taste permanently scarring her tongue.

She'd never get enough of him.

That was precisely the reason she needed to pull back.

She did, and she felt cold at the loss.

Both of them stood still, breathing hard.

God, she wanted this man. This wolf.

He shook his head then firmed his lips. "Tell me about the wolves, Lexi. We will talk about the underlying tension between us next because I have a feeling that's the part you're so afraid of. We'll let that sit for a moment, considering that's what we've been doing since you got here. Now, tell me why Parker was so scared and why you made that comment about the parents of those boys."

"Are you going to do anything about what I say?"

"What the fuck, Lex? If someone is hurting that boy or you, of course I'm going to do something about it. If they aren't hurting you but are still making you feel like you're not part of the Pack, then fuck yes, I'm going to do something about it. I already told Jasper that something was going on."

Jasper, another of North's brothers, was the Beta of the Pack. It was his job to care for the needs of the Pack on daily issues. Lexi didn't want to bother Jasper with this. She didn't want to bother anyone with this.

"Your Pack might be fighting a war with the Centrals, but they're also fighting a war with each other," she blurted then closed her eyes.

Well, that hadn't come out like she wanted.

"What do you mean?" North asked, his voice low, deadly.

"Take a look around, North. You've been fighting another enemy for so long you've had to leave others behind. Not everyone is a Jamenson wolf with something tangible at stake. Not everyone is ready to fight and not go dark. I've heard the whispers. They want to use dark magic against the Centrals, and your family won't let them."

North growled. "I've heard the whispers too, only they aren't so quiet now. My family knows about it.

We're doing all we can to keep things at bay, but it's fucking hard when people don't come to us with their problems. Now, we're going to put that topic aside for a moment because you glossed over the fact that people are treating you like shit. Tell me."

Lexi threw her hands up in the air. "Fine. Your Pack doesn't want Logan, Parker, and me. They didn't want Bay. They sure as fuck didn't want Ellie. And now they don't want us. They think we're nothing. Nothing. They think we're the enemy and all you've done is bring us into your home to take over your Pack as secret spies or something ridiculous."

He blinked then stalked toward her. He gripped her chin, and she froze, her body ceding to him even though her mind wasn't quite there.

"What have they been saying to you, my Lexi?"

"I'm not *your* Lexi," she whispered, broken. She blinked, her body going oddly numb at the words she'd spoken, the hollowness within her opening like an aching chasm of nothingness.

He traced her cheek with his other hand, keeping a firm grip on her chin. "You could be. You fucking could be."

"No, no I can't."

"Lexi," he rasped out, "let me help, baby. Please, let me help."

She tried to pull away, but he held her place. Despite herself, she liked it. The warmth of his touch on her skin radiated through her, filling the chasm for only a moment before the pain of remembering why they couldn't be one slammed into full force.

"There's nothing you can do. You can't change the minds of others. None of you can. We're dealing with what we have to, North. Just let it go. If they hurt my baby again, though, I won't be responsible for my actions."

He sucked in a breath. "I won't hold you back if they come at Parker, Lexi. You have to tell me what's happening. I'll take care of it, baby. Let me help."

"You can't help."

"You know as well as I do that we have that connection. You know we're potential mates."

She sucked in a breath as well at his words.

Fuck, he'd said it.

He wasn't supposed to say it.

Her chest shook as she choked back a sob. She felt the tears she'd held back so long slide down her cheeks.

"We're not mates," she rasped out. "We *can't* be mates."

He furrowed his brow. "What the fuck are you talking about? I have your taste on my tongue, baby. That just pushed the mating urge full force. My wolf wants you, and I want you just as much. Can't you feel it?"

She could, but she had lied to herself enough that she didn't say anything.

"Lexi, baby, tell me what's wrong. Is it because you're latent?" he asked. "I've never met an adult latent wolf before so I don't know. Can you not feel the connection because of that?"

Though his tone was gentle on that subject, almost reluctant, it still hurt to hear. Yes, she was latent. No, she couldn't feel her wolf. Damn it, though, she could feel him.

She just couldn't tell him that.

"It's not that," she whispered.

He framed her face. She bit her lip, hating what she had to do.

"Tell me. Tell me why we can't be mates when I *know* we both want it. I know we can be perfect for each other."

40

She couldn't speak.

Couldn't think.

"Is it Parker? Are you afraid I wouldn't claim him as my own? You have to know I'll raise that little boy as my own flesh and blood. I wouldn't think less of him for anything."

God, she wished that would stay true no matter what she said next.

"Is it because you still love your other mate?" he asked, and she flinched.

North didn't miss the movement. "Baby, oh baby, I'm sorry. I'm so, so sorry. Fuck. I watched Adam go through this with Anna, and it almost tore him and Bay apart. Do you still miss your mate so much that you can't think of being with me?"

He pulled back then, his hands fisted at his side. "Fuck. I didn't think of that. I mean I *knew* you had been mated before because you have Parker, and that's how wolves make kids. I didn't think of the time that had passed. It had been decades for Adam, and he almost killed himself over it. It's only been a few years for you, right? Fuck, baby. I'm so sorry. I'll leave. I'll give you space. I'll give you anything you want. Just tell me what to do."

Her heart broke, the tears spilling down her cheeks falling faster.

"I...I can't mate you because I'm still mated."

North froze.

Pain, absolute pain, arched across his face before he staggered back.

"What?" he whispered, his voice raw. "How...how can that happen? I can *feel* you baby. I *know* we can be mates. How the fuck are you still mated?"

She shook her head. "It's a long story."

A broken one.

"Tell me, please. I need to know."

She tried to hold back, but the tears in his eyes broke her all over again.

Oh God, this man, this strong man with a wolf that had to be stronger than any she'd seen from the way he shifted to the way she felt it prowl against her like an Alpha without a Pack, was crying, *crying*, for her.

For them.

Damn the Fates.

Damn.

Them.

To.

Hell.

"I'm already mated, North...but not fully."

He frowned. "I don't understand," he whispered.

"It...it's not a full mating because I didn't mark him. He...he forced me into the mating to begin with."

North's eyes widened, and then he took a step toward her, the darkness and fury in his eyes pulling at her. "What. The. *Fuck*?"

"He...Parker's father...he knew we were potential mates, and he took my will. He forced me to mate with him. He couldn't force me to bite him though, so he used a special herb and black magic to break the Fates' will as well. That's how Parker was conceived. That's how I'm mated but not. That's why I can feel you in my heart and my soul, and you can do the same. That's why we can't mate...at least while Parker's father...or sperm donor...is alive."

North swallowed hard. "Who's Parker's father, Lexi?"

She shook her head. "I can't tell you that. Please..." Her voice broke. "Please don't make me tell you."

He pulled her closer to him and gripped her chin again, forcing her gaze to his. "Tell me, Lexi. Tell me who I have to kill. I'm going to kill that man for taking you against your will. I'm going to kill that man for taking you away from me before I even knew you existed. Tell me."

He wasn't going to be able to kill that man.

No one could.

That was the problem.

They'd all tried and failed.

That's why she'd been kicked out of the Talons like the other woman before her.

Bay's mother.

The man who could have been her future held her in his arms, and she couldn't have him. No matter what he'd said, she knew he didn't want damaged goods. He wouldn't want whatever she'd become because of...that man.

"Tell me, Lexi."

She took a deep breath. This was it. She'd tell him, and her life would be in his hands. Her family would be in his hands.

She looked into those green eyes of his one more time, needing to cement that image in her mind forever. God, it could have been good between them.

"Corbin. Corbin Reyes."

He blinked at her once then left her standing alone.

It was done.

She was lost.

CHAPTER FOUR

He was going to fucking kill somebody if he didn't let out the rage, the darkness, soon. North's wolf clawed at him, aching for a run, a fight, *something*. When his wolf would calm down for a few seconds between breaths, it would howl in pain, in anguish.

Bile rose in his throat, but he ignored it, ignored the burn, the heat.

This wasn't supposed to fucking happen.

He knew how mates were supposed to find each other and find their happy endings—or whatever crap his sisters-in-law spouted. He'd thought he knew his destiny.

He was the last single Jamenson brother.

He wasn't supposed to find *her,* only to find out he would never get the chance to have her.

He'd blinked at Lexi when she'd said *that* name. Fucking blinked and walked away without saying a damn word. He left her standing in the room, her pain radiating off her like it had a tangible essence.

"Fuck!" North yelled, his chest heaving. A thin trail of sweat rolled down his back, and he fisted his hands. He needed to run on four paws and get the adrenaline out of his system. If he didn't...he wouldn't be able to control his actions.

His wolf knew this.

The man didn't want to think about it.

He stood on the edge of where the forest met the open area for the den's homes. The full moon was long past so it wasn't the goddess calling him to run. Wolves didn't need to shift with the moon anyway. They only shifted when they needed to and did on the nights of the full moon as tradition when they could.

Now, though, North needed to *move*.

He pulled his shirt over his head, toed off his shoes, and shucked off his pants in swift movements, leaving a trail of clothes behind him as he moved.

Then he shifted.

It was painful as hell—the same way it was for all wolves.

However, unlike other wolves, he didn't need to get on all fours and wait for the change to happen.

No, he could run while he shifted.

His wolf was special that way.

He took off on two feet and ended up on four paws. They pounded into the dirt as he picked up speed. He let the light of the crescent moon wash over him, touching his fur through the trees. He jumped over a fallen log and moved even faster.

He just needed to run.

To feel free.

To forget the worries that attacked his soul, his future.

North let the wolf take over, the other part of himself darker, stronger than he'd let others know. His wolf wasn't evil...far from it. No, his wolf was more primal than even the most dominant of wolves. Yes, all wolves were animals, but werewolves were sentient beings that had full-on conversations with their human halves. His wolf tended to think and act like a true wolf recognizing only prey and not-prey, and the most basic ways to fight battles. Not with words, but with claws and teeth. He knew his wolf stayed at the surface, unlike others. He knew his connection to his wolf was different. He didn't need to speak to his wolf and hear its thoughts like his brothers. No, his wolf would control him if North wasn't careful.

He was *always* careful.

He'd almost killed Maddox when they were boys because he hadn't been careful. He could still remember the shocked look on his twin's face, a mirror image of his own. North had backed off quickly then ran for his life, afraid Maddox would tell their father and Alpha that North had no control over his wolf.

He'd underestimated his twin though.

Maddox hadn't told their father what had happened only letting North know that he would if it happened again.

Their twin bond was far stronger than the familiar bonds that held their family together, and though North was grateful for the reprieve, it didn't make him feel any better about how strong his wolf was.

He ran at an unforgiving pace for over an hour, the scents of forest and its scared inhabitants rushing over him. The prey knew a predator was in their midst and were right to be afraid.

The burn in his muscles echoed the one in his heart, but he couldn't stop. He needed something more, something to take the darkness from him, but he didn't know what.

Another scent hit him hard, and he slowed down.

Logan seemed eager to join him for some reason.

Fuck.

North turned on a dime, still in wolf form, hackles raised.

Logan burst through the trees, his black wolf form large and intimidating.

Well, at least it would be intimidating for most.

North wasn't most.

Logan stopped in front of him, his fangs bared.

North lunged.

His teeth scraped against Logan's neck but didn't sink in. He didn't want to kill the man, only get rid of the rage. Logan pivoted out of the way and nipped at North's flank. North pulled back and growled, wanting, no, *needing*, to fight.

Logan nodded then moved.

North met him in the middle and clawed at him, the tips of his claws scraping against the flesh beneath Logan's fur.

They nipped, clawed, and growled at each other, both of them pulling back at just the right moment so they wouldn't draw blood.

The burn felt good across his skin as the rage poured out of him. Logan growled and started to shift to human form, surprising North.

North changed as well, though faster than the other man.

Not by much though, which again surprised him. It seemed Logan held secrets of his own.

Before North could blink, he ducked Logan's fist. The fight was over on four paws, but not two feet.

North swung his arm, connecting with Logan's chin. Logan's head rocked back before he kicked North in the thigh. North's stance didn't waver, and he punched the man in the stomach. The breath whooshed out of Logan before he twisted, and North took a fist to the jaw as well.

They fought, fists smashing against flesh, their kicks aiming at parts they wouldn't break. It wasn't lost on North that they were both very naked fighting each other, but nudity didn't matter to wolves. He didn't even know why he thought about it then.

Finally, they each took a step back, both bruised and bleeding from where their punches, kicks, and claws had hit.

"Feel better?" Logan rasped out, his breath uneven.

Considering they'd both fought to the fullest they could without actually killing each other, North was out of breath too.

The darkness, though, had receded. The run and battle had helped.

It just didn't help everything.

"Some," he said, his breath finally even.

"You want to tell me what the fuck that was about?" Logan asked.

They both sat down on the grass between the trees, not bothering to cover up since they didn't have clothing. Neither looked at the other.

"What do you mean?" North had assumed Lexi had told Logan that he'd broken her—or at least hurt her—and Logan had found him to kick his ass.

He'd have done the same to any bastard who'd done anything like that to Cailin.

"Fuck. I felt your rage from the other side of the house. I left Parker with Lexi and ran to find you."

North blinked. That hadn't been what he'd been expecting. His family usually didn't feel his rage, his darkness. He could hide it from everyone because it seemed only like the strength of his wolf. The only position in the Pack he normally wouldn't have been able to hide from was the Omega. However, since

Maddox was his twin and his brother could *never* feel him, North was able to hide.

Logan, though, there was something wrong with that.

The other wolf let out a breath. "I'm not saying that I have a power to do that, North. My wolf is just closer to the surface than most—same as yours. That's why I felt it. I was also watching out because if you were to hurt my sister, I'd kill you."

"I'm not going to hurt Lexi," he whispered, knowing that was true. No matter what happened or how he dealt with the impact of her confession, he wouldn't hurt her.

He *couldn't* hurt her.

"Are you sure about that?" the other man asked, rubbing a hand through his hair. Logan winced and looked at the cut on his inner arm. "How the hell did you cut me here?"

North ignored the first part of Logan's statement, unable to deal with exactly what Lexi's brother had meant, and raised a brow. "I'm better, stronger, faster, and cleverer than you?"

Logan snorted. "You can tell yourself anything you want so you can sleep at night, but don't lie to me."

"You don't think I'm better, stronger, faster, and cleverer than you?"

Logan let out a breath, all traces of humor gone from his face. As it was, North had long since lost the humor of this situation. In fact, there wasn't any. He was just sitting in the middle of the forest with the brother of the woman he'd not only hurt, but lost before he'd even known he'd had a shot.

Fate fucking sucked.

A lot.

"North, what the fuck happened?"

"Don't you already know?"

Logan's gaze met his, the angry burning there almost scalding. "I know what she was planning on telling you. I know that she's been through hell and back because of others. I've had to sit back and let her take it without being able to do anything about it because I love my sister more than anything. I know that I've had to kill to protect my family, and I'd do it again in a heartbeat. I know that I left Parker with his mother because she needed someone to hold on to when I came after you, but she will only comfort him and not take his comfort because she doesn't like to break down—no, she *won't*—break down in front of her son...or anyone.

"So, yes, I do *know* a few things, but why don't you lay it out for me?"

The fury slicing across North's body was nothing compared to the anguish lying beneath Logan's words. The man could do nothing for his sister more than he already had, and it was killing him.

"I'm going to kill him, Logan," North began.

"Apparently it's fated and all that shit, so it better fucking happen," Logan spat. "Tell me what happened with Lexi, not what's going to happen in the future. We'll get to that in a minute."

"You didn't just ask her?"

"No. I came after you because I felt that anger. I wanted to take care of it or at least have it directed at me rather than my sister." He let out a tired breath. "I'd do anything for my family, North."

"I'd do the same for mine."

"Then we understand each other. Tell me. Tell me what happened."

North swallowed hard and ran a hand over his face, wincing as he brushed against his cut lip. He would heal within the hour, at least that small cut, due to his strength and being a werewolf, but the pain helped him focus.

"I thought we were mates. Hell, I thought that I was *finally* going to get what my brothers had. I stayed away when she first came here, or at least as far away as I could, because you guys were just settling in, but I never expected to be forced to stay away forever."

"She told you to stay away forever then?"

North frowned. "No. Not exactly. Shit. I don't know. Jesus, Logan. How the hell could this have happened?"

"He fucking took her from our home and raped her, North," Logan spat. "The Talons, under our old Alpha at least, were weak. At least weaker than the rest of you. Corbin saw her, wanted her despite her protests, and took everything he could from her. Everything."

North moved and punched the trunk of the tree behind him, the bite of the bark a sweet elixir against the pain already running through his body, his heart.

"I don't know what I'm going to do. Shit. Corbin is Parker's father. That means Ellie's his aunt. All these connections, this web, it's getting crazy." North took a deep breath. "How the hell did Corbin accomplish this? It makes no sense."

Logan growled, his eyes glowing gold. "I have a feeling you're calling Lexi a liar."

"What? Fuck. No. I want to know *how* Corbin did it. I can feel here," he slammed his fist against his chest, over his heart, "that Lexi didn't want this. That she wanted nothing to do with it."

"At least you believe her on that part."

"Of course I do. God, my wolf knows she wants us. And I know the only good thing that ever came out of her being in this situation is that little boy."

Something then occurred to him that made his stomach tie itself into even more knots. "Does Parker know who his father is?"

Logan narrowed his eyes and gave a sharp nod. "We don't keep secrets from each other. Not when it could mean life or death. We're all we have."

"All you *had*. You're a Redwood now," North said absently, knowing there were other things on the line and saying they were Redwoods meant nothing to those who wanted to cast all evil out. The others thought the Andersons were evil because they'd been kicked out of the Talons yet no one had proof of *why* they'd been kicked out.

The Jamensons knew what had happened and trusted them but that didn't mean others would.

Lexi told him that there were those rumbling dissent, something North himself had been feeling recently. He'd have to warn his father and his family, though he had a feeling they might already know.

He'd have to warn them of a lot of things now.

There was no way he'd keep what he'd learned from his father.

He couldn't.

He just had to decide whose side he'd take if he was forced to choose.

He thought of the way Lexi made his wolf feel...of the way she made the man feel.

There was no other choice.

There *couldn't* be.

"Do you know what you're going to do? You can't mate with Lexi. Not with Corbin alive."

"I'm just going to have to kill him."

Logan nodded approvingly. "Good. I'll have your back. Now, do we have your back when you go and run to your family to tell them what you know?"

North looked up sharply.

"Lexi knew you'd be forced to tell them. You should tell them now before you go to Lexi. That way you have answers for her."

His wolf wanted her now, but he knew he needed time to tuck the darkness away...bury it deep.

"And what are you going to do?"

"Protect my sister. Even from you. Think about what you want. What you *really* want. Talk to your father. He deserves to know the threat. Not from Parker or Lexi, but from Corbin."

The thought that should have come to him right away hit him like a blow. "Does Corbin know about Parker?"

Logan met his gaze. "I don't know."

"Shit."

"Shit."

Without another word, Logan rose and ran off the way he'd come but in human form, and North went back for his clothes at a steady run, also in human form. He and Logan had each run hard, fast, changed once already, and then fought, it wouldn't make sense to spend more energy to shift into wolves so they could run harder. He made his way to his parents' home, his mind going a thousand different directions.

He needed to talk to Lexi and make sure she was okay. It didn't matter that she wasn't his mate in truth, not to his wolf, not to the man.

He staggered to a stop in front of his parents' home.

It didn't matter.

Shit.

It totally didn't.

He wanted her.

He wanted that woman in his life, his bed, his future. He wanted to help her raise Parker—no matter who the boy's father by blood was.

He wanted to have everything he could possibly have with her...even if it wasn't a true mating.

His wolf howled, and he fought the urge to howl right along with him.

"North? What's wrong?" his mother said from the open door, a frown on her face. She looked just like she had all his life. Young, fair, and yet with an underlying strength that would make most bow under it.

He went to her and wrapped his arms around her. She was short enough that she curled right in. He pressed his nose to her neck, needing the scent of sugar and home surrounding him.

His mother patted his back then pulled away slightly. "What's wrong, North?" she repeated.

He scented his father in the living room, and he moved, but kept his hand on hers. "We need to talk."

She blinked, her wolf coming to the surface with the gold in her eyes. There was a reason she was the Alpha's mate.

She was fucking strong.

"Okay, honey. Let's get going then."

He made his way to the living room and lowered his gaze in front of his father. No matter how strong North was, his father was even more powerful.

"You've been fighting," Edward said. "What happened?"

A demand.

"This was just letting out frustration with Logan."

"What caused you to need to let go of that frustration? Did he do something to Cailin?" he growled.

Pat rubbed her husband's arm. "Honey, if that's what it was, I don't think North would look so broken. Yes, he'd be hurt, but this is a different broken, my love. Tell us, baby, what's the matter with Lexi?"

Gods. No matter how old he was, his mother knew exactly how to get to the heart of the matter. He'd always envied the way his parents knew each other and their children. They knew what to say, what to do...just how to be...

Now he might not have that.

He swallowed hard, the sense of defeat all but clawing at him. This wasn't who he was...who he needed to be.

No.

He would.

Even if he had to do it in a way he'd never imagined.

North let out a shaky breath. "Lexi is already mated."

"Is?" Pat asked, her eyes wide. "I thought her mate was dead considering the way you two are acting. Sorry. I can't help being a mother and noticing when my youngest son finds his potential mate."

"You're right, Mom. At least about the potential part. I had thought Lexi's mate was dead too, but, in fact, he isn't."

Edward frowned. "How is that possible?"

This was the part that would hurt, but his parents weren't like others. They wouldn't blindly lash out because of who'd fathered Parker. They hadn't when they'd learned that Bay was the daughter of Caym, the demon who hunted them by Corbin's side.

At least, North hoped his parents would be okay.

A lot, no, *everything*, was riding on this.

"Because the man who fathered Parker, the man who mated Lexi and raped her, used dark magic to make it happen. The mating was never completed. She never marked him." It took two stages of mating to complete the bond. For the wolf, each had to mark the fleshy part of the shoulder where it met their neck.

For the human, they had to have sex, and the male had to fill the female with his seed. Two souls within one body, two connections of mating.

"Oh gods," Pat whispered, tears running down her face even as the fury raged in her eyes. "That poor girl."

"Ellie..." his father whispered.

"What?" North asked. Did his father know the connection?

"Ellie had said Parker looked familiar but couldn't place it. Parker is Corbin's son, isn't he?" The rage beneath the words didn't scare North. They comforted him that he wasn't alone in his feelings.

"I'll kill the bastard," his mother spat and stood up, her body shaking. "That bastard! He's taking too much from us, Edward. I'm going to kill him."

Jesus, he loved his mom.

Hard.

"You'll have to stand behind me, love. That little fucker has stood behind that demon and, before that, his father, for too long."

North blinked. "I take it you're not going to hurt Lexi and her family because of this?"

Edward turned his rage toward North. "I'm going to forget you just said that. She's fucking family, North. I don't care that we'll have to kill the little dick before you can fully mate her, but she's family. That little boy too." Edward closed his eyes. "And, if my little girl ever decides to mate him, Logan as well."

North closed his eyes, relief filling him.

"Have you told Lexi that you still want her?" his mother asked.

"Not yet."

Pat threw up her hands. "Then what the hell are you doing here, boy? Go to her. She's in pain, and you're here? I love you, son, but go to your mate."

North got up, hugged both his parents hard then ran toward Lexi's.

He had a mate to see.

He just had to make sure she *wanted* to see him.

CHAPTER FIVE

Four hours.

Four *freaking* hours.

That's how long North had been gone.

Lexi was pretty sure she was going to lose her mind...or kill someone. Considering she didn't really want to kill anyone in her presence, calming her mind seemed like a lost cause.

She still couldn't believe she'd just blurted out Corbin's name like that. She held back a wince at even thinking that man's name. She hated the Alpha of the Centrals more than anyone and anything.

Corbin's DNA might have given her the best thing in her life, her Parker, but that didn't stop her from wanting to see the man gutted, quartered, and burned.

She'd never forget the look on North's face when she'd said Corbin's name. When she'd said she was already mated, the look of stark pain on his face had almost taken her to her knees. The look of pure anger at the mention of their most hated enemy had made her want to curl into a ball and pray for forgiveness.

Forgiveness from what, she didn't know.

She'd told herself over and over again, just as Logan had told her, that it wasn't her fault what had happened.

Fault, though, didn't matter when it came to shame.

It didn't matter it wasn't her fault he'd touched her when she took long showers, scrubbing at her skin until she was raw, bleeding, aching, trying to get the feel of his hands banished from her memory.

It didn't matter.

It might have been years, but some days, it felt as though it had been mere minutes since it happened.

Telling North had made it all come back in a clear reality.

When Logan came back bruised, bloody, and bleeding, Lexi had frozen, her chest seizing. He hadn't told her what happened other than North was alive and would be there soon.

That had been over an hour ago.

'Soon' in man-terms meant whenever the hell they wanted it to mean.

Logan had gone back to shower then came out again with Parker in tow. The boys were going on a "camping" trip within the den wards to have some man time.

Lexi knew it was because Logan wanted her and North to have alone time—for whatever was about to happen—but Parker was smarter than that. Her son probably knew something was going on but let it slide.

She was thankful every single day her son was so insightful.

She scented him before she heard him.

"North." His name was a whisper on her lips as she turned.

He stood in the doorway, his hair a tossed mess around his head. The fading bruises on his face and on his arms only made him look more dangerous.

He might share the lightest hair of the Jamenson brothers with his twin, but right now, the darkness that emanated from his whole body made her shiver.

Whether it was a good shiver or not, she couldn't tell. At least not right then. It was probably a mix of the two.

"Lexi." The gruffness of his voice slid over her.

She couldn't feel her wolf, but she knew if she'd been able to, she'd be howling with need...with anguish.

This man was to be her mate.

Fate had proclaimed it so.

Fate had taken it away.

She opened her mouth to say something...anything, but he held up his hand.

The pain hurt more than she thought it would. Damn it. She'd had a bit of hope, something buried so deep, so far down that she hadn't even known she'd really had it. Now she knew the truth. He was going to leave her.

No, that wasn't right. He couldn't leave behind what he'd never had. He was just going to do what he should do in all reality and find another potential mate.

She'd had her shot at predestined mates—as wrong and filthy as it was.

The look in his eyes though...

She swallowed hard. She couldn't back down. She would *not* let the Redwoods kick them out or hurt her baby.

Not that she had a choice.

She never had a choice...

He was near her before she could blink, that spicy scent overwhelming her, the heat of his body scalding her.

"I left." His hand skimmed her cheek, and she forced herself not to lean into it.

"I know." God, she knew.

"I shouldn't have left."

His barely restrained anger powered over her, licking along her skin, and she sucked in a breath.

"What?"

"I shouldn't have left. Hell, Lex, baby. What happened to you wasn't your fault, and what did I do? I left you here alone. I shouldn't have done that. No matter what happens from this moment on between us, between the Pack, between *anything*, know this... I shouldn't have left."

"Why did you?"

"I'm...I'm not like my family, Lexi. I'm different."

She blinked. That hadn't been what she'd thought he'd say. "What do you mean?"

"I'm darker than the others. I hide it, and I do it well." He gave a self-deprecating grin. "I'm pretty sure your brother figured it out right away. That's something I'll worry about later though."

"I don't understand what you're saying." What had he decided? Lexi still didn't know if she should stay there and listen to his words or run from him, grab Parker and Logan, and find a way to live on the land again with nothing but a prayer for survival.

"When I get angry or feel any real emotion, I can't control it sometimes. It's not that I want to go out and kill someone, I'm not that off-kilter, but it's that I need to so...something. Something that is all wolf and not man. Something like letting myself go and not care about human rules and feelings. My wolf needs an outlet, and ripping someone's head off isn't the best course of action."

"I wouldn't think so," she whispered.

He tucked a strand of her hair behind her ear. "No, honey. I needed to leave and run out the adrenaline in my system."

"So you ran it off, rather than hurting me?" She swallowed, her throat dry.

He set his jaw. "No. I would *never* hurt you, Lexi. And there's another way I can let out the...extra energy." He grinned then, and she swallowed hard.

She blushed, knowing *exactly* what he meant. "Oh."

"Yeah, oh. So I had to leave, but I shouldn't have left. Pretty fucked up."

"Fucked up doesn't begin to cover this situation, North. What are we going to do?" Being frank had always helped her keep the craziness at bay. It had to help here.

"My wolf feels you, Lexi. You know I do too. Fate fucked up before, but it isn't fucking up now. You're my mate."

Her heart shuddered at those words, and a tear slid down her cheek. She shook her head.

"No, North. You know that can't happen."

He cupped her face and forced his gaze to hers. She melted into the jade green of his eyes, needing the pull of him, the feel of him. "Yes. It can, and it will. I'll kill him, Lexi. He deserves to die for countless crimes, but I'd kill him just to have you. I'm selfish. I want you in my life. I know we have so much to learn about each other, but I'm not going to wait to have you by my side. We'll learn each other and find a way to have our own mating...even without the bond for now."

"North..." What he was saying? God, it would kill him....would kill them both.

North closed his eyes then opened them slowly, an odd pain running through them that made her want to reach out and soothe, protect. He licked his lips and took a breath. "My wolf? He wants more. He..."

"He's darker than you let others know," she finished for him.

She watched him swallow hard, his eyes glowing gold. "He won't hurt you. In fact, he's never hurt another person that didn't deserve it...but he's stronger than the others in some ways. He's not Alpha, but I can shift faster than my father if I try and I can fight better than most. Whatever happens from here on, we'll figure it out. I want you with or without the bond. Do you want me?"

She nodded before she even thought it through fully.

He crushed his mouth to hers, and she was lost.

His tongue tangled with hers, the sweet taste dancing on her tongue. He slid his hands down her sides, cupped her ass, and pulled her closer. His rock-hard erection pressed against her belly, and she gasped into his mouth.

Holy crap, this was really happening.

He backed her against the wall, his mouth never leaving hers. She could feel the wolf within him reaching out to her, and she shuddered. It was odd, considering she couldn't even feel her own wolf, but that rough, darker energy that came from his wolf, beneath the man she cared for enveloped her like a quick lick of temptation. Yes, this man would be her mate—bond or no bond.

Her back against the wall, she arched against him, her nipples two hard points against his chest. He pulled back, letting his hands run down her sides, along her breasts, and down to her hips.

If she could have heard her wolf, she had a feeling it would be growling, nudging along her skin, wanting to touch, to taste, to *know* her mate like Lexi was doing.

"I'm going to taste you, all of you, then I'm going to fuck you hard against the wall, my Lexi."

She swallowed hard then nodded. That sounded like a great plan to her.

"Then I'm going to bring you to bed and make love to you there," he growled, his eyes glowing gold with need despite the sweetness of his words.

She nodded, needing, wanting.

He kissed her then, his tongue tracing her lips. She opened for him, wanting it harder, knowing he needed it harder too. He kept at the leisurely pace though, as if he didn't have a care in the world, as if he was going slowly for her rather than fast and hard like they both needed. Maybe he couldn't tell that she wanted it hard, wanted it hot and fast.

She would just have to make sure he got the picture.

She pressed herself against him, trying to make him go faster, but he moved quickly then, trapping her arms above her head. The action made her breasts press against his chest, and she moaned.

Yes, just like that.

"North, I need you, now."

"I'm going slow, my Lexi. You need to be cherished. Loved."

She blinked back the moisture in her eyes. "I'm not fragile, North. I know..." She swallowed hard. "I know why you're doing this, but he doesn't matter. He isn't here. You are. I am. Please don't let him come between us. It's you and me, North. Take me like you want to. You know I want it, too." She arched against him. "Please."

She knew she was begging, but she didn't care. She wanted this man, her North, and she knew he wanted her too. Holding himself back wasn't helping anyone. It was only putting a barrier between them they hadn't known existed.

"Please," she whispered.

North swallowed hard, and her gaze followed the long line of his neck before moving to his eyes. They grew darker, and he nodded.

"Done," he growled.

He kept one hand on her wrists, keeping her pinned, then ripped—*ripped*—her shirt off. She was wearing only a tank to begin with, so it fell easily, but still...

Dear. Lord.

She shivered, aching for this man, this wolf.

She hadn't been wearing a bra, so her breasts fell heavy, wanting. North licked his lips, and she panted, her chest heaving. He lowered his head and latched onto a nipple, sucking it between his lips and lapping it with his tongue. The sensation shot straight to her pussy, and she rubbed her legs together, needing release.

North growled, the sensation gliding over her skin, causing her inner walls to clench.

"No moving," he grunted and used his free hand to grip her hip, keeping her in place. He kissed around her breast then the valley between them before moving to her other nipple where he licked, sucked, and laved her. She felt her panties getting damp just from his attention to her breasts, and she squirmed.

"I love your tits, Lex. I'm going to fuck them and your mouth at the same time soon. Oh yes, my cock sliding between these pretty things? A-fucking-mazing." He moved his hand from her hip and cupped her breast. "You're beautiful, Lexi. I'm not just saying that. And, yeah, I know beautiful is such a contrived word nowadays, but I don't care. I love the way you look, the way you move, the way you breathe. Got me?"

She nodded, wanting him inside her.

Now.

"Soon I'm going to put you in something that makes these plump tits of yours even sexier, maybe a corset. Then, I will bend you over while you're wearing it and fuck you hard. What do you say about that?"

She nodded.

Okay, he was really good with the dirty talk.

Really. Freaking. Good.

Since his hand wasn't on her hip anymore, she moved so she could press against his cock. He growled and spun her around so her chest was flat along the wall, his cock on her ass.

"What did I say about moving, my Lexi?"

She swallowed hard, needing him like this, hard, demanding. Lexi craved his control, knowing when he took over, she'd feel safe, protected, and cared for. She wanted, no—*needed*—to surrender to him.

"I'm sorry?"

North chuckled, the rough sound washing over her. His hand smacked against her ass, and she let out a squeal.

"You're not sorry, but it's okay. I know you want me inside you, and I will be. Soon." He spanked her again then rubbed the sting. She was wearing jeans, so it didn't hurt as much as it would have if she'd been completely naked.

Maybe next time...

He spun her around again and let go of her hands to kneel before her. He looked up at her, his eyes filled with need and a grin on his face. She reached down and tangled her fingers in his hair, unable to help herself. He smiled big then undid her jeans. She sucked in a breath as he stripped her pants and panties off slowly, the anticipation heady.

"Spread your legs," he ordered, and she did so quickly.

He let his hands run along her thighs, and then he was there, his thumb on her clit, his face between her legs. He licked, nibbled, and sucked along her lower lips and clit, her inner walls slick, ready for him.

"North," she panted. "Please!"

He growled against her clit, the low rumbling shooting straight through her. She came hard, her inner walls tightening on the tip of his tongue. He licked and sucked her as she came down from her high. Finally he stood, and she watched him undress for her in a hungry haze. She wanted more, but she wasn't sure she could voice it. Her body was too full and yet empty without him.

She licked her lips as her gaze raked over the long, lean lines of his body. He wasn't as bulky as most of his brothers, but he was muscled and damn sexy. He had a scattering of blond chest hair and that little happy trail below his belly button that went right to his cock.

Oh, sweetness.

He was long, not too thick, and curved slightly so he bobbed against his belly as he bent over her. His hands slid up her sides then one went around her neck, softly but still in control. Her eyes widened, and then she relaxed, knowing what was coming.

"Ready, my Lexi?"

"Always."

He moved quickly, cupping her ass with his large hands, and she immediately wrapped her legs around his waist. Slowly, oh so slowly, he entered her, their eyes never leaving each other.

He pulled out then let out a breath, slamming back into her. He gripped her tighter and pumped into her, their breath coming in pants. She arched her back, taking him deeper. One hand moved from her ass to flick her clit, and she came again, but this time around his cock. She screamed his name then kissed him before leaning back against the wall as he continued to fuck her.

She swallowed hard, knowing that no matter how precious this was, no matter how hard he gave it, there wouldn't be a bond. The tears she'd tried to hold back fell down her cheeks, and North leaned over to kiss them away. As he moved back, the tears on his own cheeks just about broke her.

Gods, they wanted their bond.

The deserved it.

But it wasn't for them.

At least not yet.

He flexed his hips again, this time shouting her name as he came within her. She sucked in a breath, loving the way he felt. Without leaving her, he pulled her closer then walked them to the bedroom.

Before she could blink, she was flat on the bed, and he was over her, still pumping into her, still hard because he was a wolf and could last longer than a human. He cupped her face, and she slid her hands down his back, bringing him closer.

This time when they came, it was together, beautiful yet bittersweet.

Yes, she had her North, and he had his Lexi, but they weren't mates.

Not fully.

He kissed her hard and then softened it. She melted against him, needing him closer than she'd ever thought possible.

It didn't matter, she told herself. It didn't matter there was no bond. As long as she had North, she could make it.

She had to.

CHAPTER SIX

North was pretty sure the best way to wake up was wrapped around a woman, and that woman being Lexi just made it all that much better. The warm body currently snuggled into him made his wolf howl, and the man wanted to beg to bury himself even deeper.

"She's ours. No matter the cost. She's ours."

North silently agreed with his wolf, even though the dull ache of not completing the bond stayed with him. He had a feeling that ache would always stay with him.

At least until he killed Corbin.

His hand fisted in the sheet, and a soft growl escaped him. No, he shouldn't be thinking about that. Not now. Not when the woman he wanted to be with— the woman he *was* with—was so close, so his.

Her light lashes lay against her pale skin, beautiful, restful. Her blonde hair looked mussed— something he knew he was responsible for and liked. He brushed a strand away, careful not to move too fast and wake her up.

He liked her here, sleeping in his arms as if they didn't have a care in the world. Oh, he knew the overwhelming issues of their war and Pack would come soon, but right now, in this bed, all he wanted to do was pull her close, taste her skin, and then sink his already hard cock into her heat.

His dick twitched at the thought, and a small laugh escaped the woman in his arms.

"You're faking it," North whispered then nuzzled her neck, biting down slightly. Again, he ignored the pain that it wasn't a mate mark, that there might not be a chance for a mate mark ever. He had to take the happiness as it came and ignore the ache for now. "You've been awake, haven't you?"

Lexi turned in his arms and smiled. "I couldn't help it. You're so warm, and I love the way your hands move over me."

He grinned then captured her lips. "They could have roamed over you even more if you hadn't been feigning sleep, baby."

His hand brushed over the curve of her belly, stopping over her mound. She arched into him, and he smiled.

"I'm going to like waking up with you in my arms. I might just have to wake you up in the future by filling you up and rocking you awake."

Her brows rose, and she smiled. "That'd be one hell of a way to wake up, but I'm a light sleeper. Being a mom sort of took care of that for me."

North froze, a thought slamming into him that should have come to him before.

Wolves could only have children with their mates. Shit.

If he didn't kill Corbin—and he *would,* damn it— he'd never watch Lexi grow round with his child. He'd never hold their baby in his arms and watch it grow up. He'd already missed Parker's first words, first steps, first change...first everything.

Jesus.

Corbin had taken everything.

Lexi cupped his cheek, and he nuzzled into the touch. "Don't look so lost, North." Her words were hoarse, the pain woven so deep he could feel it as his own.

"I love you being in my bed, baby." His wolf nudged along his skin, wanting to be closer.

Lexi swallowed hard, the line of her throat slender. "I swear I could almost feel your wolf dance along my skin."

He frowned, and his wolf howled. "I told you he was close to the surface. I can control him, Lex. He would never hurt you."

She punched his arm. "Hey, did I say that? Did I say I was afraid of him? No. I was only sad that my wolf can't come out to play with him. He's got to be in pain. I *know* the two of you are more entwined than most, and I like it. It almost makes up for the fact that I can't hear mine."

"Fate's tricky like that."

"Yes, and she's a bitch too." North joined in her laughter and kissed her throat. "I have an idea, Lex."

"Does it involve you sliding between my legs and saying good morning?"

He licked along her neck and gently bit down. She shuddered, yielding. "That's the next idea." He pulled away so he could see her eyes. "I was actually thinking about your wolf."

Lexi frowned. "What about her?"

He ran a hand through her hair, trying to soothe. "I want to see if there's something I can do."

"North, I'm latent. There's nothing you *can* do."

"No, there's nothing that's been done. That's different. I've never heard of an adult latent wolf, Lexi. Not more than a whisper here or there. I'm a doctor."

"And you need to fix things," she finished for him, her tone dead.

He kissed her hard. "No. You aren't broken."

"I'm the definition of a broken wolf, North."

"Shut it. Don't put yourself down that way. I'm a doctor, meaning if I see someone in pain, I want to help. Okay? Let's see if there's anything to be done. If there isn't, then we'll continue on as we have."

"I don't even know if I can mark you as my mate if we get to that point."

That now-familiar pain arched over him, but he pushed it away. "We'll deal with that then."

She took a deep breath, her breasts pushing against his chest. "For you, I will."

He nuzzled her. "Thank you, my Lexi."

"You don't think we're moving too fast then?"

North held back a snort. "Hell, I waited on the sidelines for months while we tiptoed around each other. I'm not waiting anymore. If I had my way, you'd be in my bed in my house every night and we'd move Parker in the guest room and make it his own."

Her eyes filled with laughter, pushing away the sadness, at least for now. "That would be moving really fast. We haven't even told Parker about us."

"I think he has an idea, Lex." The kid was old for his years and extremely observant.

"Having an idea and having you in his life in a new way are two completely different things. We're going to have to be careful around him."

"I would never hurt that boy. I want him to be part of my family just as much as I want you to be part of it. It was never a question for me about whether I'd want to help you raise him. Not that I have any idea what I'm doing in that situation. You and Logan seem to be doing a great job on that front, but I want to help. I want to be there."

Tears filled her eyes, and she reached up to kiss him. He lowered his head and met her halfway. She melted against him, and his wolf howled.

"You're a good man, North Jamenson."

He moved so he was hovering over her, his cock right at her entrance. "I'm *your* man, Lexi Anderson." He couldn't wait until she was Lexi Jamenson, but that would be moving a little too fast.

The door opened behind them, and North froze. "Mom—oh."

North closed his eyes as Parker mumbled something about breakfast while Lexi shook beneath him.

Jesus. He was officially going to scar the kid, and the woman beneath him was probably quaking in fear. He looked down at her, only to find her laughing.

North moved so he was by her side, pulling the sheet up over both of them. It had already been around his waist, so technically Parker hadn't seen anything.

But still.

"Parker," Lexi said in her best mom-voice. "What did we talk about concerning knocking, honey?"

The kid looked down at his bare feet and shuffled. "That I need to knock so I give you some privacy since living with me and Uncle Logan takes away all your privacy on most days."

Despite the awkward situation, North bit his lip to hold back his laughter. Jesus, the kid was a hoot.

"If you can recite my whole speech back to me, Park, why are you in here without knocking?"

"I forgot?" Parker still hadn't faced them. Good, since North and Lexi were still naked in bed together.

Hell, this was fucking awkward.

"Go on out and pour yourself some cereal, Park. I'll be up in a minute. Okay?"

"Okay. Morning, North." The kid ran out, closing the door behind him, and North blinked.

"Well, shit," he mumbled.

"So much for being careful around him," Lexi whispered as she slid out of bed, taking the sheet with her.

North reached for his jeans and slid them on. "Have we scarred him for life? I mean, I know sex is a natural thing, but I don't think the best way to introduce me to him as someone more than just a friend is to find me between your legs in bed."

Lexi pulled a shirt over her head, the rest of her already dressed. "There's nothing we can do about it now. One thing being a mom has taught me is to roll with the punches. Honestly, North, Parker is a wolf. He scented you here when he walked through the door this morning and probably heard us mumbling." She blushed, and North walked around the bed to take her in his arms.

"Hey, we'll deal with this together, right?"

Lexi nodded, her head on his chest. "He was just testing the boundaries, something he'll have to do differently next time, or I won't be so calm. He's a little boy, but he's also old enough to know better. You're also the first man I've had in my bed since he's been born so..."

North growled softly. "I'm the last man who will be in your bed as well." He kissed her hard then moved back. "I'm going to give you some time with him this morning, and then we can eat together tonight. I want to be part of both of your lives. Logan can come too if he wants."

Lexi raised a brow. "Logan does what he wants to do, so we'll see. I'd love to have dinner with you and Parker tonight. He's hanging out with Cailin and Noah today by the way."

"Noah? Why is Cailin hanging with him?" His baby sister better stay away from all men. Even Logan.

Lexi snorted. "Your sister is a grown woman, and I don't think she and Noah are sleeping together. At least not anymore." She whispered that last part but from the slam of a cabinet in the kitchen, Logan had heard. "Crap."

"Cailin will be staying pure until she's a hundred. I'll have to watch this Noah." Once he got his brothers on the job, this Noah wouldn't be a problem. Who was this punk kid to think he could touch or even *think* about touching his little sister?

"Oh, honey, you're so cute to think that your sister, who is in her twenties by the way, is still all sweet and innocent. I won't burst your bubble though. As for why she's taking Parker today, well, she asked. Logan and I have to go to your mother's to work on something with Mel. I'm not sure what, but when the Alpha and Heir's mates tell us to jump, we jump."

His thoughts still on the fact he would have to kill this Noah for putting his hands on North's innocent baby sister, he almost missed the last part of Lexi's statement.

"You don't have to jump, Lex."

She raised a brow. "Uh, yeah, I do. They're the dominants in this game. They know this. I know this. It's okay, North. They never ask us to do things we don't want to do, but they wanted us over to help them with something, so we're doing it. Even if it wasn't an exact order, we're still going to do it. We owe them."

He slid his hand through her hair, pulling slightly so she was forced to meet his gaze. She let out a little gasp, and he held back a smile at that beyond-sexy sound. "You owe them nothing, but do what you'd like, Lex. I know you feel like you owe them, so do what you must. As for Cailin, I'm going to have to watch her. I don't want any wolves messing with my baby sister."

Lexi rolled her eyes. "She's watching my son today because she wants to get to know him. In this weird way, she might be his aunt."

He warmed. "Because you're mine."

She smiled. "I meant because of her and my brother, but yes, because I'm yours." She swallowed hard. "At least as much of me as I'm able to give."

He kissed her hard. "I'll take it all and give you more."

Her smile went wobbly, and then she shook her head quickly as if to clear it. "Go play doctor, North, and leave your sister alone. I will see you for dinner. Okay? I'm going to talk to Parker before he goes with Cailin and Noah first though. I want to make sure he's good to go for the day and talk about what happened this morning."

"And make sure he's not scarred for life? Because walking in on me about to fill you is an image no kid should see."

Lexi raised a brow. "We were covered, so he didn't actually *see* anything. And, yes, I will talk to him and see what he's thinking." She reached around and smacked his ass. "Now go."

He took her lips again then left the house. He could hear Logan and Parker in the kitchen talking but didn't stop to say goodbye. No, he wasn't sneaking out of the house—as wolves, the other two could hear him—but he had a feeling everyone needed a moment to breathe.

He and Lexi had taken a huge step the night before, and it would take time for everyone to get used to it. One thing North would not be doing though would be to move back and let others rule his life. He was going to take all he could and find a way to make their non-mating mating work.

However the hell that could work.

"Looks like you've found your mate," Patrick said as North made his way toward his house.

North stopped and looked around, confused as to why Patrick was around the Jamenson area, considering his place was on the other side of the den.

"What are you doing here?" He didn't like the fact that Patrick seemed to be everywhere recently, and he sure as fuck wasn't happy that the wolf knew where he'd been the night before.

It wasn't as if North was ashamed of being with Lexi, far from it, but some things were meant to be private. Sleeping with one's mate for the first time was right at the top of that list.

"Out for a jog with Jeffery," Patrick raised his chin at the other wolf as he came out of the trees.

North frowned between the two men. They both wore running clothes and seemed to be doing what Patrick had said, but it still didn't sit right with him.

"Is there something you need?" North asked.

"Just wanted to say congratulations." Patrick frowned at North's shoulder, and North glared. "I don't see a mark though. Taking it slow?"

"Mating is a private thing, Patrick. Keep your thoughts to yourself. If we're done here, I need to head home to shower."

Patrick just smiled. "Sure thing, Jamenson. Have a good day." He and Jeffery loped away, leaving North with an uneasy feeling washing over him.

Something was going on with that wolf, but North didn't know what—at least not yet.

Annoyed at this thought, he slammed into his house then cursed. Maddox and Jasper sat on his couch, their brows raised.

"What the hell are you two doing here? Does this look like a community center? No. This is my home. The clinic is attached to the side, but that doesn't mean you can just walk in whenever you please."

He left them before they could answer and stripped off his clothes. He jumped in the shower, anger at Corbin, whatever the fuck Patrick was up to, and frustration radiating off him.

He had too much going on in his mind to think straight. Patrick was acting odd, Corbin was being way too fucking quiet, and fate had kicked him in the balls. He and his wolf wanted to act, to fight, but other than running headfirst into a situation they didn't understand and getting themselves killed, North wasn't sure what to do.

He cleaned himself off quickly then turned off the water. He pulled back the curtain, only to curse again.

Maddox stood with a towel in his hand and a frown on his face. A face that, but for the scar marring it—thanks to an up-close-and-personal attack from Corbin himself—looked exactly like North's.

"You done being an asshole and throwing your temper tantrum?"

North grabbed the towel and dried off. "Is there a reason you're in my house?"

Jasper, who stood in the doorway with his arms crossed over his chest, and blinked. "Mom and Dad told the rest of us about Corbin. Kade had wanted to tie you down last night so you didn't run off halfcocked and get yourself killed trying to protect Lexi."

"I'm not a fucking idiot." He stormed past them. Sure, the thought had come to his mind, but he needed to make plans before he went after Corbin. He wouldn't go without thinking it over first.

Oh, he'd be going to Corbin personally, but not until he got the lay of the land.

Not that his brothers needed to know that last part.

"He never said you were," Maddox said smoothly as North pulled on his clothes in jerky motions. "But that doesn't mean the thought didn't cross your mind."

"Of course it crossed my mind. That bastard fucking raped my mate, Maddox." His voice broke on the end of the sentence, and he had to pause to collect himself.

Maddox narrowed his eyes, his eyes glowing gold. "Yes, North, I happen to know exactly what you're talking about. Keep it in check."

North closed his eyes, and bile filled his throat. Fuck, he hadn't meant to sound so callous. Ellie had been kept prisoner by Corbin for most of her life and had been raped by the bastard's friends. She was healing now, but he knew it would be a long path until the broken remains of her spirit were finally put back together again, even if they never healed fully.

"I can't feel her like I should, Mad. I can't bond with her like I should. I don't have the connection you have with Ellie, that Jasper has with Willow. I just have my wolf aching for his mate and a woman I can have beneath me, beside me, and with me, but no bond. That bastard wolf has taken everything from us, Mad. Everything."

He sank onto his bed and let his face fall into his hands, his body shaking. The bed dipped beside him as Jasper pulled him into a hug.

"You're right. Corbin's used a deal with the devil himself to take everything from our Pack, or at least he's tried to. You know the prophecy says you will kill him, and we have to believe in that."

"The prophecy didn't say that you'd live through the process though," Maddox whispered, and North leaned back, his eyes closed.

"I know. We keep ignoring that subtle fact. But if I can break Lexi and the Pack free from him, isn't it worth it?"

"I'm not going to comment on your death wish, brother, but I still don't know how you're going to accomplish killing him when he's so ensconced within his den beneath the dark magic wards. We can't break in."

North rubbed his face. "I have no fucking idea what to do. We're at a standstill because we have no way to win. This defeated feeling makes me want to scream. The Centrals are winning because they are killing themselves in the process. We're not them."

Jasper let out a curse. "Of course we aren't them. It's been the same thing over and over again, hasn't it? We fight, and we win a battle, and they come back and kill us because they can cross the boundaries we can't. We've taken away their connection to hell, taken away their Alpha, and have hurt Corbin and Caym greatly. But is it enough? Fuck no."

"It's never enough," Maddox mumbled.

"And while all of this is going on, we're rotting from the inside," North added.

Jasper turned sharply. "I know. Fuck. We're letting our Pack down because we have to focus on the perimeter and the outside forces. But what about what

I'm doing, huh? I'm the fucking Beta, and I can't help all of them. I don't know what to do, North."

"You're doing all you can. You're trying to help them all, but you can't do everything."

"There are rumblings," Maddox said, his voice a growl.

"I know. Something is happening, and I don't know what," Jasper said.

"We're going to have to find out who is hurting our Pack from within and make sure that our family is safe."

"And that includes the Andersons," Maddox added, speaking of Lexi, Parker, and Logan.

"They're mine," North whispered. "I don't want them to feel like they aren't part of the Pack, but something is going on. Something I can feel, but I don't know what it is exactly."

"I know. We'll just have to be careful." Jasper stood and ran his hands through his hair.

"We're always careful," North mumbled. "That's all we do."

"We'll have to do better," Maddox said.

Yes, better. That's all they could do, but for some reason, North had a feeling it wouldn't be enough.

Not this time.

CHAPTER SEVEN

Her hands were shaking.

Lexi fisted them then closed her eyes. She had to do better than this. She wasn't going to die. At least she hoped not,.

She'd promised North she'd go to his clinic and have him check her over. Rather than getting naked and sweaty with the man she knew she was falling in love with—a whole other topic she would think about later—she was going to get naked and clinical.

So not even in the realm of the same thing.

North wanted to help her with her latent wolf. She knew his heart was in the right place, but she couldn't put any hope in the situation. He was a doctor and a Jamenson, meaning if he found something broken, he needed to fix it.

Oh, he'd said she wasn't broken, but they both knew that she was, even if he wanted to call it something else.

He wanted to find her wolf.

Damn it, so did she.

Finding it might kill her though.

She *knew* that.

There were very rare occurrences of latent wolves for as long as there had been werewolves. Almost as soon as latent wolves were discovered, attempts had been made to study them. These studies were made more difficult because most latent wolves didn't make it past puberty. Those who were lucky enough to survive puberty almost always died as young adults, victims of the added adrenalin, hormones and changes to an already fucked up central nervous system.

She had no idea how she'd lived through it, other than the fact she hadn't wanted to die.

Logan called her the most stubborn person he knew.

He wouldn't be wrong—though her brother gave her a run for her money.

The fact that she had lived made her an exception to the rule. As far as she knew, she was the oldest living latent. At fifty, that was saying something. She'd also had a pure werewolf child who could shift and was a dominant.

She was living on borrowed time, and it wasn't a secret.

If North could find a way to help her so she could actually have a future, not only with him, but in general, she'd take it.

She'd made it to the porch of the clinic when North opened the door. He stood there, wearing jeans that rode low on his hips and a button-down shirt that made him look sexy—though he looked sexy wearing just about anything—or nothing at all.

His hair curled slightly on his neck as if he'd had a long day and had run his hands through it repeatedly. He leaned against the door jamb, his arms folded over his chest.

"You ready for this, baby?"

"No," she answered honestly.

He straightened immediately and walked toward her. He gripped her chin and forced her gaze to his. A simple touch made her relax and tighten like a coiled spring at the same time. Having him close made her feel safe, but the anticipation of what his touch meant made her want to brace for the pounce.

"If you want to stop this and never look at it again, I'll do that for you, Lex. You know I'd do anything for you."

Yes, he would. He'd back down and step away for her. He was already subjecting himself to a life where he would never have children, never feel the pull of a mate bond...never fully reach the true nirvana of mating.

He'd do this all for her.

The least she could do was try to live longer and find her wolf. Maybe if she had her wolf, she'd be stronger. If she was stronger, maybe she could help fight and bring down the Centrals. Yes, her mind worked in mysterious ways, but she'd do anything for North.

Anything.

"I'm just freaking myself out. It's just a physical, North. I'm fine."

He kept his grip on her chin but used his other hand to brush her hair behind her ear. "If you're sure."

"I'm sure. Let's get going."

He nodded then moved to hold her hand, leading her into the clinic. It was a three-room place, complete with waiting area. His house seemed small in comparison to the attached clinic, but it suited North. She knew he loved helping people and having his work area so close would help not only him but his wolf.

The place also didn't smell like a normal clinic or hospital. Sure, there was that underlying scent of antiseptic that came with a place of healing, but it didn't feel sterile or hollow. She could scent North around the place, as well as other Pack members and Jamensons. It felt like a part of his home, rather than a place she should be afraid of.

Not that she was holding back all the fear today.

Once they were in the exam room, he stepped away from her, his doctor mode firmly in place.

"Strip down and put on that robe."

She raised a brow but didn't object or tease him. She could tell he wanted to keep the exam professional. Not only would it help her with her nerves, but it wouldn't cross that imaginary line she knew North had with patients. Though in reality, he already had crossed that line since he treated family and friends. He was the only doctor though and even though Hannah was the Healer, she was family too.

He turned his back and did something with a chart so she stripped down quickly. Getting naked for a physical seemed very different than getting naked for him in her bedroom.

Thank God.

She really didn't want to think about how many women must have gotten naked for him in the past.

She closed her eyes.

Nope. Not going to think about that.

His movements were swift and clinical. They talked about Parker and what she was feeling, but he seemed detached, as if he didn't want to get too close and show his emotions while he was working. She was fine with that considering she was freaking out that he wouldn't find a way to help her and she'd die in pain because she couldn't find a way to let lose all the energy building and locked within her.

Okay, so maybe she held out a little hope that he could save her.

Shit. That wasn't good.

When he was done, she dressed quickly then sat back down on the table, crossing her legs in front of her in yoga style.

"So..."

He moved closer and sat down on the stool in front of her. "Your body is definitely different."

"Just what every girl wants to hear," she said dryly.

He grinned at her, and she relaxed. That was the North she knew and was falling for. "You're cute. Once we leave this room, I will tell you exactly what I feel about your body. As for what I found, I'm going to talk with Hannah about it, too. Is that okay?"

"She's our Healer, so sure."

He grinned again, a little light entering his eyes to clear out the darkness. "I love that you said *our*."

She tilted her head. "I'm a Redwood now. It's a little strange getting used to, but I'm trying."

"Good. I'm glad you are. Okay, as for what I found, right now, I have the facts but I need to put them together to make sense of them. Your blood pressure and heart rate are slightly elevated. I don't think that's because of the exam itself, but more because your body is under chronic stress. Your eyes are dilated a little more than most people's. That could be because you were scared about what we were doing today, but I don't think so. I've noticed in the past your pupils slightly larger than other's, but I never picked up on it like I should. I think the excess hormones and adrenaline in your system might cause this. I'm not sure yet."

"Is that bad?"

"The dilation? I don't think so. You don't have eye strain, do you?"

She thought about it. "No, not really. Only if I read too long, but that's normal."

"That's what I'm thinking. The excess chemicals in your body though might be an issue. When we shift, we use up that excess adrenaline and power. That's why, though it's a painful process, it's a relief too. You have all those extra chemicals in your body with no way to relieve them. Well, at least not like you would when you shift." He grinned broader this time. "We could find another way to relieve that tension."

She snorted, her muscles relaxing like he'd meant them too. "Shut it, you."

"Just saying, Lex."

"Tell me what else you found and maybe we can talk about how to relieve tension."

"What I'm looking at more though is your elevated heart rate."

She sighed. "That's the symptom that really sucks."

He cupped her face, and she leaned into his hold. Damn the restrictions they'd put between them while they were in this room. She needed to be held.

"Your body is taxing itself, baby. I'm not sure how you are controlling it to the point you're not always tired, but you need to relax."

"I'm *trying*."

"I know, baby. Your reflexes and strength are just as good as someone who can shift though. That's good."

"It's helped."

He pulled away, and she felt the loss of his touch. "I'm going to try one more thing."

She nodded.

He reached around her shoulders and pinched her pressure point on her shoulder. The arcing pain slicing through her body made her feel as though she was on fire. She screamed and pulled away from him, tears running down her face.

"Shit, baby." He pulled her into his arms, and she tried to get away, the pain still rocking her body as though someone had electrocuted her.

"Fuck, Lexi, I'm sorry. I didn't know it would hurt that bad."

She finally stopped wanting to throw up then leaned into his touch. "What...what was that?"

"Everyone has a few pressure points. Usually when I do that it's like a little knee jerk reaction or even a calming one if your body is in tune with itself. But since you have all that excess pressure..."

"I freaked the fuck out."

He nodded then kissed her forehead.

"Shit. That's not good, North. It's another weakness."

"One we're not going to tell anybody about," he growled, and she nodded.

She knew better than to advertise her weakness. As it was, others thought she was a submissive wolf because she couldn't shift. Oh, she knew she wasn't as high ranking as others within the hierarchy of the Pack, within *any* Pack, but she wasn't submissive.

Well, she was submissive to North in bed, but that was a whole other topic.

"There's one more thing." His voice rumbled against her cheek, and she sucked in a breath, his scent washing over her, calming her.

"What is it?"

"I don't have magic, not like Hannah, but I can use the fact I'm so in tune with my wolf to help me with my diagnostics." She must have given him a blank stare because he continued. "I can sense things when I'm really trying that others miss because they can't feel their wolves as much as I can. Baby, my wolf can feel your wolf. Do you know what that means?"

She froze.

"That means your wolf is there, baby. She's *there*."

Tears filled her eyes. "I know she is, but I don't know what she wants. What she needs."

He swallowed hard. "She's in agony. I got a huge dose of that when I pressed that point on your shoulder. Baby, we're going to figure out a way to get her out. Not only for her but for you. I hate that you can't feel your wolf like you should. We will fix this."

"We have to," she whispered.

"Let me take you to my place tonight, okay?" North asked as he rubbed a hand up and down her back. "I just want to be with you."

She smiled against him, surprised she could even do that. "Logan already knows he's taking care of Parker tonight. Plus...I have a surprise for you at your house. I...uh...kind of broke in earlier to leave my things."

North moved her so he could look her in the face then threw his head back and laughed. "You don't have to break in, Lex. What's mine is yours. But you leaving things at my place with that little devious look on your face? That is one awesome surprise, baby."

"That's not the surprise," she whispered.

His eyes glowed gold. "Well then, let's go see what you have in store for me."

She grinned. "I hope you'll like it."

"I can scent your arousal, my Lexi. I have a feeling I'm going to fucking *love* your surprise."

"It's your surprise, North."

He pulled her to her feet then out of the exam room. Before she could blink, he had her pressed against the wall, his mouth crushing hers. His hands gripped her ass, pulling her up. Her legs wrapped around his waist, and she kissed him back, his tongue tangling with hers.

He wrenched his mouth away, leaving them both panting. "I wasn't expecting to kiss you like this here. I was going to smooth into it and seduce you."

She licked her lips, and his gaze followed the movement. "Let's get to your place, and you can seduce me."

She was going to lock away the fear and anger that came from what they didn't know. Oh, it would always be there. She would worry about the fact that her body was killing itself and the war that raged around them, but not right then. Now she needed to be with the man who should be her mate and remember that there were many worthwhile things out there.

Then, only then, would she plan her life with this man, her son, and everyone else.

She'd fight for them and maybe even die for them.

First, though, she would live for them.

CHAPTER EIGHT

North stood in his living room, his hands in his pockets as he tried to remain patient. He'd already tried to be the patient one in his family, the one who stood back but was always there when they needed him. He'd tried to be the one who stood back and kept from meddling when necessary and facilitated the necessary steps that would lead his siblings to their happy endings.

Now he was getting his own happy ending.

At least his version of it.

He swallowed hard and tried to think about what surprise Lexi could have for him, but his mind kept going to the paleness of her skin and the scream that had gone straight to his bones when he'd touched her.

He'd known it would be difficult to exam her, look at her as though she was a patient and him merely her doctor, but it had been even tougher than he'd expected. Though he'd kept his face carefully blank in that exam room, with each poke, prod, and scan, he'd forced himself to keep the wolf—and the man—at bay.

Lexi had been in pain, *was* in pain, yet she'd taken it in stride.

Frankly, she'd done better than he had. He'd practically crawled out of his skin trying to calm and soothe her, though he knew she wouldn't have wanted that.

His mate might have melted in his arms in bed, but she was strong and steadfast when it came to anything else. He'd never really thought about who his mate would be beyond the idea of her. He'd never pictured her with blonde hair, curves that fit his hands, and a personality that not only proved she was a fierce momma wolf but was fragile beneath the tough exterior.

No, fragile wasn't the right word.

She'd fight to the end and never give up.

His wolf just wanted to care for her as if she was fragile, knowing she could take care of herself too.

She was the perfect woman for him, and he was damned lucky he'd found her.

He just didn't want to lose her.

North scented the sweet sugar and peaches before he heard her enter the room. One look at Lexi and all thoughts of loss, war, and her wolf fled his mind.

Sweet moon goddess.

He was one fucking lucky man.

"What do you think?" she whispered, her voice low, unsure. "You like your surprise?"

North couldn't quite form a response as most of his blood had gone farther south.

Lexi stood in the doorway wearing a black lace-up corset with little pink bows on the side that he wanted to untie with his teeth. The corset was so tight that her breasts almost spilled out. He could just see the pink of her nipples every time she took a breath.

The action alone made him shift in his jeans, his cock pushing against the zipper.

The little pink bows were tied to a garter belt and stockings that had little skulls etched into them. Totally fucking hot. The black pumps she wore had little lifts on the bottom of the soles making her legs look even longer and sexier than they did on a normal day.

Considering he loved Lexi's legs, that was saying something.

One thing she was missing though was panties. Shit.

She was completely bare for him except for that little trimmed patch of hair. He swallowed hard, taking her in.

His gaze raked over her again and met hers. Her long blonde hair cascaded around her face, slightly curled as if she'd done it quickly while she'd been getting ready for him. He couldn't wait to wrap it around his fist as he fucked her...or let it trail across his body as she leaned over him as he fucked her from beneath.

She bit her lip, uncertainty filling those hazel eyes he loved so much.

He swallowed hard, not knowing where to start. What to say.

"How the hell did you get that corset to fit you just right?"

"Oh good, that was a great way to tell her you want her," his wolf teased.

His could just shut up.

Lexi blinked then licked the spot she'd bitten on her lip. "Bay helped. She knows her way around them."

North closed his eyes, trying to burn out images of his brother, Adam, and Bay exploring the uses of said corset.

"Never mind," he grumbled. "Jesus, baby, you look fucking amazing."

She grinned at him, her eyes lighting. "Really?" She turned for him, and he about lost it. "I wasn't sure if I should wear panties or not since you hadn't mentioned them when you were fucking me against the wall, so I went without. You know, easy access."

North closed his eyes, begging for control. It wasn't easy with his mate in front of him looking like a siren beckoning him closer.

"Turn around for me again, but slowly," he ground out, his wolf coming to the surface.

She grinned that little grin of hers then did as she was told. She turned on one foot then looked over her shoulder like some kind of pinup.

"Stay there," he growled when her body faced the wall.

He stalked toward her but stopped just short so he couldn't touch, only tease. The heels had made her ass high and pert—well, more than it usually was—and he couldn't wait to squeeze, lick, and fuck.

He closed his eyes again.

No, he wouldn't act like an animal, but he wouldn't go soft either.

Not tonight. Not with his Lexi.

"Why did you wear this, Lexi?" he asked, his voice low.

She swallowed then blinked. "Because you wanted me to. I thought you'd like it."

He let one hand go to her waist, holding her still, and then licked her lips. He pulled back when she moaned for more. "I fucking love it."

"What...what are you going to do about it?" she asked on a breath.

"Everything," he said then grinned when her eyes widened.

He turned her around again then walked her back to the wall next to the doorway she'd come through, careful since she was in her fuck-me pumps. Oh, he'd make sure those heels lived up to their name and then some.

"You look amazing, Lexi."

"I'm glad you like it."

"I like when you're wearing ratty jeans and a tank after working all day with the enforcers, I like when you're wearing a towel after you just got out of the shower, I like when you're wearing a nice dress when you go to dinner at my parents', and I like when you're wearing a corset because I said I wanted to see you in one. I just like you, Lexi. I like everything you wear because I like you."

"So I didn't have to wear this thing? Because it's kind of hard to bend over without leaning on something."

He grinned, letting a little growl come out. "Oh, baby, I fucking *love* you in this thing, and we're going to have a lot of fun with you wearing it. And as for bending over? Oh, I'm going to fuck you hard bent over while you're wearing it, so we're just going to have to make sure you're leaning on something." He looked over his shoulder. "Hmm, how about the couch? Can you walk over there in those shoes, or should I carry you?"

She let out a shaky laugh, but he could scent her arousal flare. "I can make it to the couch, but that's about it. I'm not really a heel kind of girl."

He traced her cheek with his finger, and she leaned into the touch. "You're anything you want to be, Lexi. Remember that."

She gave a sad little smile. "Whatever you say, North."

He reached around and slapped her ass. She made a little sound on a breath, her eyes darkening. "Don't placate me, Lex. Now walk to the couch, slowly. I want to watch that ass."

"Then what do you want me to do? Bend over?"

He thought about it then shook his head. "No, sit on the arm if you can."

She frowned then widened her eyes as if getting his meaning.

"I can do that."

She walked carefully to the couch, swaying on the heels so her hips moved from side to side. North's gaze trailed over her back and her ass, watching the way the globes moved with each step.

Hell, his mate was hot, and she didn't know it. Not enough. He'd make sure she understood though.

He stripped off his shirt as he walked to her then toed off his shoes and socks. Her eyes never left him just as his never left hers. When he reached her, he stood between her spread legs and took her chin between two fingers.

"Can you breathe sitting like that?"

She nodded then licked her lips.

The couch was low enough and he was just tall enough that she was the perfect height for what he had in mind. He pulled his hand away, undid the button on his jeans, and then slowly unzipped the zipper.

He hadn't bothered to put on underwear that morning since he'd shifted for a run, and as soon as he unzipped, his cock sprang out, ready for his mate's lips.

"Ready?" he asked.

In answer, she licked the crown of his cock, and he groaned. Just that little touch almost had him going. If he didn't hold back and rein it in, he was going to come right away, and he didn't want that to happen.

He twisted her hair around his fist like he'd wanted to the first time he'd seen it then flexed his hips. Her mouth opened, and he slid in.

"Hell, your mouth is perfect, Lex."

She hummed in response then sucked him down to the back of her throat on the first shot. He held her there for a moment before pulling her back. Her cheeks hollowed as his dick slid from her mouth. Before he could take control, however, she'd swallowed him down again then bobbed her head, gaining a rhythm that made his balls tighten. Her hands went to his ass and massaged, pressing, spreading. He felt her fingers dance to the crease, and he pulled her back.

"You do that right now, and I'll blow. I don't want to come down your throat tonight, not when I want to come in you. Okay?"

She gave a wicked little grin then nodded, letting his cock go with a pop. "Whatever you say, North. I trust you."

His heart warmed, even as his dick throbbed. He took a step back, stripped out of his jeans fully, then pulled her to her feet. "Ready?"

"Always."

He grabbed the back of her head and brought her lips to his in a hungry kiss. Their teeth collided at the roughness, and their tongues fought for dominance. His little wolf was feisty tonight, and he loved it.

When they pulled away, they were both breathless and beyond ready. Lexi turned, took two steps to the back of the couch, and then bent over. She looked over her shoulder and grinned.

"Okay, Doctor. You're up."

North threw his head back and laughed. "Hell, woman, only you can make me laugh by playing naughty nurse or patient or whatever you are right now after what we just did and what we're about to do."

"Shut up and fuck me. Okay?"

He shook his head and smiled then gripped her hips. She opened her mouth to speak again, and he slammed into her in one stroke. He held there when they both gasped. She was so fucking tight around his cock he could barely think.

Once they were both able to breathe, he slid out then pumped at a steady pace that had Lexi bucking against him and sweat rolling down his back. He leaned over and kissed her shoulder, nibbling at her neck and the spot he so desperately wanted to mark but knew he wouldn't—not until he could do it in truth.

The darkness at that thought pulled at him, and he moved, twisting Lexi and lifting her so she was sitting on the edge of the couch.

"North," she panted as he pumped into her. She wrapped her legs around his waist, her heels digging into him, but he didn't care.

"I needed to see your eyes. Needed to see you," he grunted, his pace never slowing.

She framed his face with her hands and kissed him. He leaned into her, tasted her, and came at the same time as her, his Lexi.

His everything.

They broke apart, sweat-slick, aching, and in tune with one another.

"Loved the corset, baby," he rasped out.

She smiled and kissed him again, shifting slightly on his cock. "I know."

"Best surprise ever."

CHAPTER NINE

"So, tell us all about North," Hannah said as she sat down next to Lexi on her own stool. They were in Hannah's greenhouse the morning after she'd totally rocked North's world. Lexi smiled at just *how* she'd done that and how he'd reciprocated.

"Oh! I know that look," Melanie said as she sat down on the stool opposite of them. "She totally got some."

Lexi felt her cheeks heat up and cleared her throat. "So, uh, we're here to grind plants, right?"

Hannah nudged her with her shoulder. "Oh no you don't. This is the sacred ritual of women bonding here. We want to know all about North and how he put that look on your face. Well, not all about him."

Thank God.

"We'll wait for the really juicy details for when Willow, Ellie, and Bay are with us. I'd say Cailin too, but since North is her bother that might be a little awkward."

"Just a little," Melanie agreed, a devious grin on her face.

Lexi hadn't had real girlfriends for almost a decade. Even within the Talons she hung out with Logan and his friends. Sure, she was friends with the Talon princess, Brynn, but it had been a long while since she'd had a chance to dish with the girls.

"Um...it's good?"

Hannah threw up hands. "Oh please, you're so talkative. It's like I can see every detail in my mind." She narrowed her eyes. "Now give us the deets, woman. We all know North has to have some secrets in bed. He's all dark and swoony."

Melanie laughed. "Geez, woman. You have two men for yourself, and you want the dirty details on North? Are you looking for another for your harem?"

Hannah threw a plastic baggie filled with seeds at her sister-in-law. "Shush, you. I'm very, *very* happy with my men." She grinned. "Oh, yes, mated to a wolf and a partial demon? Best. Ever. But we're not here to talk about my tremendously amazing sex life. And it is that. Tremendously amazing. We're here to talk about Lexi's sex life. She's a Jamenson now. She has to share."

"I didn't know that was part of the code," Mel said wryly.

Lexi swallowed hard, that slight pain that had always been there arching.

"Hey, I didn't mean to make you cry," Hannah whispered. She wrapped her arm around Lexi's shoulders and brought her in for a hug. Mel hopped off the stool and came to Lexi's other side to hug her as well. "What is it, honey? I can back off. We're just so happy North's found someone and now we have another woman in our club."

Lexi pulled away to wipe away the tears she hadn't known had fallen. "I'm sorry. I guess I'm just a little emotional."

Melanie moved so she was in front of Lexi. "Tell us what's wrong. It's not about us prying, is it?"

Lexi let out a breath. "I'm not a Jamenson."

Hannah tilted her head. "Well, no, not technically. But you and North are mates. You're an unofficial Jamenson until we party and make it legal. You're part of us."

Melanie frowned. "You know we don't care about who Parker's father is, don't you? I mean, we care in the sense we want to gut that motherfucker for you, but Parker is innocent in all of this. *You're* innocent in all of this."

Well then.

It looked like the cat was out of the bag.

Oh, Lexi had known the Jamensons had been filled in on her past, but it was a whole other thing to have it out in the open like this. She'd never talked about it, not really. She'd told North, and that was it. She and Logan had always tiptoed around the actual topic of conversation.

It was too hard to deal with otherwise.

Lexi let out a shaky breath. "I might not ever be fully mated to North. You understand that, don't you?"

Mel nodded. "I know that you might not be able to fully bond with North. We all know that. We also all know that Corbin will die. There's no other outcome for him and not just because of this situation. No, he's deserved to die for a long time now and has used pain and dark magic to keep living. We're in a standstill now with the Centrals, but that won't always be the case. When he dies, you and North will be free to mate fully."

Lexi shook her head. "But what if that doesn't happen?"

"If you have to look negatively on that, then know that it won't matter to us if you don't fully bond with North," Hannah said. "Yes, it will matter to you because, God, the pain, but to us? You'll be our sister-in-law. In fact, we pretty much already think of you that way. And if the bond doesn't happen, and you can't have babies, you can always adopt." The pain in Hannah's eyes looked fresh at the thought of not having babies. She didn't quite understand that, considering Hannah had twin babies, but that seemed like a whole other story.

Lexi ran a hand over her face. "Let's start over for the day, shall we? I need to not be so emo, I guess."

Mel cupped her face, the Heir's mate's eyes glowing gold as her wolf rose to the surface. "Honey, you're entitled to feel whatever you want. This situation? It sucks. God, that's not even a good word for what's going on right now. I know what we need to do to fix it, but I don' t know how to get there. At least not yet. But no matter what happens, know this, you're ours. You're a Jamenson in our hearts if not in bond or in name. It might be working too fast for you right now in some respects, but remember, we aren't human. We're wolves. I learned the hard way about what happens when you try to slow things down for fate, and I don't want you to go through that too. So just breathe and be with North as you can now, and we'll all work on a way to make that permanent."

Both women hugged her hard then started back to work. Today they were grinding up some of the leaves and plants that Hannah had been growing in her greenhouse. As wolves, witches, and partial demons, in Josh's case, they couldn't use normal human medicines. Yes, as the Healer, Hannah could Heal wolves and the like, but it was costly. Each time she used her powers, she drained herself and had to wait to recharge herself using the bonds with the Pack and time. She would do it daily if she could, but everyone knew she needed time to rest.

So Hannah would only Heal those who truly needed it.

As they were at war, that need increased daily it seemed.

The medicines they made were old recipes handed down for generations. They would be too potent for humans, but for wolves, they helped alleviate pain, headaches, and other small things.

They were also very time consuming and annoying to make.

Cailin used to make them on her own for almost five years because she wanted to shoulder the burden. The Pack hadn't had a healer or a witch within the Pack who dealt with herbs on a primary basis, so Cailin had stepped up.

Lexi had a feeling the young wolf had wanted to prove herself, though to whom she didn't know. Being the Pack princess had to be hard, considering everyone thought she had everything yet needed to earn it more than others.

Or, at least, that's what Lexi thought.

It would be interesting to see how Logan and Cailin would actually fit together if they ever stepped over the barrier they'd put in front of themselves.

"So, where are those beautiful babies of yours?" Lexi asked as she curled her lip, grinding the pestle in the mortar with a little more vigor than she should have. The plant smelled disgusting, and the quicker she got rid of it, the better.

Hannah grinned. "Kaylee and Conner are both with their daddies at the moment. They wanted to have a kiddie date I think."

"I love the fact that Reed and Josh are a couple too, you know?" Mel added in as she bagged up her herbs.

Hannah smiled, that dreamy, in-love look on her face heart-warming. "I know. Plus, it's fun to sit back and watch them get all hot and sweaty together."

Lexi barked out a laugh. "What is with you and sex today?"

Hannah shrugged as Mel shook her head, a smile on her face. "Last night and all day today it's been all about the men. They don't get much time alone since we all like to cuddle together, so I get I'm a bit lonely. Not that it's their fault. We all need time together and apart as duos and as a triad, but I'm spoiled."

Lexi snorted. "Yeah, honey, just a bit."

"What can I say? I like being the creamy center of that cookie."

Melanie threw her head back and laughed, almost falling off her chair. "Oh hell, I can't sit here in this room and deal with that smelly herb anymore. Let's go to Willow's bakery and get some cookies." The Heir female winked, and Lexi choked on a laugh.

"Uh, I think I'll get a cupcake and leave the cookies to Hannah."

Hannah rubbed her hands together. "Sounds good to me. Come on, ladies. Willow is working today and has Bay with her I believe. Ellie is off with Maddox and Charlotte doing...something. And Cailin and Noah have Parker for the day, right?"

Lexi nodded. "Yep. Parker loves Cailin, and she loves him like the little brother she never had. I don't mind them hanging out when I would need to find someone else to watch him anyway if I'm working."

They made their way out of the triad's home and toward the den center. The den was situated in the middle of the forest between two rock faces. It kept them safe on three sides, and the wards, usually, kept them safe on the other. Since the Redwoods would conceivably be living with each other for centuries, they'd done their best to leave tons of space between homes. The Jamensons all lived near each other in one corner of the den and were either a long walk or a short drive to the center, where the school, shopping, and other amenities were located.

Today they decided to walk the distance, needing the fresh air.

"I'm glad you decided to help today," Hannah said a few minutes into their walk.

Lexi smiled. "Me too. You two are hoots."

Mel laughed. "You wouldn't have thought so if you'd met me before I mated with Kade."

"Oh shush," Hannah admonished. "I bet you were just as adorably dorky as you are now. You're just getting some."

Lexi tripped over a root, laughing so hard. "Oh my God, Hannah. Those men need to get home soon so you can get laid."

Hannah huffed out a breath. "I know. It's been like thirty hours or something like that. I'm shriveling up."

"Jesus, Hannah," Mel mumbled through her laughter.

"What? I'm still waiting to hear the deets on North. Just saying."

"Yes, why don't you tell us the *deets* on the man you stole," a voice said from behind a tree.

The girls stopped walking. Melanie put herself in front of Hannah while Lexi took the other side. Hannah was a witch with powers connected to the earth, but she couldn't Heal herself. Lexi might not be able to shift, but she was still stronger.

Melanie could kick ass if she had to, but Lexi hoped they wouldn't have to.

"Colleen? Is that you?" Melanie asked, her voice cool, dangerous.

Three women walked out from the trees, smirks on their faces and looking as though they were out on the prowl for trouble. Lexi had seen them around the den but hadn't spoken to them. For the most part, the wolves she didn't know stayed clear of her.

After all, she was just the new addition to the Pack with the shady past.

Honestly, Lexi didn't blame them for their hesitation to welcome her and her family with open arms. The Pack had been beaten and culled through battle after battle. Lexi was a threat because she was an unknown.

Picking a fight, though, was too much for her.

She might deserve space from others, but she didn't deserve whatever these women were about to dish out. Melanie and Hannah for sure didn't deserve it.

"So tell us, Lexi, how is it with North?" Colleen spat. "You come into our Pack and take the last remaining available Jamenson? What kind of shit do you think you're trying to pull? You're nothing but trash."

Melanie growled, the sound crawling over her like a sweet chill. "Marissa, Sandra, go if you don't want to be part of this with Colleen. If you stay, you'll all be forced to deal with me."

"And me," Hannah added. She stretched her fingers, the soil around them rippling like small waves, the tension in the air rising.

"Guys..." Lexi didn't know what to do. Yes, she was more dominant than the non-Jamensons by far, but as a latent wolf, the others wouldn't know that.

She didn't want anyone to get hurt because others were prejudiced or whatever the hell was going on with them.

"We'll stay here," Sandra answered, an ugly glint her eye.

"Yes, it's about time we deal with the Jamenson bitches," Marissa added. "The three of you came into this Pack and took our men. Melanie had to be turned. She's not even a born wolf like us. Hannah is a fucking witch. And you, Lexi? You're not even a real wolf. You're just a broken joke."

"Shut your fucking mouths," Melanie ordered, her power flaring. Lexi swallowed hard, the power washing over her like a warm blanket. Though she couldn't feel her wolf, she could feel the comfort that came with being with another wolf that was there to protect her. The other women's eyes widened, and their knees buckled. Lexi knew Melanie hadn't put out too much of her power, but shit, she was strong. "We're Pack. We're family. Why they hell are you spouting nonsense and trying to break that?"

Lexi had been right when she'd thought the Pack was changing from within. The Jamensons had spent so much time protecting their members from outside evil they hadn't been able to see the poison within.

"You're nothing," Colleen yelled then charged. Her claws spouted from her fingertips as she swung at Melanie. Mel ducked then punched the bitch in the face. Colleen attacked back and tried to pounce on Mel, but the Heir female would have none of that. Mel kicked and punched, showing how strong she was compared to the lower-ranking female.

Sandra came at Hannah, her fangs bared. The Healer pulled up her arms, bringing the earth with her. A heavy wave of soil, leaves, and roots slammed into Sandra, and the other woman screamed.

Marissa attacked Lexi, her claws out, ready to maim. Lexi didn't have claws or fangs. No, but she had strength plus the fact she'd been the underdog her whole life.

She ducked then used her shoulder to slam into Marissa's gut. The woman let out an oof, but Lexi didn't stop. She pushed Marissa to the ground, twisted the woman so she was on her stomach, and then pulled her arms back so Marissa screamed out in pain.

"Yield."

"Never, you bitch!"

Lexi pulled harder, and Marissa screamed louder.

"All of you, stop it." Melanie's voice held a thread of power, sending shivers down Lexi's back.

The sound of people running toward them reached her ears, but Lexi didn't face them. She could scent the Jamenson men coming for them, but she had to focus on keeping Marissa pinned.

They didn't need the men fighting for them, considering the three of them had kicked ass all on their own.

"Melanie."

"We're fine, Kade." Melanie pulled Colleen by the hair so she lay between Marissa and Sandra. "The three of you have shamed the name Redwood." Her power flared again, and Lexi lowered her eyes.

Jesus, the woman was strong.

"I'd kick you out of the Pack right now, but unlike you, I'm not an ignorant bitch. I'm calling a circle."

Shit. Calling a circle would force the women to be put in the center of the entire Pack and shown their punishment handed out by the Alpha.

Some of the Pack already hated her, and Lexi didn't want others to be hurt because of it. "Melanie..."

"Not now, Lex."

Lexi closed her mouth.

She felt a hand on her hip and risked a glance over her shoulder. North stood behind her, the heat radiating off him mixing with the metallic taste of his anger. She knew the darkness he feared was close to the surface, but he was holding on.

For her.

She leaned back, letting herself need him as much as he needed her.

She heard the three women on the ground gasp at the movement, jealousy all by pouring off them.

Whatever.

With North's touch and her movement, they were claiming each other in front of the Pack with more than words and the scent she'd carried from their lovemaking before.

They were making a statement, and she'd be damned if she'd let the others ruin it for her.

"The Alpha will decide your punishment; I'm too angry deal with you," Melanie ordered.

Kade came up from behind her and put his hand on her hip as well. He didn't speak. He didn't need to. The women had this down.

Lexi could tell the others around them—Adam, Maddox, and Logan—were holding themselves back so they wouldn't make the women look weak.

There was no way anyone would mistake them for that now.

No way.

North's other arm came around her, and she let out a breath.

This was her new family, and they'd stood up for her.

She just had to get used to that.

CHAPTER TEN

"It's just dinner, Lex." North smiled as she paced around her bedroom in her fifth outfit for the night. He loved it when she was all jittery because that meant he got to soothe her.

He'd been needing to soothe her more and more over the past few days. Lexi had been on edge ever since the attack where Mel, Hannah, and Lexi had not only kicked ass but also shown they were stronger than others thought.

He knew she didn't feel comfortable being the center of attention, and with the Pack circle coming up after the full-moon hunt, there was no hiding behind others. While North understood Lexi's reluctance to be part of the Pack circle to see the women's punishment, he had no such qualms. He wanted to see what his father would do to the wolves who would not only attack those they thought weaker, but attack family.

It was past time to show that the Jamensons ruled for a reason.

"It's not just dinner, North," Lexi answered, bringing him out of his thoughts. She wiggled out of her sweater dress, leaving her in thigh-highs, heels, her bra, and panties.

Unable to help himself, he walked up to her, pulled her flush against his body so her ass was against his crotch, and slid his hands up her sides.

"North, we don't have time for this," she said breathlessly, but tilted her head to the side anyway.

Good girl.

He inhaled her scent and rocked against her. "You smell so fucking good, my Lexi. I want to bend you over the bed, tuck your panties out of the way, and fuck you hard while you wear these high heels."

She shuddered in his hold but didn't move away. His hand slid up her stomach and chest so he could collar her neck. She sucked in a breath, her body going lax against him.

He kissed her temple then moved away, annoyed they didn't have enough time.

"When we get back from dinner, I'm going to taste every inch of you."

Lexi blinked at him, her gaze glassy. "Now I really don't know how I'm going to do this dinner. I used to be nervous, but now I'm nervous *and* horny as hell."

North barked a laugh and shook his head. He moved to her closet, pulled out another sweater dress he knew looked good on her, and handed it over. "Put this on. It makes your ass look amazing."

She raised a brow. "I'm not sure if an amazing-ass look is what I'm going for tonight."

North shrugged then moved to the bed so he could stretch out and watch her dress. He cupped his hands behind his head and grinned. "The dress covers you so you'll look as demure as you'd like, but I'll know what you're wearing underneath. Plus with your ass looking fuckable, it'll give us something to look forward to."

She snorted as she pulled the dress over her head, careful not to mess up her hair. "You're not fucking my ass tonight, North."

He licked his lips. "Not tonight, no, we're still preparing you for that. But soon."

She shivered, and he ran a hand over his cock through his pants. Shit, his plan of making her think of something other than her nerves had backfired. Now he'd have to get rid of his hard-on before sitting with his family for dinner.

Having a mate seemed to lead him into whole new situations, and he fucking loved it.

"You look beautiful, Lex," he said as she patted down her curves.

"Thank you, but I'm still nervous."

"You've had meals with my family before."

"But this is different."

Yes. This would be the first family meal with Lexi by his side.

He couldn't wait.

A knock on the door pulled him out of his thoughts.

"Come in, Logan," Lexi called as she walked into her bathroom doing whatever women did when they were getting ready.

"I don't know why I have to go to this family dinner," Lexi's brother grumbled as he fixed the sleeves on his button-down shirt.

"Because I need my family there," Lexi said from the bathroom.

"Lexi, you're going to be there with my family, which is now *your* family," North said softly, and Logan smiled.

"Thanks," the other man mouthed, and North nodded.

Lexi came out, her eyes filled with tears.

He jumped up to his feet and ran to her. "Hey, I didn't mean to make you cry." He pulled her into his arms, and she pushed back.

"I'm fine, really. That was just really sweet of you to say."

"Okay, you can stop with the sap now," Logan added in, deadpan.

"Does that make me family too?" Parker asked from the doorway, and North turned to the kid he wanted to claim as his own.

"Of course. You know me and your mom are mates, and that means we mix our families together." He hoped the hell he was saying the right thing.

"So that means I can call Cailin Aunt Cailin?" the kid asked, and North held back a laugh. Yeah, the kid had it bad for North's sister.

"Yep. I think she'd like that. You're family. So is Logan." North raised a brow at the man. Unsaid was that Logan was family through Lexi, not Cailin. If the man even looked at North's baby sister in the wrong way he'd end him.

Slowly.

"I don't have to call you dad, do I?" Parker asked, and North froze.

"Uh..."

"I don't know if I'm ready for that."

North nodded, his throat suddenly very dry. "You can call me North, Parker. I won't force you to do anything that makes you feel uncomfortable."

Parker bit his lip then nodded.

Hell, North needed a drink, not that wolves could get drunk without copious amounts of alcohol. He could use one nonetheless.

"Okay then, we need to go now, or we'll be late," Lexi said, her voice unusually high.

It might seem like an insta-family to some, but North would take it. He just wasn't exactly sure what he was going to do with it when he got it. It wasn't as if he'd ever been a dad before.

They piled into his Jeep then made their way to his parents' house. The Jamenson family dinners were not only summonses. They were times when they could all talk about things that were going on within the Pack and their individual families.

Before Kade met Melanie, seeming to start the cascade effect of the rest of the brothers finding their mates, dinner used to be a little quieter, a little shorter.

Now there were added mates, babies, children, and chaos.

North knew his mother was in grandmother heaven.

As soon as they made it to the porch, his mother opened the door, a bright smile on her face even with the wariness that came with war in her eyes.

"You're late, North Jamenson, but since you've brought me this little guy, I will forgive you. Come in."

Before North could blink, she had Parker in a tight hug. Her murmurs and squeals at him reflected Parker's being there as part of North's family rather than a normal guest and made him smile.

"You know, Parker, Finn used to be the oldest cousin, but now I think you are," Pat said as she pulled him in for another hug. "Are you ready for that responsibility?" she asked, her tone solemn.

"I'll take care of the other kids. I promise," Parker answered, his tone equally solemn.

Yep, North had just fallen in love with the kid.

Lexi wrapped an arm around his waist, and he pulled her close.

He loved the kid's mom just as hard.

"Go sit at the children's table. Your Uncle Reed will be sitting with you since he decided to use one of my vegetables as a weapon."

"It was *one* pea, Mom! And Kade was egging me on," Reed called from the other room, and North laughed.

As old as they were, he and his brothers had never grown up.

"Shut up, Reed. Lexi, it's good to see you." She kissed Lexi's cheek and hugged her before moving to Logan. "And, Logan, I'm glad you could come."

Logan looked like a fish out of water but let the smaller woman bring him into her arms.

Once they got through the foyer, they made their way to the dining room where everyone already sat, drinks in front of them and the food in covered dishes on the table.

He felt Lexi freeze beside him, and he pulled her closer.

"I'm sorry we're late," Lexi said, her voice small.

"I waylaid her, but we're here now," North added in before she could blame herself.

His family laughed and gave knowing glances.

"We're glad you could come," Willow said, her eyes bright. "Now you can tell us all about those details Hannah said you were holding back."

North frowned and looked at Lexi as they sat down. He noticed out of the corner of his eye that his mother had put Logan across from Cailin, but the two wouldn't even look at each other.

Interesting.

"What details?" he asked as Lexi blushed red.

"Uh, nothing. I'll talk about it later, Willow."

Hannah and Melanie threw their heads back and laughed while the others looked around, confused at missing the joke.

North shrugged it off, knowing he'd tease Lexi's real answer from her later. As soon as his mother sat, they began serving the roast, chicken, veggies, and sides family style. He loved his mother's cooking and knew that no matter how hard he tried, he'd never be as good as her.

"Can you cook?" North asked, his voice low. That seemed like something he should know. Yes, they'd had meals together before, but he'd never really thought about it.

Lexi raised a brow. "Yes, though not as good as Willow and your mom. If you're asking if I'm planning on being your cooking slave, that would be no."

He could feel every eye on them, and he swore he could also feel a blush running up his neck.

"That's not what I meant."

Lexi leaned toward him and captured his lips. "Good."

"Whipped already. I like it," Kade said then rubbed his side where Melanie had elbowed him.

"I'll show you whipped, Kade Jamenson."

"Lexi, as long as you can cook better than Reed and Hannah, you're fine," Josh said and then kissed Hannah's temple.

"I heard that!" Reed called from the kiddie table.

Hannah just shrugged. "Reed's the one who caught that towel on fire. Not me."

Josh raised a brow. "No, you only burned a hole in the bottom of my pan while boiling water."

Hannah blushed hard, and Josh pulled her close for a kiss.

North smiled then leaned back so he could hang an arm around Lexi's chair. He loved eating with his family now more than ever. Sure, he'd enjoyed it in the past with the inside jokes and ribbing, but now that he had his own family with him, he liked it even more.

He looked across the table at his twin, who had his head lowered while talking to his mate. Maddox had to be feeling all the emotions of the people in the room but looked as though he was finally at peace rather than holding in the strain as he had before.

North knew his twin had Ellie to thank for that.

Maddox looked over and smiled at North. He raised a glass, and North did the same.

Yes, things had certainty changed over the past few years...though not all of it good.

Once dinner was over, they cleaned up their dishes, served coffee, and sent the kids to his mother's kiddie room. Armed with baby monitors and an observant Parker, the adults left the kids to their own devices—at least those who were awake. The babies, at least, were sleeping.

Now was the time to talk about what had been bugging North from the start.

The rot within the Pack.

And the oily ruination of the Centrals.

North sank into the end of one of the couches and pulled Lexi onto his lap.

"Hey," she whispered.

"I'm just saving room," he said back, and she rolled her eyes.

"Sure, brother mine," Cailin said as she sat, squeezing between him and Maddox.

North looked up at Logan, who just gave Cailin a hard grin then sank to the floor in front of her, essentially trapping his sister's legs against him.

Every single male Jamenson gaze landed on Lexi's brother, but he did nothing but look at them all and raise a brow.

Oh, they'd be having a talk about his intentions.

Soon.

Lexi elbowed him in the gut, and he looked down at her. "What?"

She kissed his jaw then shook her head. "Stop it. We're here for more important things. Worry about castrating Logan later."

Hmm, castrating didn't sound like a bad idea.

"Hell." Cailin wiggled out from Logan's weight and rolled over the back of the couch. "I'm going to go watch the babies. Parker shouldn't have to do it on his own. Let me know what you talk about and what I need to do to help."

She walked away, her chin held high.

"Great job, boys," his mother muttered, a frown on her face.

"What?" all six brothers and his father said in unison.

"What's on the table for discussion tonight?" Mel asked, apparently ignoring the odd tension in the room.

His father sat forward, placing his forearms on his thighs. "Our scouts have come back from the Centrals' borders."

North sat up. "We had scouts?" Why the hell hadn't they said anything?

Edward raised one finger, his power arching out as he did so. North sat back and pulled Lexi closer, needing her warmth.

"Kade and I sent out scouts. And, no, we didn't tell any of you because it's something the Alpha and Heir needed to do. I used my own enforcers and kept them in secret. We didn't want word to get out to anyone within the Pack in case we have another mole. We kept it from the family because, as we will talk about soon, others in the Pack think the Jamensons wield too much power. I'm doing what I need to in

119

order to protect my family and my Pack. We don't tell you all we do, but we do tell you most."

"Is that where you went that night?" Hannah asked Josh. Josh might have been one of her mates, but he was also one of Edward's enforcers.

Josh gave a slight nod but didn't say anything, merely tucking Reed and Hannah closer to both his sides.

Adam growled, and Bay put her hand on his chest. "What did you find out?" As the Enforcer, it was his job to protect the Pack from outside forces, so not knowing there had been a mission must be pissing his brother off even more than it pissed North off.

"The Centrals are up to something. Something different," Kade answered. "I'm not sure what, but they're tightening up their forces, and we believe they have an ace up their sleeve. I'm not sure what it is yet."

He felt Lexi stiffen. "What is it, baby?"

"Word must be out that I'm here, right?" she said, her voice shaky.

North pulled her close and put his nose to her neck, inhaling her scent, needing her there.

Edward gave a slight nod. "They know. They also know Parker is here, Lexi."

North tugged her closer, the fear radiating off of her tangible. "We knew that would happen, baby. When you came to the Redwoods to save my life and for protection of your own, we knew the Centrals would find out."

"You're Pack, Lexi. We won't let the Centrals have you or the boy. No matter what claim Corbin might have."

"But—"

Logan cut Lexi off. "No. We're here, and we'll fight with the Redwoods. Fuck Corbin."

Pat snorted. "Well, that about says it all, doesn't it?"

Logan ducked his head, a blush creeping up his neck.

"We don't know what the Centrals are up to, but we're all on edge. We all are," Edward said. "That doesn't mean we're sitting back and doing nothing. We're all building up and keeping the Pack secure. Our enforcers are out and learning what they can about the Centrals. We can't attack head-on, not when we don't have or want to use the magic they use, but we're not standing still either. That's not our only problem though."

The others in the room mumbled, and North growled.

Edward took a breath then began again. "We've been fighting the Centrals for so long without real progress. At least that's how it seems to others. I believe the fact we've slowly won each battle with them means something. Others don't believe that. There are rumblings."

Jasper cursed. "It's Patrick and his crew."

"That fucker?" Maddox asked. "He's the one who wanted to kill Ellie without cause."

"Maddox, he thought I killed Larissa and Neil, so I wouldn't say that was without cause," Ellie said, and raised her hand to stop Maddox from growling. "I'm not saying he was right then with his thoughts, but they didn't come out of nowhere. However, it didn't stop there. He didn't listen to those more dominant than him then, and he hasn't changed, has he?"

Jasper shook his head. "No, he's getting worse."

Edward growled, his eyes glowing gold. "And now he's bringing others with him. He was the one who encouraged Colleen, Marissa, and Sandra to attack you. Marissa finally spilled that tale."

North cursed.

"Why haven't we put an end to him yet?" Reed asked, anger in his tone.

"Because we're waiting him out, making sure he hasn't done anything else," Edward explained. "There's no tangible proof he has done anything that would warrant a Pack circle or death. I don't plan on letting him get that far. We're having a circle for the women who attacked you, but as there is no proof that he egged them on or did something close to that, we're stuck. He and his friends seemed to have forgotten the Pack hierarchy and how strong we Jamensons are."

"Things are going to hell," North mumbled, and Lexi leaned back, resting her head against his.

"We're not like other Packs, beating and killing those who think or talk out of order," Edward said. "Even if that kept some dissension out of the ranks, it would only put larger targets on our backs. We're keeping up the fight against the Centrals and keeping an eye on Patrick. The Pack circle where I deal out the women's punishment will be a deciding factor I believe."

"That comes after the full-moon hunt," North said, and Lexi burrowed closer.

"We're ready for them," Edward growled, and the others in the room growled with him.

They were family. They were Jamensons.

They would not fail.

He squeezed Lexi tight.

No, they wouldn't fail. Not when they had so much to fight for.

CHAPTER ELEVEN

"**A**re you sure you're going to be okay tonight alone?" North asked, and Lexi just gave a small smile.

Seriously, the man needed to stop worrying about her feelings about not being able to shift. It wasn't as if she wasn't used to the fact others would be out on the hunt tonight and she'd be left alone.

Again.

Okay, so maybe he had a reason to worry and be cute about it, but still.

"I'll be fine. I have Brie, Micah, Kaylee, and Conner to keep my company." She would be babysitting some of the Jamenson kids while their parents were on the hunt. Usually Josh and Hannah, who didn't shift, would do it, but they wanted to be together as a couple. Since having the babies, the triad seemed to be finding interesting ways to be together as groups of three or two.

Parker was already out with his Uncle Logan. She had a feeling the little guy was doing his best to hang out with Cailin and Logan, not only to play matchmaker with her and North but with the other two as well.

North brought her close and trailed a finger along her neck and shoulder. She tilted her head, giving him more access.

"What time do they get here?" he asked, his voice low.

"We're alone for another two hours, I think," she answered huskily.

North grinned.

Oh yes.

She loved this man.

Not that she'd told him yet.

He picked her up, and she found herself on her back, the soft bed cushioning her fall. He pulled off her clothes and his in a mad rush. They were acting like freaking teenagers who never got laid, but she didn't care.

He pulled away, his cock against his belly and a wicked grin on his face. "Okay, we've done against the wall, over the couch, on the couch, in the bed, on the floor, in the shower, on the table...what are we missing?"

"We're not going backdoor, North Jamenson," she teased.

His eyes darkened, and his hands went to her ass, brushing her hole, and she froze.

"North..."

"Not yet, we will though, soon."

That tantalizing excitement she hadn't known she'd feel with that idea filled her. Sure, she'd tried that before, but not with North. It also hadn't been that great, but considering most sex before North paled in comparison, she was willing to bet anything with her mate would rock.

"Soon," she agreed, and he licked his lips. "Um, what haven't we tried? We don't have much time to get too adventurous."

His eyebrows rose. "I have an idea." He lay beside her on the bed, and she frowned.

"We're taking a nap? That doesn't sound like the best use of our time since I thought we'd be getting sweaty, but if that's what you want to do..."

"Minx. Now straddle me but face my feet."

"Seriously? That's what you want to do?"

He went to his side and bit her lip. "I want you to ride my face while I fuck yours. Have a problem with that?"

"Well, in that case." She laughed then did as he asked. "Now—" She swallowed her words as he went to town like a hungry man at a feast.

Dear gods, the things that man could do with his tongue could drive any woman to insanity.

Since his cock was right there... Okay, who was she kidding? She loved his cock. She licked along his length, the salty taste settling on her tongue. Then she kissed down around the base, sucking his balls into her mouth one at a time then letting them go with a pop. He groaned into her pussy, and she shuddered.

"I love when you do that."

He nibbled her clit in response, and she swallowed hard, her inner walls fluttering. She went back to his cock, swallowing him a little at a time, knowing he liked it when she went slow at first. She breathed through her nose then let her jaw relax so she could take him to the back of her throat.

Finally her nose reached the coarse hair at the base of his cock, and before she could gag, she pulled away, hollowing her cheeks as she did so. Using her hands while she sucked the crown, she set a hard rhythm that matched his mouth. She could feel his balls tighten and the first hot shot of his seed coating her tongue. She swallowed quickly as he came in her mouth, not letting a single drop go.

He growled her name then bit down on her clit as he pumped two fingers into her. She pulled away from him, his cock still hard, and came, little flashes of light dancing behind her eyelids as she did so.

Out of breath, she kept her eyes closed and didn't complain as North moved her to her back. She gasped as he entered her, his cock rock hard.

"I don't know how you can do this again so quickly," she whispered, her once satiated body rising again to meet him thrust for thrust.

He kissed her hard, their combined essence mingling on her tongue. "I'm a wolf," he answered simply.

He pulled her legs to rest on his shoulders and pumped into her, playing with her clit at the same time. She tried to hold back so she could crash at the same time he did, but it was a lost cause. She needed it too much. She moaned, her pussy clenching around him as she fell, and North finally followed, his rasp a sweet temptation for the already tempted.

North leaned his head against hers, panting. She swallowed hard and squeezed her inner muscles around his softening cock.

"Jesus, woman. Stop that, or we'll have to start all over again." He kissed her softly. "We need to get ready because the others will be here soon."

She grinned, and he slipped out of her, leaving them both moaning.

"I still don't know a better feeling than my cock inside you, my Lexi." He pulled her to her feet, slapped her ass, and then pushed her to the shower. "Go get cleaned up. I'd join you, but we'd never get out on time if I did."

She rolled her eyes but did as he said. Once she was out, he ducked under the spray behind her, and she laughed, loving the way they were acting—not like a new couple, but like a couple set into their positions and feelings.

She just hoped that they'd have a bond to cement it all.

Dressed and ready to watch the Jamenson babies, Lexi let out a breath.. Brie and Micah, both around two, would be sleeping hopefully. Brie would be shifting within the year as well, which was exciting. Both Kaylee and Conner were eight months old, and Hannah had said they were sleeping through the night now, but that could change at any moment.

So Lexi would be within the confines of North's home with babies in portable cribs. Logan already had Parker with him at their house, so they were getting ready for the hunt. Since she'd been with North, they'd been alternating which house they slept at. North had to be close to his clinic, but Lexi didn't feel comfortable leaving Parker alone with Logan overnight every night.

Soon she'd have to figure out if they were ready for her to actually move in full time—Parker included. She knew Logan could use the space to himself, but as she was a mom and not alone, she had to think about her son first, not her own desires and feelings.

Parker might seem okay with her seeing North now, but living with him was an entirely different matter.

"What's put that frown on your face?" North asked as he wrapped his arms around her waist.

He was always doing that, touching her and pulling her close. While she liked it, she still had that annoying fear that she'd depend on it too much. What if he finally gave up on them because they didn't share the bond?

Sure, he hadn't done a single thing to warrant that fear, but it didn't stop her from thinking about it. The man deserved to have a full mating bond and have that connection. Considering the one she was currently mated to—even though it wasn't a full bond so she couldn't actually *feel* him—was his greatest enemy, it only made sense that she should worry.

North turned her in his arms. "Hey, stop with the doubt."

She swallowed hard. "I know I need to. I'm sorry."

He framed her face. "You doubt us, you doubt me. You got that? You have no cause for that. We're going to make this work, damn it."

He kissed her hard, and she closed her eyes, keeping the tears at bay. She was stronger than this, damn it. The stupid ache in her belly had nothing to do with North but her own insecurities and the fact that Corbin was still out there, alive...waiting.

Once he was dead, she could live again.

Or at least find some peace.

North pulled away, a frown on his face, but didn't say anything.

Soon the house was filled with babies, and then she was alone again while the adults and children who could shift were on the full-moon hunt. Lexi closed her eyes as she sat in front of one of the windows. The moon danced along her skin and called to her.

As with every full moon she'd experienced, this one hurt.

Not that she ever told anyone that.

Her emotions went haywire during the full moon. It was like PMS on steroids. She knew that was one reason she was freaking out about being with North and worrying that she'd rely on him too much.

The moon made her crazy—at least a crazy that could be controlled. Watching the babies usually helped her find her calm.

The madness seeped into her soul while the pain from not being able to shift only intensified as she got older. North had told her the chemicals in her body were fighting each other and herself, but she didn't know of a way to free herself from it.

She was dying, and she knew it.

Other latent wolves died much younger, unable to handle the madness and overbearing pain of not being able to shift.

If they didn't figure out a way to stop the pain, she might not be able to fight it anymore.

The door opened to her right, and she stared at North, shirtless, his body slick with sweat.

"What are you doing here?" she asked as she stood on shaky legs. "You should be on the hunt. You know your wolf needs to be let out."

North shook his head then stalked toward her, a predator with his prey in sight. He grabbed her, pulling her to his chest then crushed his mouth to hers.

Her pulse quickened as she opened for him, a moan echoing through the room.

North finally pulled back, his hands still clenched around her upper arms. "My wolf might need to run, but he needs to be by your side even more."

This man.

"I did a short run, and now I'm here because I'm not leaving you alone. I shouldn't have done it in the first place. I knew this night would be hard for you emotionally, but I'm a fucking idiot in that I didn't think about the physical aspects."

He ran a finger along her cheek. "It's hard, but I'm okay," she lied.

"You can tell me what's wrong. I can hear the babies are asleep, Lex. We have time before the others come back from the hunt, so you can talk to me."

"I'm fine."

"No, you're not. You're in pain because you can't shift, and you're doubting everything you've had because of the emotions running through your system like a freight train. You're allowed to lean on me, Lex. I'm not going anywhere."

Oh, how she'd love to do that fully, lean on the man she knew would catch her if she fell, but she knew that wasn't in the cards for her. Not until she lost the chain around her neck tethering her to the Central Alpha.

"North...I don't know if I can lean on you," she whispered.

He growled then cupped her face. "Why not?"

"I...it's not as though I *need* to lean on you. You know that, right?"

"Jesus. Yes. Of course I know that. You don't need anything, Lexi."

She pulled away. "No, that's not what I mean. I only meant that I've learned to stand on my own, but the fact that I *know* you'll be there is something completely different. I know that you'll be there if I need to fall, to let go. I know you'll catch me. That's not the issue. I trust that you'll be there."

"Then what's the problem?"

"What if you're the one I hurt when I fall?" Her voice broke.

North let out a breath. "Baby..."

"I'd rather be broken in a million pieces than be the one to hurt you. I'd rather fall and bruise, break...*bleed*...than make you succumb to the pain that follows me. I would never do that to you. I don't want you to fall for me. I couldn't bear it."

"Lexi, I've already fallen for you, just not in the way you mean. I love you so fucking much, Lexi Anderson. Don't hold back to try to keep me safe. Go all in, and we'll keep each other safe."

She sucked in a breath at his words and licked her lips. "You...you love me."

North kissed one side of her mouth then the other. "Of course I do, silly woman."

"But...I thought you'd need a bond for that."

North growled. "Seriously? For fuck's sake, Lexi. No, we don't need a bond. Would I like one? Yes. Of course I fucking want to have that connection, but that's not all we have. A bond doesn't equal love. Mating doesn't equal love. Just because I can't have you every single way being a werewolf allows doesn't mean I can't love what I have."

Lexi closed her eyes, and swallowed hard. "I'm an idiot. Aren't I?"

"Yes, but I love you anyway." He grinned, and she punched him.

"I love you too, you butt."

North rolled his eyes. "Nice, I go all romantic and heartwarming, and you call me a butt. I can see our future together is going to be rife with love."

"You better believe it," she said then took a shaky breath.

"Now, the babies are asleep, and I think I still have a little tension to get out of my system. What do you think of us necking on the couch while we wait for the others to finish their hunt?"

Lexi snorted, the pain in her joints and heart slowly fading to the background with North by her side.

She was stronger than she thought she was.

She just had to believe that.

CHAPTER TWELVE

North ran hand through his hair and looked out among the circle that had been part of his life and Pack for as long as he could remember. He could feel the magic and memories along his skin as if they were living things, rather than echoes of something far greater.

The circle was where centuries of decisions, judgments, meetings, celebrations, and wakes had been held. His father was only in his mid-two hundreds while the Pack was almost a millennia old. The Alphas before his father had ruled with iron fists yet also with justice embedded in their cores. Edward was another version of them, an Alpha wolf in modern times, who not only had to deal with the Pack and a war with the Centrals, but the secrecy surrounding their existence.

Before the war, others, like himself, could go out into the human areas, live among them, and return to the den to hide out until they were no longer remembered. This way their lack of aging would never be found out.

Modern technology and the war between the Packs were forcing the Redwoods to stay close and almost cage themselves into the Redwood land.

North wasn't sure how much longer wards and secrets could keep them apart.

He didn't want to think about what discovery would mean for his people, his family.

He let out a breath.

Now wasn't the time to think about their existence coming into the limelight. No, that thought would always be in the recesses of his mind, but he needed to focus on what was in front of him.

Namely, the punishment of the three women who had attacked his mate and his family.

With that punishment would come the iron fist his father was known for, even if he didn't use it regularly.

North and his brothers would have to keep an eye out for Patrick and his goons. The lower-ranked wolf would be at the circle, as would almost all of the wolves who didn't have a patrol or young children to watch.

The Jamensons would be making a statement.

He just hoped the others would listen and take note.

Now wasn't the time to fight among themselves. No, now was the time to come together against a greater enemy. The Redwoods just needed to remember that.

He took another step into the circle and inhaled, letting the wash of centuries of memories seep into his soul. The circle itself was made of dirt and stone—a place where wolves could fight in dominance battles, and in some cases, like Kade's, it became a mating circle. Around the circle, stone seating rose up, much like in a coliseum, the stone long worn down and smooth from ages of meetings.

There were two entrances into the circle at ground level. The grassy area around the circle was marked by small stones that had wards within them. This would allow whoever was fighting to keep magic out. The wolves would use their own power and strength to fight, not the magic of others—or, in the cases of those connected to the moon goddess, themselves.

Since it was a circle, there wasn't a true head or foot of the area, but the Alpha's platform and the Jamenson clan's box was situated so the mountain was behind them. It was the place of power, and North had always loved and hated it.

Loved because it meant he was close to his family.

Hated because it meant his wolf was closer to the power that made the darkness just that much harder to control.

With Lexi at his side though, tonight would be okay.

He knew it.

The woman in his thoughts pressed her hand to his, and he looked down.

Yes, everything would be okay.

"Ready?" she asked, not hiding the nervousness in her tone.

He moved so she was against his side and his arm was wrapped around her, his hand resting on the curve of her ass. He leaned over and kissed her brow, and she let out a breath, relaxing. That his touch alone could calm her left him breathless.

"I'm ready," he said then squeezed her a bit tighter. "I'm glad Parker is with Emmaline tonight."

"Me too."

Emmaline was an elder whom Bay and Adam befriended awhile back. The shy woman was just now emerging from her shell and had offered to watch all the Jamenson children so none of the parents would miss the important evening.

Usually one or two of them could miss a circle because of their children, and no one would bat an eye. However, tonight was the night the Jamensons would stand tall and try to reconnect their Pack so they would once again stand united against the Centrals. Uniting as one against those who had harmed his mate made a powerful statement as well.

Sometimes even the smallest of acts could prevent disaster.

He hoped.

They made their way to the box, the other Jamensons already there. It seemed North and Lexi were always the late ones. Honestly, he couldn't help it considering it always took them forever to get themselves out of bed.

North liked having Lexi there.

The murmurs within the crowd reflected nervousness. It wasn't often a punishment circle was held, but in this case, three women attacking another group of three women and losing, without relenting or apologizing, warranted it.

Edward stood up on the platform, and the crowd silenced.

At least most of them.

North looked over at Patrick and his crew of five wolves. They weren't speaking, but they were still rustling about, making just enough noise that they walked a fine line between respect and disrespect. Something would have to be done about that.

Tonight.

Edward growled, and Patrick froze.

Good.

"We're here tonight because our Pack is losing what we've always had as our backbone, as our foundation. We're losing our unity. We cannot allow this to happen."

His father's words washed over him, and his wolf perked up, sensing the Alpha and basking in his presence.

Edward lifted his chin, and the three women were brought out. Each one kept her head down, but they weren't shackled or tied. No, they walked into the circle on their own.

"Colleen, Sandra, and Marissa, you three attacked Pack members with no cause," Edward accused, his voice low. "You used claws and teeth against two members who could not shift. You used brute force against our Healer and Heir female. You tried to kill one of the newest members of our Pack rather than welcoming her into our fold. What do you have to say for yourselves?"

Marissa and Sandra fell to their knees, their wolves unable to stand against the Alpha's words.

Colleen alone stood tall and then lifted her gaze. "We're tired of waiting," she whispered, her voice shaky.

"What?" he heard Willow whisper behind him, but he didn't answer her.

No one did.

His wolf went on alert, and he stood with his brothers as Patrick and his five men broke from the group and stepped into the circle.

Shit.

"You may speak, Patrick," Edward drawled, seemingly bored, but North knew better.

"We're taking over the Pack. We're tired of sitting by while you precious Jamensons sacrifice those that are weaker—or at least those you *think* are weaker—so

136

you all can live. It's bullshit. If I had been leading the war, we'd have won a year ago. But, no, we're forced to sit back because you're too afraid of dark magic. Fuck that."

North growled, his brothers making the same sound, low, deadly.

Patrick wasn't done. "We're tired of dying because you're too *weak* to do anything about protecting us. We're done."

Edward raised his chin. "Is this really how the entire Pack feels? That I'm too weak to rule?"

"Yes," Patrick answered.

"No," screamed most of the Pack.

Edward raised a brow. "It seems you're mistaken, Patrick. But if this is a true challenge, then let's both of us meet in the circle. I'll show you how Alpha I am."

North turned to his father. A dominance fight? Shit. He had every confidence in his father's fighting abilities, but that didn't mean he wanted to see his father hurt, even a little bit. Plus, though Patrick might think winning would make him Alpha, that wasn't the case. It was the moon goddess who chose the Alpha. Meaning Kade would become Alpha since he was the Heir, not Patrick. Patrick would have to kill every single one of the Jamensons to find a way to take over the Pack fully.

Something the other man seemed prepared to do from the way Patrick's friends looked with their side glances and tension rolling off of them in waves.

Well, shit.

"And when I win, old man, we'll beat the Centrals. Something you've failed at doing for far too long."

"How do you expect to use dark magic and not become tainted like the Centrals have?" Kade asked, pure anger lacing his words.

"We're stronger than them," Patrick spat. "We're the fucking Redwoods. We bow to no one."

"That arrogance will get you killed," Jasper put in.

"No, your ignorance in leading will get us killed," Patrick said. "Now." He held up his arm, the glint of steel catching North's eye.

North pulled Lexi behind him even as the shot rang out, overpowering the screams and shouts around him.

North could only watch as his father lurched, putting his body in front of his mother—the intended target—and take the bullet to the chest.

"Dad!" Maddox screamed, along with the rest of the family.

Edward growled, his body taking the hit but still standing. Blood poured from the wound, but he didn't fall. His eyes glowed gold, and a sense of deadly calm rolled over him, his claws slicing through his fingers— a talent only a few of their family could do. With one last look at his wife, the Alpha jumped from the platform, landed in the dirt circle, then stalked toward his prey.

No one had ever used a gun within the Pack circle before.

No one had ever *shot* the fucking Alpha during a circle before.

North would fucking kill the bastard who thought he could get away with trying to kill his mother and shooting his father.

He kissed Lexi hard then ran out to the circle, his brothers following. From the corner of his eye, he saw Cailin trying to come with them, but Logan pulled her back.

"No, protect those weaker than you," the other man shouted. "I'll help you. Let your father and brothers take care of those pieces of shit. We'll protect the Pack."

"That's my family out there!"

"And your Pack needs you."

North would have smiled at any other time when Cailin nodded and went with the Jamenson women and Logan to protect the other wolves and make sure Patrick and his men didn't have another plan waiting in the wings. That was the plan he hoped. The Jamensons had always made plans for something like this though they had prayed it would never happen. People scrambled away, screams and shouts echoing in the air. Chaos erupted and people held some back, urging some to safety while others moved forward, trying to find a way to help their Alpha.

He turned back to the circle and growled, ready to fight.

Sandra and Marissa had run off when the chaos had started, but Colleen was standing with the men, ready to fight. She screamed and lunged at Jasper, who didn't care she was a woman. He fought back.

She was trying to kill their Pack.

She was the enemy.

Another man, Jeffery, came at North, his teeth bared. North growled and punched the bastard in the throat. His wolf howled, wanting to spill blood, but he stopped himself. There wasn't any call for killing those other than Patrick, at least not yet. Not until they got all the information they could out of them.

Then, if his Alpha demanded it, he'd kill them.

Kill them all.

He reached out and grabbed Jeffery by the throat, keeping him pinned. Adam had another wolf down while Maddox was fighting another. Reed and Kade each had their own wolf while Jasper had Colleen pinned. Each of their enemies fought and spat, trying to claw back, but they were nothing compared to the Jamensons—something all others should have known.

His father stood above Patrick, his face pale from blood loss, but he looked strong—like the Alpha North had always known he was, but North was still in awe to see it.

"Yield, Patrick," Edward growled, a sadness in his tone that North wasn't sure anyone other than family could have picked up.

"Never. I'm through being your pussy. I'll never quit trying to take care of this Pack. You're *nothing,* Edward Jamenson."

Edward let out a sigh. "So be it." Before North could blink, his father had his hands around Patrick's neck. The quick snap was loud, the resulting silence deafening.

Patrick died instantly; the coup was finished.

His father turned to the others, his eyes glowing gold. "I give you all one last chance. Yield and accept your punishment of hard labor at the bottom of the hierarchy or death. There will be no banishment. I'll not have you go to our enemy."

"We yield," Jeffery gurgled, and the others murmured their assent.

"Take care of them," Edward ordered his enforcers, who rushed to their sides. They'd been in the fray with the Pack, doing their duty to protect their Alpha's back while the Jamenson sons protected his sides. "Know this, you lot, every time you come near another wolf, you'll bow or fall to your knees. If you don't, I'll know and you won't get another chance. Your lives will be forfeit. We have no tolerance for disobedience and cowardice. You understand me? You're lower than any other wolf in our Pack. You'll have to earn your rank back, if you can, through loyalty and service, not strength. You will serve the submissives and ensure their happiness. I will add hard labor—rebuilding what was torn down from the attacks on our den and other things needed within our community at a later time. Do I make myself clear?"

The wolves nodded, and Edward walked away, giving his back to the wolves he'd deemed less than nothing. With the enforcers and his sons, the Alpha wouldn't have to worry about his safety.

North looked at Kade and lifted his chin. "Get to Lexi and make sure she's all right, okay? I'm going to go take care of dad."

Kade nodded and loped off in a run, the rest of his brothers following.

"You want me to get Hannah to Heal him?" Reed asked.

North looked to where his father had gone. "No, I don't think he'll allow that."

Reed frowned. "He doesn't have to take on the pain and scar."

"I think he thinks he does."

Reed shook his head but went toward his mates. North would go to Lexi and Parker soon. First, though, he needed to care for his father. He went behind the platform, got the first aid kit, and ran.

He made his way through the forest to where his father sat on a rock, his hand over the wound on his chest.

"Let me see, Dad."

Edward let out a breath and dropped his hands. North winced at the angry wound, but it didn't look too bad. It was a through-and-through and was closer to his dad's shoulder than his chest.

He cleaned it up and made sure it would heal on its own. His father was the Alpha and was stronger than all the others in the Pack, meaning he'd heal quickly, but without Hannah's help, it would be painful.

"You don't have to do this, you know," North said as he patched his father up. "Hannah could Heal this quickly."

"Let her be with her mates, North. I need to do this on my own."

"It wasn't your fault that Patrick went crazy."

"Wasn't it?" Edward asked, his gaze in the distance. "He almost killed your mother because I was too arrogant to deal with the people in my own Pack."

North blinked. "You've always put the Pack first, Dad. Always. You know everyone's names, birthdays, and sometimes what they ate for dinner the night before. You take care of this Pack better than any other Alpha I know."

Edward let his gaze rest on North's. "And what has that gotten me? War and fighting within."

"Dad..." North had never seen his father look so...defeated. It chilled him to the bone.

"Ignore me. I think seeing that bullet come after your mother scared me more than I thought."

North liked that his father was actually being truthful about this feelings and not hiding them because he thought he had to, but he wasn't sure what he should do next. "Why don't you go to Mom?" he suggested.

"I just needed a second to breathe. Plus, she doesn't like seeing me bloody. Two hundred years together, and it still hurts her."

"She's your mate, Dad." There really wasn't anything more he could say.

"That she is. Take care of your Lexi, North. I know you don't have the bond, but you don't need it to love like you do."

North smiled. "I will, Dad. You want me to walk you home?"

Edward shook his head. "I'm old and wounded, but not dying. I'll make my way." The sound of someone stepping on a branch and the scent of warmth and cookies reached them. "Or my mate will be here to get me home."

"Damn right, Edward Jamenson." She walked right up to him, cupped his face, and then kissed him.

Hard.

North looked away. "Uh, I'll just go to Lexi then."

"Do that, son. Let me take care of my mate who thinks he can dodge bullets."

"I didn't dodge. I just blocked it from you."

North winced. Yeah, that wouldn't help his cause.

"Edward Jamenson, you do *not* step in front of bullets for me."

"You're my mate."

"Yes. I am. And as your mate you get to listen to me, Edward Jamenson. Let's get you home, and I'll make it all better."

The suggestive note in her voice made North run a little quicker away from them. There were some things a son didn't need to hear or see.

He hoped that over time he and Lexi would be like his parents. He also knew that if the situation arose, he'd step in front of a bullet for her.

She was his mate.

There really wasn't another answer.

CHAPTER THIRTEEN

"You're sure he's okay?" Parker asked as he squeezed his hands together.

North held himself back from pulling the kid into his arms and soothing him like he would with one of his nieces or nephews...or if Parker had been his biological son and not just the boy he thought of as his son. They were right in the transition phase of getting to know each other, and most days he had no idea what he was doing, let alone what he thought Parker would want him to do.

Being a parent was hard.

He closed his eyes. Oh, yes, that was an elegant thought right there. Lexi would probably laugh at him if he ever told her that.

So he wouldn't mention it.

North cleared his eyes and looked into Parker's hazel eyes, eyes that looked so much like Lexi's it was a bit scary.

"The Alpha is going to be fine, Park," he finally answered. "He was resting yesterday because my Mom made him, and the Pack knows that if the Alpha female says to rest, you rest. He wasn't sequestered or anything."

Parker furrowed his brow. "What does sequestered mean?"

"It means hidden away for a awhile," North explained then finally sat down next to the kid on the couch. They were in North's home and had been for the night. It had also been Parker's first night staying over in the guest room, which would one day be his room in truth—a big step for them. Lexi was in the shower, leaving him and Parker alone in the house. It was awkward and a little scary.

Hopefully that would change soon.

"So he's really okay?" Parker asked. The kid looked so scared that North was afraid he'd have to take him to the Alpha's house right then and there, even though North's mom might hurt him since she'd told the entire family to give them space.

North let out a breath and wrapped his arm around Parker's shoulders. The kid stiffened for a moment then sank into him. North's wolf nudged along his skin, savoring the feel, as if Parker was theirs and comforting was their duty.

North squeezed Parker closer for a bit then let him loose, not wanting to frighten him. "My dad's fine, Parker. I promise."

"But he was shot," Parker said, eyes wide. "How can you be all right when you're shot?"

North swallowed hard, remembering his father's pallor and the defeat on his face when they'd been alone. The war was wearing on Edward, but the Alpha would never acknowledge that.

His father was stronger than all of them.

"He's a wolf, Parker. The Alpha at that. You know we can heal faster than humans and can live through most wounds when others couldn't make it. My dad's really strong, bud. Really strong." North let out a breath, trying not to think about how things could have been so much different if the bullet had been a couple inches to the left. "He's healing and will be back to top form probably today knowing him. When Mom lets us, we can go over and check on him. Will that make you feel better?"

Parker nodded, his head rustling against North's arm. "Yeah. I know I'm being a baby, but I want to make sure he's okay, you know?"

"You're not being a baby. Get that out of your head. You're a dominant wolf—or at least will be when you get older—who wants to make sure his Alpha is okay. All that means is that your wolf is strong and the person that holds that wolf is even stronger. You care for others. That's not a bad thing." North paused. "Plus, in a way, my dad's your family too."

Parker turned toward him on the couch, his eyes narrowed. "Because you and my mom are mates? You already said I can call Cailin, Aunt Cailin." He grinned. "And I think she likes that."

North chuckled. "Yeah, she would." Though if she was called that through her connection with Logan, it would be a whole other matter. "And yeah, you're my family, Parker. I know we haven't made anything formal, but your mom and I? We're the forever kind of mates." At least he hoped they had a forever to look forward to, but that was another talk for another day.

A light shone in Parker's eyes, but he still frowned. Oh hell, had North not said the right thing? Was this too soon? Where the hell was Lexi? She could handle this way better than him, though at this point a monkey with a banana could handle this better than him.

"So...you're not leaving? *We're* not leaving?"

North couldn't speak, his throat too clogged with emotion. Parker had never had a home, not really. He'd been on the run his entire life, and now people were telling him the Redwoods was his home. How was he supposed to believe that? How was he supposed to trust in that?

How was North going to make sure Parker knew there was no backing out of this—that they were family, no matter what happened with the mating bond and the war around them?

"Parker honey, this is our home," Lexi said from the doorway, her hair wet and her eyes filled with tears.

North had been so involved in his conversation with Parker he hadn't noticed the shower turning off or Lexi padding into the living room area. With all that had happened with the revolt and other wolves, he needed to keep alert if he was going to protect his family.

He sucked in a breath.

Yes, Parker and Lexi were his family and it was time they made it official.

"But, Mom, what if we have to leave again because someone's found us? How can this be our home if we have to leave?"

North closed his eyes, at a loss for words.

"Oh, baby." Lexi's voice broke as she came to the couch and sat on the other side of Parker. She wrapped her arm around him and leaned closer so she and Parker were essentially leaning on North.

North moved so he was now holding the both of them. His wolf nudged him, needing to have their scents on him and vice versa. This was his family now, and he had to make sure everyone knew that.

"Parker, we're not going anywhere." Lexi let out a shaky breath. "We're here to stay. I know we haven't done that before, and things are a little crazy right now, but we're not leaving."

"How can you be sure? We always leave when they find us," Parker whispered.

"You didn't have us behind you, Park," North interjected. "We're not going to let the others hurt you. No matter what happens, know that we're here for you. We Jamensons stick together."

"But I'm not a Jamenson," Parker whispered.

Lexi met his gaze over Parker's head and smiled. "No, we're not Jamensons in name, but..."

"But you're my family, Park. We just talked about that. Your mom and I are mates, meaning we're going to be together for a long da— time." He felt the blush creep up his neck. He'd have to work on not cursing he supposed. "You and your mom are a package deal."

"So why are we still staying at our place and only visit over here?"

He felt Lexi stiffen, and he grinned. Well, it looked like the waiting period was over. "Do you want to stay with me? I didn't want to move too fast for either of you, but I'd be...honored if you and your mother would move in with me."

"Maybe this is something you and I should talk about privately," Lexi said tightly.

Parker looked up at his mother. "But shouldn't I have a say too?"

She ran a hand through her son's hair, and North chewed on his lip. Maybe putting that out there like that hadn't been the best idea. What did he know though? He'd never done this before, and his brothers hadn't been in this situation before either.

Kids were complicated.

"Yes, you do. I guess we should talk about this, huh?"

"That seems prudent," Parker said deadpan.

North threw his head back and laughed. "Where did you learn to say that?"

Parker turned and grinned at him. "I heard Aunt Mel say that to Uncle Kade. Uncle Kade said that he loved when his mate talked all smart like that."

That sounded like his brother and his mate for sure.

"If we're done talking vocabulary—prudent, by the way, is a great word, honey—can we talk about our plans then? Since we decided to have this conversation all together, let's get it done."

North wasn't sure if Lexi was mad or scared about the way this had come about—he was guessing both—but he wasn't going to let her run away from it.

"I'd say that we should make it official. Why should we alternate between houses when you can just stay here?"

"But this is going a little fast, don't you think?" Lexi asked.

North shrugged. "We're wolves. Everything moves a little fast for us."

"And I can stay here too? With you and Mom?" Parker asked.

North ran a hand through Parker's hair. "I'd like that a lot. I have the guest room we can make into yours."

"But what if you have guests?"

North grinned. "Then it looks like I'll have to build on. I had always planned on doing it anyway when I found my mate and made a family. I don't really want to move to a bigger place since the clinic is attached, but we can make it work."

"And Kade and Jasper would help build it, right? I think that's what they do."

"Yep. It helps having contractors and architects in the family. Though I do know how to do a lot of it myself. Once we have time, we can build on." There were a few more important things to worry about first, but he'd be damned if he let go of his future to dwell on them.

Parker turned toward Lexi. "Can we move in, Mom? I want to know we can stay. Plus, I think Uncle Logan is getting all growly with Aunt Cailin and needs space."

Out of the mouth of babes.

"Come on, Lex. We don't want Logan to get all growly."

Lexi narrowed her eyes. "Seriously? You're gonna try that on me?"

Parker leaned into North, leaving him grinning. "See? Parker wants to stay. I want you to stay. No, I *need* you to stay. We can figure out everything as we go, but I think it's time we take this next step. Plus, you'll be closer so I can protect you."

His wolf growled happily at that.

Lexi rolled her eyes but he could see the sheer joy on her face. "Okay, if that's what my boys want, we'll move in."

Her boys.

Yeah, he liked the sound of that.

Parker leapt off the couch and whooped. "This is so cool. I can't wait to tell Aunt Cailin." He paused. "What about Uncle Logan though? I don't want him to be lonely." The kid snapped his fingers and grinned. "I know! I'll tell Aunt Cailin that she needs to watch out for him so he isn't so lonely." The kid threw his arms around Lexi then North then pulled away. "I'm going to go call Aunt Cailin." He whooped again and ran to the kitchen, presumably to get the phone.

North's body was shaking as he tried to hold back his laughter.

"Oh God, poor Logan."

"Hey," North said, affronted. "Poor Logan? What about poor Cailin?"

"Those two don't have a chance in hell with Parker playing matchmaker," Lexi teased.

"So..." North began but stopped, not knowing what to say.

"So..." Lexi repeated. "Looks like we're living together, which was what we sort of were doing anyway since we haven't spent a night apart since we've been sleeping together so I guess this works. I just don't want to move too fast and hurt Parker. You think this is a good idea, really? What if we're doing the wrong thing? What if—"

North crushed his mouth to hers, effectively shutting her up. He pulled away then ran his thumb over her cheek.

"Stop worrying. We'll make this work."

She sucked in her lips. "If you say so."

"I do say so."

There was a knock on the door, and North inhaled, scenting Logan's presence on the other side. Well, it looked as though they were breaking the news of their new living situation sooner rather than later.

"I'll get it," Parker called as he ran past them. It seemed the kid was already making this place his home. That suited North just fine.

Logan casually walked into the room, his brow raised. "Looks like you guys have settled things."

"And why do you say that?" Lexi asked.

"You guys look more relaxed, and Parker just answered the door like it was his own home."

"It is his home now," North said, and Logan grinned.

"About time. Now I get to make the old place my bachelor pad."

"I wouldn't do that, Uncle Logan. I already talked to Aunt Cailin, and she promised me she'd take care of you." Parker's face scrunched up and looked away so he couldn't see his uncle's face go pale. North held back a laugh at the sight. "Though it took forever for her to say yes to that. I don't know if she likes you. You'll have to fix that though, okay? Because we're all family."

North watched Logan as he swallowed hard and gave a small nod. "I'll work on that, buddy. In fact, let's go get started on that now. I was going to ask if you wanted to work with me on a project for Mel and Pat. You wanna come? We'll stop by Cailin's on the way."

Parker's face brightened. "Okay. Let me get my shoes." He froze mid-step. "Oh, can I go, Mom?"

"Sure, have fun, baby."

Soon Lexi and North found themselves alone in the house—*their* house. "So, Lex, how do you want to celebrate our new place?"

Lexi blushed, and she shook her head. "You are in so much trouble, North Jamenson. Next time you want to make a huge decision like that, you don't get to do it in front of Parker. If you're going to help me raise him, then you need to learn that some parenting happens out of earshot of said kid."

North collared her neck softly, loving the way her eyes darkened. "I'll do better next time, I promise."

"You better," she rasped out.

"So, have any ideas?" he repeated, loving the small gasps coming from her throat.

"North, we should plan out all the details of the move." Her eyes darkened as he traced her cheek down to her neck. "We...we need to make sure we have things for Parker's room and move over my things slowly or something so I'm not taking over the bathroom or anything."

His free hand slid down her back, cupping her ass. "You can have as many drawers as you'd like. We'll buy more."

"North."

"Let me love you, my Lexi."

She closed her eyes, her head falling back as pulled her closer.

"Okay, but I don't like how you make me all swoony with just your touch."

He chuckled then brought his mouth down to hers, taking her lower lip between his teeth. She stiffened for a moment before sighing. He nipped lightly then licked where his teeth had been.

"You do the same to me, love."

She rolled her eyes. "I don't think we've ever sounded so cheesy."

North tugged at the bottom of her shirt, and she immediately held up her arms. He pulled it over her head then went to work on her jeans.

"Well then, if we're too cheesy, I suppose I'll just have to fuck you hard to make up for it."

He knelt before her, sliding her jeans down her legs, and she held on to his shoulders for balance.

"I think that idea has merit."

He looked up at her standing in nothing but her panties and bra and grinned. "Good."

Before she could blink, he lifted her off her feet, and she wrapped her legs around his waist. As he walked them to the bedroom, he licked and nipped along her neck. She tilted her head to the side, giving him more access.

He dropped her on the bed, and she bounced, her eyes going wide. "I can't believe you just did that."

"You said I was cheesy." He stripped off his clothes then leaned over her, capturing her lips again. God, the taste of her on his tongue would never be enough.

He kissed his way down her body, taking off her bra slowly so he could watch the goose bumps rise on her flesh. He latched onto one nipple, sucking hard and biting down. When he let go, her nipples were red, wet, and perfect.

"Look at those tits," he whispered. "Fucking amazing."

"You're a sweet talker for sure," she whispered, her body arching over him.

He lavished attention on her other breast, licking the same way he had with the other, and trailed his hand down her stomach at the same time. His fingers slid deftly under her panties, and he spread her so he could rub against her clit.

Lexi moaned for him, and he let go of her breast so he could trail kisses down her stomach. The lace of her panties brushed along his skin as he pulled them down her legs, leaving her bare.

"Goddess, you're a sight."

She spread for him, and he grinned. "I take it you want to come?"

She raised a brow, sliding her hand along her mound. "I can take care of that myself if you have a problem with it."

He gripped her hand then pulled it over her head. "Give me the other one." She did quickly, and he kissed her hard in reward. "I get to make you come. Got it?"

"Only if I can do the same for you."

"Deal. Keep your hands there. Don't make me tie you up."

She blushed at that so he filed that little tidbit away for later. He moved down to the edge of the bed, pulled her ass closer to his face, and lapped her up. She bucked against his face, egging him on as he fucked her with his tongue, going as deep into her pussy as he could go before licking up to her clit and biting down. His fingers dug into her soft thighs, keeping her still as she screamed his name, coming on his tongue.

She was still writhing as he stood up and pulled her to his chest. He crushed his mouth to hers, and she wrapped her arms around him. Their breathing quickened, and he pulled away, his cock aching.

"Get on your knees and grip the slats on the bottom of the headboard," he ordered when he pulled way.

She nodded and did what she was told, leaving her ass high in the air. He gripped his shaft, roughly sliding up and down it a couple of times, needing to feel the rush before he sank into her heat.

"Ready, my Lexi?"

She looked over her shoulder and grinned. "You know it."

He gripped her hips and thrust into her waiting pussy with one stroke. They both called out at the penetration, her inner walls still swollen from her past orgasm, and he froze, waiting for her to accommodate him.

When she pushed back against his hips, he pulled out and slammed back in, repeating the movement over and over and setting a rapid pace that left sweat rolling down his back.

"Fuck, North. Jesus, you feel good."

"You gonna come again for me, Lexi?"

"Hell, yeah. If you work it."

He let out a harsh laugh at her tease then moved his hands so they were on her breasts. He plucked and thrummed her nipples, rolling them into hard little points as he fucked her from behind. His balls tightened, and he knew he was close, so he pinched her nipples hard. Her pussy clenched around him as she came, and he followed right behind her.

While he filled her with his seed, he pulled her back against his chest, gripped her chin, and lowered his mouth to hers.

Finally, he let her go, resting his head against her shoulder. "Am I cheesy now?" he said on a breath.

"Only in the sexiest of ways." She laughed so he bit her shoulder, not hard, just enough to show her who was in charge.

She wiggled her ass, and he moaned.

Okay, so she was in charge.

But she didn't have to know that.

CHAPTER FOURTEEN

"**W**hy are we going to the elders' camp again?" Lexi asked as she stepped over a fallen log.

It had been almost two weeks since she and Parker had officially moved into North's home—no, *their*—home, though she wasn't used to calling it that yet. Parker seemed to be settling in nicely, considering a new home and a new move were nothing out of the ordinary to him. However, she knew her little boy wasn't quite ready to lean on North as a father or whatever Parker wanted to call him.

She and North might have professed their love for each other, and they were working on finding out how their mating would work, but that didn't mean things were easy.

Far from it.

They each had their own insecurities about where this was heading, not that they'd actually talked about it with each other. No, of course not. Why act like reasonable adults when they could act like scared teenagers when it came to emotions?

Honestly, after what had happened in her past, she'd never thought she'd actually find a man she could love and who would love her back. Once she had Parker, she'd never really thought about how their lives would adjust to having another man in the house. North was cautious, not acting like a father per se, but a father figure. Parker didn't come to him for permission to do things, but she had a feeling that her son would soon be testing the boundaries of how their relationship would work.

She and North needed to learn how to be a mated pair, they'd have to learn how to raise and, if necessary, discipline Parker. She wasn't sure how that would all work out, but she knew that the situation would arise soon. There was no way she could have an eight-year-old in the house and not deal with issues. Issues were par for the course.

North would just have to deal.

She shook her head. Damn it. She was counting him out before he'd even had a chance. North was great with Parker, and she needed to believe it would stay that way—even with a few bumps along the way.

North grabbed her hand, and she froze. "What?" she asked.

"I answered your question, yet you weren't listening," he said as he faced her. He tucked a piece of hair behind her ear and tilted his head. "What's going on in that head of yours, baby?"

"Just thinking," she mumbled.

"About? Come on. I can't help if you don't let me in."

"I was just thinking about the adjustments you've had to make since we found each other."

"What do you mean? You think the fact that I've had to change a few things around is a problem for me? I love it, baby. I love you."

Her heart warmed as she heard the words again. "I'm just a little lost."

"Then I'll find you," he whispered, and he took her lips. She melted into him, needing his touch, his taste. She could drown in him and relish it.

He pulled away, and she licked her lips, needing his flavor on her tongue for just that much longer.

Wow, she had it bad.

"So, what was your answer to my question?" she asked.

"What was your question?" North teased.

Lexi rolled her eyes. "Why are we going to the elders' camp?" North had come to her that morning with an odd light in his eyes that she couldn't quite figure out, telling her that they were going to go see Emmaline, an elder who was friends with the Jamensons, to talk about...something. North hadn't been too helpful in the details, and by the manic way his wolf was coming through his eyes and his growls, Lexi hadn't asked too much about it, worried she'd hurt him by doing so.

North gave a small smile, but Lexi could see the strain behind it. "We're going because I've asked Emmaline to take a look in the archives—the ones that only the elders can use—to see if she can find anything about being a latent wolf."

Lexi froze. The sound of the wind brushing through the trees, the birds in the air calling for each other, and the scurrying of prey on the ground reached her in almost slow motion.

She'd known North had been looking into what to do with her situation. She also knew he was doing it to save her life and not because he felt she wasn't worthy of him, but still, it unnerved her.

It'd caught her by surprise, and she didn't like that. She shouldn't have been surprised that North would do *anything* for her. He'd told her that, yet she hadn't put two and two together.

"Oh," she finally said, the sound of her pulse in her ears finally slowing down.

"I know I should have told you more about it when I was talking to Emmaline, but I was afraid to get your hopes up, considering mine were up too."

"So she found something?" She chewed on her lip, worry washing over her.

North rubbed his thumb over the place she'd bitten and took a deep breath. "That's what she says. She said she'd already talked to my father a couple days ago and now was the time to tell us. I'm not sure what that means. I had wanted to bring her to us, or at least to my parents' place to talk, but the other elders are being asses about 'elder knowledge', so they wouldn't let her leave."

"She's a prisoner then?"

North growled. "Maybe. I'm not sure since the elders are a league of their own within the Pack. At least it seems like that. Dad's not going to stand for it though. Come on. I don't want to be late. The other elders might make Emmaline stay away from us or something."

Lexi nodded and gripped North's hand. Soon they found themselves in another part of the den, where a small grouping of houses surrounded a stone circle.

Emmaline, a beautiful woman with blonde hair and faraway eyes, came out and greeted them. "It's good to see you," she said, her voice soft. "I've found something that might help, but I don't know if it can be done."

Well, that was straight to the point.

She led them into her home, and Lexi gripped North's hand as hard as she could.

"Tell us what you've found, Emmaline."

The elder looked off into space for a moment before blinking away whatever she'd been thinking of. Lexi wondered what it would be like to live so long and to see so much. It was no wonder that Emmaline seemed not of this world, more Fae-like than any of them.

"I've been reading all I can because I've personally never heard of a latent reaching adulthood, let alone having a child of their own." She frowned. "At least I don't remember knowing. Sometimes things get jumbled after so long." She shook her head again and gave a small smile. "I promise I'm not crazy, just a little lost."

Lexi reached out and gripped Emmaline's hand. "It's okay. We all get that way sometimes."

Emmaline turned her hand to return Lexi's grip. "Thank you for being so kind. Now, what I've found about latent wolves isn't pretty, not by far. There's only one way in all that I've read that actually will set the wolf free."

Lexi started. "There's a way?" Hope filled her. This could be what they'd be waiting for.

Emmaline gave a sad smile but nodded. "Yes, but it is not easy."

"Tell us."

"It's said that a latent wolf is so buried beneath the human that it takes two parts of a whole to bring it forth. It takes two Packs, two Alphas, two slays, and two acts of brutality to let the wolf roam free."

Lexi swallowed hard. That didn't sound good at all. No, in fact, it sounded downright scary as all fuck.

"What does that mean?" North asked, his voice low, dangerous.

Emmaline met Lexi's eyes. "It means that latent wolves are doomed to die by fate's decree unless there is one who is of two Packs. Talk to your father, North.

He'll know what to do. It won't be easy, and death might be the only way to relieve the pain, but it's an answer."

"You're saying she'll have to go through a change like a human turning into a wolf."

"Yes."

Lexi swallowed hard. Turning a human into werewolf wasn't like it was portrayed in books or movies. It took an act of brutality so gruesome that most didn't do it. The human had to be near death in order for the enzyme within the wolf's bite to work. It also usually took an Alpha wolf and their power for the change to take hold. Though Willow had been able to survive on Jasper's bite alone, it was almost unheard of for other wolves to make the change happen.

"What's this about two Packs?" she asked, her voice a little too shaky for comfort. North wrapped an arm around her, but she didn't lean into him. She was so scared that if she did so, she'd break down.

Emmaline tilted her head, looking more wolf than human. "You were born within one Pack and are now of another. You're of two Packs like the books say. Not all wolves have that option. It seems, though fate has taken much from you, it has given you this...loophole."

"You're saying the Alpha of the Talon Pack needs to change me just like Edward will? That's so not happening. Joseph, the Alpha, is a cruel man. He kicked me out, remember?"

Emmaline smiled. "You cannot be bitten by a dead man, sweetie. You'll need the Alpha of the Talon Pack to bite you."

Lexi froze. "Joseph's dead?" she rasped out.

"How do you know this?" North asked, sounding just as shocked.

162

"I don't remember," Emmaline said as she shook her head. "I'm sorry I'm not much help. I'm reading through all I can to keep the Centrals away and now looking into this. I don't remember where I learn things all the time."

The woman looked so distressed that Lexi couldn't help but want to make the woman feel better. "It's okay. North…" She turned to her mate. "We need to talk to your father. If Joseph isn't the Alpha anymore, that could mean something for the Redwoods." And they would need to talk to Edward about her changing into a wolf.

"Thank you, Emmaline. Thank you." Lexi stood and hugged the woman hard. Emmaline seemed surprised for a moment then hugged back.

"I'm sorry I couldn't be more help. I hope it works out. I'm going to go back to the stacks and look up ways to bring those dark magic wards down now. The Centrals' put up those wards right after they took Hannah and Reed before they mated and found Josh. The wards seem to be getting stronger as time passes. At least that's what the scouts tell your father. I think it has to do with the fact that the Pack is dying. As time moves on, the wards use their specific magic and the life essence of the Pack members to maintain the ward's strength. In other words, the demon is using the Pack to protect the den, but killing them at the same time by using their souls to keep the dark magic alive, rather than using the inherent power that emanates from the Pack."

"My goddess," Lexi whispered.

"Indeed," Emmaline agreed. "I'm still looking for ways to break them. There's got to be something."

"You're doing great, Emmaline. Thank you so much."

"The Redwoods are my Pack," she said simply.

They left the elder part of the den and made their way to North's parents' house. North called on the way, telling them what they'd learned. Who knew how much time they had or how much time had passed since Joseph had died. They needed all the time they could muster to figure out what to do. His father told them cryptically that plans were being made and that they should come over...quickly.

Other than the phone call, they were silent on their way back. There really wasn't much they could say without breaking down. Before they had never had a true hope, and now, they did.

It just wasn't the ideal solution.

She'd either die because her body was giving out on itself when it couldn't release the extra energy and chemicals accumulating in her body because she couldn't change, or she'd die like so many others before her trying to force the change.

"Can you make sure Parker is there at some point?" she whispered right as they arrived in front of the Alpha's home. It had taken almost an hour of walking to get there since they couldn't use a car to get to the elder's part of the den, so she'd had a lot of time to think.

North stopped her and looked down. "Should he be here for this conversation?"

"I...I think he needs to be told what's being done but not be there for it."

North nodded. "I'll tell Mom when we get inside."

They walked inside without knocking and found Logan talking with Edward in the living room while Pat poured iced tea.

"Let me help you, Pat," Lexi said when they walked in.

Pat waved her off. "I need to do something with my hands. Go sit down. You guys had a long trek from the elders' area."

Lexi looked down at Pat's hands and frowned. The Alpha's mate wasn't shaking, but her tension seemed high.

"What's wrong?"

Pat looked over her shoulder at Edward, who gave her a nod. "It seems we're having visitors here any minute now. As soon as North called to tell us about the Talon Alpha, Edward called the Brentwoods."

The Brentwoods were the ruling family of the Talons.

"Is Gideon Alpha then?" Lexi asked. Gideon had been the eldest son of the Alpha and was therefore Heir of the Pack. He and his brothers had also fought to keep her and her family in the Pack but had failed because Joseph had ruled the Pack with an iron fist.

"Yes, though it had happened only a few days ago, hence why I wasn't told yet. Gideon had wanted to ensure the Pack wouldn't rise against him once he took control. He was very interested to know how I'd heard, but I didn't mention Emmaline's name."

North let out a low whistle. "Lots of change. And I'd like to know how Emmaline knew as well, but I think it has to do more with magic and the moon goddess than with a mole."

Edward nodded as Lexi sat down next to North. "I agree. She's always been more connected to the voices in the wind than most. I'm glad she listened to them this time and was able to warn us."

"Wait," North said. "You said visitors. The new Alpha is coming here? So soon after taking control?"

Logan let out a growl. "Apparently the Brentwoods want to make good with the Pack and ex-Packmates they've ignored for so long."

"Logan," Lexi admonished, "Gideon and his brothers and sister were always good to us. It's not their fault they had shitty parents."

Logan snorted. "I didn't see them caring for us and trying to help us."

"They let us leave the Pack without being hurt, and it was Gideon who made sure Joseph didn't kill me as soon as they understood what had happened to me and what was growing within my belly. Remember that."

North growled beside her, and she leaned into his hold. "It's okay now," she soothed, even though she was nervous at seeing any of them again. "The Brentwoods... at least these are good ones. I saw two extra glasses, Pat. I take it Gideon and another are coming then?"

"Yes, Gideon rather than Ryder, the Heir, because the Alphas need to meet, and he was also told of your...situation. Emmaline told us a few days ago, Lexi. I'm sorry we didn't tell you. We wanted to make sure that we could actually do something about it and not leave you wanting." Tears filled Pat's eyes but she blinked them away.

Lexi sucked in a breath but didn't say anything. How could she when all they had wanted to do was help her and not get her hopes up.

"Also, Gideon's cousin, Mitchell, who is the Beta, is coming with him since the Alpha shouldn't travel alone."

Lexi nodded. It made sense, but it was still a bit scary to think about. She hadn't seen any of the Brentwoods since she'd been kicked out of the Pack. She wasn't sure how they would receive her. She might not be looking for approval from them since she was in her new home now, but deep down she knew she still wanted it. Sure, she'd told Logan that the others hadn't hurt her and had even gone to bat for her, but she'd still had to leave.

She'd still been banished.

North squeezed her knee then moved so they were leaning with their foreheads together. "If Gideon is coming here, then this might happen sooner rather than later." She watched his throat as he swallowed hard. "Do you want to wait?"

Lexi let out a breath. "I...I think that if they leave their den and come all the way over here, then we should get it taken care of. I'm ready to do this."

North closed his eyes, his nostrils flaring. "I will be by your side the entire time. We will do this and I won't let you leave me. I just found you. I know you want to find your wolf and I know it's time to do it. If we wait...well then it might be too late. I'd rather you do this now, when you're strong. I won't leave your side."

She cupped his face. "I trust you with everything I have, North." She met his gaze, knowing he'd see the tears there that hadn't fallen yet. "So, yes, I want to figure out if I can find my wolf. If I can't...well, you know what will happen. You know I can't last much longer like this." She tried to smile, but the pain in his eyes made it hopeless.

Logan growled beside her, and she turned. "You, sister mine, need to let me in on your medical issues." The betrayal on his face surprised her. "I...I always knew we were lucky that you'd lived past a certain age, but you never told me it was this bad. You never told me you were in such need of your wolf that you're about to risk dying by mauling in order to achieve it."

"Logan," she started then stopped herself. What could she say? She'd hidden her pain and wants for years because she didn't know what to do with them. There hadn't been any real hope, so she hadn't wanted to make Logan worry more than he already was. Then they'd been on the run and they'd had to raise a baby and learn to live on their own, in hiding.

"Drop it, okay? I'll watch them tear into you and hopefully save you. Then I'll stand back and let you raise your son and I'll be the best uncle I can be. If the worst happens?" He growled. "If the worst happens, then I'll die inside, but Parker won't be alone."

"Well, it looks like Logan's stolen my lines," North said, his voice gruff with tears.

Her own tears, the ones that she'd held at bay, finally fell. Great, she was falling apart, and she hadn't even told her son what she was doing yet.

She took a deep breath, inhaling the scents around her and froze, noticing a scent that had been there all along, but she'd missed it. "Parker's here?" She gasped as she stood up. She's been so stuck in her own head she hadn't put the pieces together.

Pat nodded. "Logan brought him over, but he's upstairs." The woman came over and kissed her cheek. "Go tell him your plans and be strong, baby."

Lexi gripped North's hand and dragged him upstairs. There was no way she was doing this without him.

Parker sat on the bed reading a book and looked up when she walked through the door. Tears streamed down his face, but he didn't say anything.

Her baby was way too smart and clever for his own good.

"Parker..."

"I don't want you to die."

It was like a kick to the solar plexus, but she walked to him, sat on the bed, and pulled him into her arms. He went willingly, and she broke down all over again.

"I don't want to die either." There was no use making empty promises she wasn't sure she could keep.

"I know what you're going to do. I heard them talking when they didn't know I was there."

Lexi closed her eyes tight. "You shouldn't eavesdrop."

"I had to. I was afraid you'd keep it from me."

She pulled him back so she could cup his face. "Never, Parker. I would never do something like this and hide it from you."

He swallowed hard. "Just come back. Okay?"

She choked on a sob but didn't lie to him, only held him while North held her. She didn't know how much time had passed before Cailin walked in the room.

"Hey, Parker. I'm on my way to Willow's bakery. Want to join me?"

Parker nodded against Lexi's body, and Lexi gripped her son tight.

"I love you, Mom."

"I love you too, my Parker."

She kissed him and let him go. Parker stood then went to North, throwing his arms around his neck. North looked surprised for a moment before hugging him close.

"Take care of her, okay?" Parker whispered.

North ran a hand through Parker's hair. "Always, Parker. Always."

Soon Lexi found herself in North's clinic, a robe wrapped around her while she sat in North's lap. Though it might look odd considering they were both on the exam table, they didn't care. He hadn't wanted to let her go, and while she might have wanted to stand on her own, she knew North needed this.

Once Cailin had taken Parker away, Edward had said he would be meeting with the Talon Alpha with Jasper and Kade in attendance in another part of the den. It was their protocol, and he didn't want Logan or Lexi near them in case the resentment was stronger than they feared.

"Well, son of a bitch," Logan mumbled, and Lexi turned.

Gideon and Mitchell stood in the doorway, looking the same as they had the last time Lexi had seen them. That only made sense considering wolves didn't age, but it was still a bit jarring. It was as if no time had passed, yet looking into the pain and darkness in their eyes, Lexi knew they'd missed a lot.

Logan, who had been off to the side, walked right up to them, and before Lexi could blink, Gideon was cursing at his bloody nose, and Mitchell had Logan against the wall by his throat.

"Logan!" Lexi scrambled off North's lap—not an easy thing to do in only a robe—but was pulled back by her mate.

"Let them handle it," North whispered.

"Men. Stupid, stupid men."

"Let him go, Mitchell," Gideon ordered.

Edward strode in with Kade and Jasper behind him. "Well, that's a great way to start this," the Alpha mumbled.

Mitchell growled then let Logan go. "Keep your hands off the Alpha, Logan."

"Always the Brentwood bastard," Logan spat. "You might be one too, but you weren't the son of the Alpha. You're the cousin. Remember that."

"Stop it, Logan. Just stop it!" Lexi screamed. "Getting into fist fights and acting like stupid cavemen won't help it. Were Gideon and Mitchell part of what happened with Joseph? No. Are they here now to help me?" She looked at Gideon, who nodded, the blood on his face making him look even more dangerous than usual. "See? They're here to help. Stop acting like an idiot and keep your hands to yourself."

A laugh boomed from Edward. "I love the women in my family. They stand for no shit. Let's let that one punch and subsequent strangle be the end of this." He let out a long breath. "Now I have to do the one thing I hate more than any other as an Alpha. Gideon. I'll have to be the one who bites first and last since she's of my Pack now."

Gideon looked at Lexi. "Is that what you want? To be a Redwood? We'd have you back, Lex."

North growled, low and menacing.

"I'm a Redwood now, Gideon. But thank you for the offer." Really, what else could she say?

The Talon Alpha nodded then pulled off his shirt. Lexi blinked and turned to her mate. She wasn't in the mood to look at any naked man but North. Plus, she was scared out of her mind.

He cupped her face then kissed her. Hard. "I love you so fucking much, Lexi. Don't leave me. Please."

She sniffed then kissed his jaw, the rasp of his unshaven beard scraping along her lips. "I love you too, and I'll do all in my power to come back to you. I promise you."

He nodded then looked over his shoulder. "While Dad and Gideon are shifting, help me tie her down with the chains so she won't fight the attack."

Lexi sucked in a breath.

She hated this part.

They chained her down, apology in their eyes, but she let it happen. She'd taken off her robe so the Alpha's teeth had direct access to her skin when they bit down—something she really didn't want to think about.

Soon the room began to fill with Jamenson men and women. Each with a role that would be assigned to him shortly or there for moral support. Though she knew it would hurt them to watch, she also knew they wouldn't be anywhere else. During the painful process, they would stand united.

This was just one more reason why Lexi knew she was in the right Pack and doing the right thing.

Hannah came in, her body stiff but determination in her eyes. "I helped Melanie through this, and I will help you through it as well," she said then gripped her hand. Pat came in and gripped the other.

The Alpha female looked at them individually, Kade, Jasper, Mitchell, Adam, Reed, and Josh. "You have one job," Pat said, her voice firm. "Hold back Logan and North to keep them from stopping this. They are both going to want to stop her pain, and it will only make things worse. They have to be in here or their wolves will take over, and that will be worse than anything, but they need to stay away. We've done this before. We will do it again." She cupped North's face then Logan's, murmuring into their ears. Then she came to Lexi's side. "I will see you when you wake up, my darling. This will be painful, but you will survive. You're my daughter now. I won't lose you."

Lexi licked her lips then nodded. The fear overwhelmed her, but she had to stay strong. She had to do this.

She met North's gaze and never wavered.

Out of the corner of her eye, she saw two wolves prowling in the room, but she didn't focus on them. She focused only on her mate.

She screamed at the first bite again with the second, then went limp with the third.

Through it all she kept her gaze on her mate, who screamed with her and tried to fight off his brothers.

They were stronger though in numbers and kept him back.

The fiery pain scorched through her, rendering her helpless. She felt the burn with each bite as the enzymes seeped into her skin like hot pokers. Bile filled her throat, and darkness swept over her—much too slowly.

The agony ripped through her, but it was nothing compared to the pain in her lover's eyes.

He kept her sane.

He kept her alive.

The darkness filled her, and she fled the pain, finally tumbling into unconsciousness.

CHAPTER FIFTEEN

"She'll wake up soon," North whispered to himself—the same thing he'd done hundreds of time over the past four days.

He rubbed his hands over his face and cursed softly. Why hadn't she woken up? He could still hear the screams, not only from her but from himself and Logan. He could still smell the copper scent of blood and taste the acid on his tongue as he fought not to vomit.

Thank the gods she'd passed out only a few minutes into the process. As soon as his father and Gideon were done, the Alphas had shifted back, pale and looking as if they each wanted to crawl into a hole and die. His mother had taken his father home while Mitchell had taken the Talon Alpha back to their own den, their part in helping Lexi over.

North was sure that wouldn't be the last time they heard from the Talons, but that wasn't his main concern right now.

No, all he wanted to do now was see his Lexi open her eyes.

"North?" Parker whispered as he walked in the room.

North raised his head and held out his hand. The boy immediately tucked himself close to North and sat in his lap, not too big to need comfort.

North would take all the comfort he could get at this point.

He tried to remain strong, though, because this boy, his son in every way but blood, needed him to be.

"Why won't she wake up?"

North closed his eyes, praying for strength. "It takes a lot of energy to heal and become a wolf."

"But she won't even know if she changes into a wolf until the next full-moon hunt, right?"

"Yes. Once she wakes up," and she *would* wake up, "it takes the first full moon to bring on the change."

"So even when she wakes up, her wolf could still be hiding? So all of this could be for nothing?"

North squeezed too-knowing Parker tighter. "We would have at least tried, Park. That isn't for nothing."

"There are my boys," a soft voice said from the bed.

Parker and North both looked up, holding their breaths.

"Lexi."

"Mom."

She was pale, too pale, but her eyes were open. Thank the gods.

Parker was up in a flash, softly putting his arm around Lexi's shoulders. She didn't raise her own arms, but North could see that she wanted to.

Parker pulled back. "Am I hurting you?" he asked, his voice small.

"No, baby, I love your hugs."

"What about my hugs?" North asked through his tightening throat. His knees shook in relief that she was alive and breathing. He didn't know how to hold back his emotions anymore, didn't know how to remain the calm Jamenson. All he wanted to do was throw back his head and howl in utter relief.

"Come here," his mate whispered, and he went to her willingly.

He leaned down and brushed his lips against hers softly, not wanting to hurt her in any way. He didn't care that his tears fell on her cheeks. He was just so happy she was awake. They'd made it past one more step. Now they just needed to ensure that she would be the wolf she'd always wanted to be.

North also had another step to take, but this one wouldn't be with Lexi by his side.

His wolf growled, eagerly anticipating their next move.

Lexi blinked up at him as Parker got into the bed with her, cuddling to her side, the pup needing his mother more than ever before.

"What is it, North?"

He tucked a piece of hair behind her ear then cupped her cheek. "Everything's fine. I'm going to go get Hannah and make sure you're really okay. I love you, my Lexi."

Lexi studied his face, but he made sure she wouldn't see any hints of what he planned, of what he needed to do.

"I love you too."

He kissed her again, ran a hand over Parker's head, and then left the room, ready to carry out the next part of his mission. He couldn't stand by and let those who wanted to hurt his family continue to act as if they had not a care in the world. He'd waited for a plan, a way to make what needed to be done easier, but he knew it would take more than blind luck for fate to run its course. His mate was with her son, and would hopefully find her wolf and live a long life.

Now it was North's turn to take another step on fate's path and kill the man who'd taken so much from them all, from his family, from him.

Yes, this would be personal... beyond personal.

He would find Corbin and kill him. The prophecy that they all believed in foretold he'd be the one to kill the Alpha of the Central Pack, and now it would be up to North to ensure that would happen.

As his brothers had pointed out, there hadn't been any mention that North would live through the process. That didn't matter though, not as much as the lives of his family and Pack. He'd already had to stand by and watch the Centrals kill Adam's first mate, attack and torture Willow, kidnap Reed and Hannah, make Josh a hybrid, including a piece he had only a semblance of control over, take Adam's leg, take Bay's pride...and so much more.

Year by year, his family had stood strong for their Pack, and North had lost nothing but his hopes.

Now he would fight for them, fight for his mate, fight for himself.

"Where are you going?"

North stood by his front door, his hand frozen on the doorknob. "You know where I'm going, Maddox." His twin had been tortured and scarred because Corbin had thought Maddox was North. North would have done anything to have taken his brother's place.

"You're going to get yourself killed."

"Then I'll take the bastard down with me."

"North, think about what you're doing."

North spun on his heel, his wolf on edge. "I have been, Maddox. Ever since you told us what Corbin told you all those years ago, I have been. It's been on my mind every day, every second. I can't let him come here and hurt my family. I'm going to take him out."

"Then you're a fool."

North raised his chin. "Then I am. But I have to try. I can't sit back and wait for him to come to me."

"Then don't go alone."

Both Maddox and North turned to Logan, who walked into the living room, a frown on his face.

"This is none of your concern," North growled.

"Isn't it? You're my brother-in-law, my Pack mate, and hopefully, one day, my friend. I don't have a mate bond like the rest of your brothers, so if I die beside you today, then I won't hurt another." His mouth set in a grim line, and North had to hold himself back from mentioning their sisters.

If they died today, both men knew Lexi and Cailin would find a way to kill them both again in the next life. .

"Lexi can't lose both of us," North countered.

"Then let's make sure we don't get killed, shall we?"

"You're both idiots. However, I'll stay here with Lexi to make sure she's safe." Maddox gave both men a quick slap on the back then hugged North hard. "Don't get dead."

North sucked in a breath, gave Logan a nod, and then went outside. They climbed into his Jeep and made their way through the den in silence.

It would take almost an hour to get to the Centrals' den, but North wasn't going to go directly there. No, he wanted to go only part way and see if he could find any of Corbin's enforcers around. The bastard had a way of knowing where people were going at all times—thanks to his dark magic.

"So, got a plan? Or we just winging it?" Logan asked.

"Go to the halfway point. Find an enforcer. Kill him. Wait for Corbin to find out I'm there, which should take, oh, ten minutes, then kill the bastard. If we aren't *inside* the den, we have a better shot. And, this way, we're less likely to get any other Redwoods killed."

Logan was silent for a moment before he whistled softly. "Getting Packmates killed sounds like something Corbin would do, so you're banking good there, but going out without knowing exactly how we're going to come back whole and not knowing even if Corbin will come like we hope? Sounds risky as all hell. Why didn't you do this earlier if you could just do it like this?"

North gripped the steering wheel until his knuckles were white. "Because I didn't want to risk anyone else's life, and I was scared, okay? I'm not looking to die."

"Doesn't sound like it from your plan so far."

"Fuck you. I'm supposed to kill him."

"Yeah, did they say when? Because right now doesn't seem like the best time. Not when your mate is lying in a bed after almost dying."

"She'll be okay." She had to be okay. "We'll live through this. I don't have a death wish. I just want her free of Corbin so we can move on."

"I was waiting for that."

"What?"

"You're allowed to be selfish here. You're allowed to want to feel that mating bond. I can't wait until I fucking feel that." He held up a hand. "No, don't ask. I'm not going to talk about my mating. However, we can talk about yours. You want to kill Corbin so you can mate with Lexi in truth and have all those babies you Jamensons seem to like making, and as a bonus, get one step closer to having the Centrals taken down?

Sounds like a plan to me. Just be honest with yourself about your intentions. Okay?"

"Just don't die on me."

"Ditto."

North pulled the Jeep off to the side of the road. They were still in the middle of the forest and would be for a while yet. The three Packs of the Pacific Northwest were all bunched up together with neutral territory between them. The Redwoods, Centrals, and Talons had generally been at least friendly to one another, if not having outright alliances. The Centrals, though, had always wanted more, and since they were between the Redwoods and Talons, they fought with whichever group they could. The Talons had been far enough away from the Redwoods that it wasn't until the modern age that communication had been more than a passing glance through Mediators—wolves that went between the Packs to negotiate treaties.

North had chosen to come to the neutral territory where he'd known the Centrals had put enforcers, breaking their treaties. However, since the Centrals invaded and killed when they wanted, the neutral territories were a small matter.

No, nothing to the Redwoods was small. If his family could, they would find a way to take out the whole Pack, but in doing so, they would kill what they stood for — their honor, their peace, their magic. Since they were also not using the dark magic the Centrals were, they might even kill themselves as well.

There wasn't a way out of this situation. Not with the demon amongst the Central's ranks.

He punched his steering wheel and cursed.

"Let the rage settle right beneath your skin," Logan said smoothly. "I can smell the enforcers." He took a deep breath. "Can't you?"

North growled then nodded. Yes, he could smell the bastards prowling around them, thinking they had the upper hand. They weren't as stealthy as they thought.

With one look and a nod toward Logan, they both got out of the Jeep, claws bared.

Four Central enforcers came out from behind the tree line on North's side and pounced. Out of the corner of his eye, he saw another four wolves attack Logan.

Eight on two, not a bad deal.

They were fighting as men since it would take too long to shift. However most of them held the power to be able to use their claws and fangs while in human form.

Logan was strong enough to stand on his own and fight, so North focused on his own battle. He clawed at the wolf closest to him, getting the bastard in the neck. The tips of his claws sank into flesh, tearing it as he pulled away. The man screamed, clutching his neck as he tried to turn into his wolf form. He wouldn't make it, not with the wound North had delivered. The man would be dead before he hit the ground.

Two other wolves came at his side, and he twisted, letting them go past him. One clawed along his side, but it was a necessary wound so he could get to the fourth wolf. He lowered his body and rammed his shoulder into the man's gut. The other man let out a grunt as North slammed him into the ground. He stepped on the other man's neck, holding him down as he turned to grip one of the other wolves by the neck. He squeezed hard, feeling the wolf's spine crack under the pressure. The dead wolf went limp in his hands, and he threw him down. North stepped harder on the wolf on the ground and twisted his foot, killing the wolf instantly.

Finally, the last wolf came at him, and he punched out, digging his claws into the enforcer's belly. The other man screamed, and North pulled away, his hand and forearm covered with blood.

The wolf blinked, looked down at himself, and fell to his knees.

"You made quick work of them," Logan said as he walked toward North, a spray of blood on his shirt, but otherwise he looked like he was on an afternoon stroll.

However the gold gleam in his eyes of a wolf on the hunt told another story.

"You were quicker." North looked down at his side and winced as his body started to heal the light claw marks. "And didn't get hurt."

"Mine didn't use their claws as much. Idiots." He looked over his shoulder then turned in a circle around them. "So, where's Corbin?"

"He'll be here." North rolled his shoulders then looked at the dead at their feet. "Let's pile them up and put them in the forest. The Centrals aren't stupid enough to let humans know about wolves, but leaving eight dead bodies around isn't smart."

"No, it isn't smart," Corbin called out. "I suppose we'll just have to leave two dead bodies instead."

North and Logan both pivoted toward the Central Alpha, who stood about twenty yards from them. He looked the same as always, dirty and oily, with a sneer on his face. North's wolf clawed at him, wanting to kill the bastard now for ever laying a hand on Lexi, but he held him back. This wasn't the time, not yet. Not when he didn't know his surroundings or whether the demon was with the bastard.

Corbin alone North could take. Add in the demon and there was a problem.

"I see you got our message," North said, his voice oddly calm.

Corbin snorted. "I knew the minute you stepped off Redwood Pack land. You think my demon doesn't know all? Fuck you."

Interesting that the bastard called Caym his demon, yet it sounded to North as though the demon was the one that held all the power.

"Are you ready for this?" North asked, beyond ready. Out of the corner of his eye, he saw another four enforcers come through the trees. He didn't tense up, though he'd have liked to. Logan gave a small nod, and North gave one back. Logan would have his back like they'd planned.

North would have to take Corbin...finally.

"I suppose it's time to see if fate's right...or just a cruel liar," Corbin sneered.

North growled and charged, Logan coming up behind him. Acting as his defense, Logan took down the enforcers one by one, staying behind to kill them. North had eyes only for Corbin, who stood still, grinning like a fucking idiot.

Corbin pivoted at the last second, but North was faster. He gripped the bastard's arm and wrenched it. Corbin let out a scream and tried to get away, but North held tight. The two clawed at each other, and North took him down, punching and kicking while Corbin tried to get away.

The details from where Lexi's brother fought, trickled in like bursts of images from a movie while his attention was somewhere else. Logan growled, the sound a menacing tear along the eerily quiet of the rest of the forest. The animals in the area had long since run for cover, knowing the wolves were the predators to fear. Logan moved to claw at one wolf, his shrieking cry broken off abruptly as it died. With the grace of a wolf much smaller than he was, the Anderson wolf turned and kicked out, catching another wolf in the side. That enemy wolf went down hard, but still fighting. Logan sank his claws into its neck, killing it instantly.

Logan jumped while North ran, ramming two more wolves together, blood pouring from his side as another wolf clawed at him. North could hear the other wolves dying around him as Logan won his own battles, but he kept his focus on Corbin. He had to. If he looked away for too long, or lost his concentration for even a moment, Corbin would run. The bastard always ran.

Corbin had relied on others for too long. He wasn't the wolf he thought he was.

North wrapped his hands around Corbin's neck and squeezed. "Fuck you," he whispered.

The Alpha gurgled below him, his eyes bulged, the scent of death surrounding him.

"I think not, young Redwood," a voice said from behind him before red-hot fire scorched over his body.

The blast threw North in the air, his body twisting and turning at odd angles, and bones broke, muscles rending. He screamed, the agony forcing bile up his throat. Below him, Logan lay prone on the ground, blood pooling around his too-still body.

Caym stood by Corbin, laughing with that twisted sneer on his sharply angled face.

The demon snapped his fingers, and North slammed into the ground, the impact shocking his body. The darkness slid over him, and he knew he'd lost.

He'd lost it all...and for nothing.

CHAPTER SIXTEEN

"**H**e went where?" Lexi screamed as she scrambled out of bed. That damn wolf. How could he even *think* of doing this? And her brother? Oh, she'd kick both their asses when they got back. And they would get back because if they didn't, she'd find them and kick their asses even harder.

She choked on a sob then cursed at herself. Really? Crying? This wasn't the time to cry; this was the time to be pissed. The man she loved and her brother had taken it into their own hands to try to end the war. How idiotic could they get?

"Lexi, you should be resting," Maddox said.

"Fuck resting," she rumbled, and she put on her jeans in jagged movements.

"Mom!" Parker whispered, and Lexi shut her eyes, counting to ten. Freaking out and cursing were the appropriate actions when male wolves acted as though they knew better when, really, they only had death wishes. But she wouldn't do either in front of her eight-year-old son.

Ellie, Maddox's mate, walked into the room then with Charlotte, her newly adopted daughter, by her side with their hands clasped together. Technically, Charlotte was Ellie's sister; therefore, both of them were Parker's aunts. The weirdness of all the family trees made Lexi's head hurt.

"Okay, Parker. Come with me so your mom can worry about North and Logan. Okay?"

Parker gave her a hug then went with Ellie. He stopped at the doorway, though, and turned to Lexi. "Make sure Cailin is safe. She'd go after Logan if she thought no one was looking." With that, her too-wise son left with the sister of the man Lexi hated more than anything, and Lexi fell back to the bed, needing to breathe.

"I don't know how much more of this I can take, Maddox," she said, rubbing a hand over her face. She was still weak from the attempt to bring out her wolf, but with each passing hour, she was almost back to full strength. She couldn't feel or hear her wolf yet, but she'd never thought that would be a possibility at this point. She'd have to wait for the full moon for that to happen.

"I could have held him back, Lexi, but he'd have found another way to go. North's determined like that."

Lexi narrowed her eyes. "All you men are the same way. Add a little dominant wolf and you go freaking crazy. How long have they been gone?"

Maddox looked at the clock on the nightstand. "Four hours. The family and our enforcers know what happened. We're looking for them now."

"They were stupid." Her gaze left his. She knew she might have been spitting angry, but it only covered the worry and panic that her mate could be out there dying and she wouldn't know.

She didn't *have* the mating bond.

She couldn't feel him...not even to know if he was alive.

The shaky breath that left her lungs echoed in the room.

"Yes, and they'll be reprimanded for that."

Lexi growled. "Well, they better get their butts back here so they can actually *be* reprimanded."

She heard the front door open, scented the husky scent of her mate and the coppery tang of blood, and ran.

"Need some help over here," Logan grunted, limping into the room, covered with blood and holding an unconscious North in a fireman's carry.

"Give him to me and follow us to the clinic," Maddox ordered, taking his twin. He didn't struggle under the weight, but carried his brother as if he were precious crystal.

Lexi followed them to the clinic, picking up the phone on the way. She called Pat to tell her what she knew so far and that they needed Hannah right away. North's mother would know what to do from there.

"What happened?" she asked through her tears. Damn those tears. She couldn't fall apart, not now, not when she didn't know what the future held.

Maddox had North on the table, her mate's body a ravaged semblance of broken bones, odd angles, torn skin, blood, and dirt. Logan sat on a chair beside the table, his hand clutching his side, his face pale.

"We almost had him," Logan rasped out, his voice sounding as if his lungs were full of fluid. From the way he was breathing, Lexi wouldn't have been surprised if that were true. "We only got away because Corbin left us. Don't know why. The fucking wolf mumbled something about Caym saying it wasn't the right time. I don't even know anymore." He let out a shaky breath and widened his eyes like he was trying figure out how to use his lungs again.

She would worry about exactly what Corbin meant later. The implications of the Central Alpha letting the one fated to kill him go meant something. She just didn't know what. Either Corbin had a plan that was more involved than she thought, or Caym did.

Knowing both of them, she was afraid what that plan could be.

Right now though, she needed to focus on her mate and brother. She swallowed hard, putting the thoughts of what was to come away and looking to the present. If she didn't compartmentalize, she'd scream, cry, or do both.

"North!" Parker yelled from the doorway, and Lexi spun on her heel. Her little boy looked stunned, his eyes wide, his face pale, his mouth open.

"Go back into the house, Parker." He looked ready to revolt. "Please, baby. For me."

He nodded, gave one last look at North and Logan, and then headed back to the residence area of the building. She could hear him pad his way there, very reluctantly. She made her way to North's side so she could be between him and Logan. This way she wouldn't have to make a choice of who to comfort. No, Lexi needed to be by both men to make sure they would heal and that they wouldn't do something as crazy and stupid as what they'd just done again. She wanted to hold her mate's hand but was too afraid to touch him.

"North..." Her voice broke, so she stopped speaking. She had to remain strong. If she let her emotions breach the shield she'd put up, she'd break down. Her gaze met Maddox's, who looked as if he'd been sucker-punched, and she cursed.

Maddox was the Omega. He could feel the emotions of the entire Pack—save his twin, meaning he could also feel everything Lexi was feeling and trying so hard to hide.

"I'm sorry..." she whispered.

He held up a hand. "Don't be. If you weren't feeling like this, you wouldn't be the mate my brother needs."

"Oh goddess," Hannah said from behind them. "Reed, help Logan get in a better chair. I'll help you soon, honey." The Healer sent everyone to work and lay her hands over North.

"Hannah, baby, can you fix him?" Reed asked the question they had all wanted to ask but had been too afraid to.

"I'm going to try."

Heated energy filled the room, and little pinpricks of sensation danced along her skin as Hannah went to work. Her hands glowed, and her eyes were set on her charges, determination on her face. Lexi went to her brother's side and did what she could with the wound. Cailin came in while she was dressing the wound and set about helping without a word.

Lexi sensed the pain and anger radiating off the woman at seeing both North and Logan hurt, and she knew it mirrored her own.

"Stupid men," Lexi whispered, her throat constricting.

"After they're healed, we'll yell together," Cailin mumbled back, and Lexi closed her eyes, knowing she wasn't alone in her agony.

What seemed like hours passed, but Lexi wasn't sure how long exactly. Before she knew it though, she was sitting on a chair beside the bed where she'd been lying that morning. Only this time, North was the one unconscious, and she was the one praying to the moon goddess that her mate would wake up soon.

Logan had gone back to his place—her former place—with Cailin by his side. The duo hadn't spoken a single word to each other, and Lexi was too tired to worry about what was going on between them.

Parker had fallen asleep in his room after Pat held him and read him a story. Lexi had tried to join in but was told to go do what she had to do and to stop spreading herself so thin. After all, she'd just been brutally attacked—on purpose—and was still healing herself.

She ran a hand over her face, unsure of what to do just then. She could go and find another family member to sit with, go try to force herself to eat, as the others had tried to do earlier, or just sit there and stare at her unconscious mate.

She was just so...*angry*. What right did he have to do this? He didn't have to go out and look for trouble. Not when trouble always seemed to find him and his family. He'd gone out there because he wanted to protect her, she knew that, but she didn't like it. Didn't understand it.

It pissed her off to no end that he thought his life was worth less than hers...less than anyone else's in the Pack.

That's what it came down to.

He'd risked himself to try and force fate's decree faster than she'd thought possible. So what if some hack had foretold it was North's *destiny* to kill Corbin?

So. Fucking. What.

It wasn't his duty to die for something that might not even happen. Fate and paths changed daily with just a new thought or action. She didn't believe that, no matter what happened, *one* way was the only way.

He didn't have to throw himself into the fire in order to make something happen.

She let out a breath.

If he hadn't done it though, he wouldn't have been the wolf she loved.

Damn it.

The man risked everything for those he loved, and this act was no different. The fact that Logan had gone with him didn't change things. Her brother was the same as North in that they protected what was theirs.

They just didn't protect themselves as much as they should.

Lexi clenched her hands and tried to take a deep breath. If it weren't for Parker, she'd probably have done the same thing herself, and it killed her to admit that. As a whole, the Pack had been on the defensive against the Centrals for far too long, and they knew it. With each strike, they won what they could and held strong. However, the time would come when the Redwoods would need to go on the offensive.

They just needed to make sure they had the magic and power to back it up.

With the demon in control like he was, Lexi wasn't sure that would happen any time soon.

"Still sleeping the day away?" Edward asked as he walked in the room.

Lexi gave a small smile and gestured toward the empty chair next to her. "Sit. You're healing just like the rest of us." She winced at her tone and lowered her gaze.

The Alpha chuckled then sat next to her, patting her knee. "You're fine, Lexi. You know you're family when you tell me to take care of my health." He rubbed the part of his chest where the bullet had hit, and she bit her lip, not knowing what to say.

She looked over his features, already knowing North looked more like his mother in some respects than his father but still looking for similarities. Her mate had his mother's light hair, but he had his father's build and eyes. Right now, the Alpha's jade-green eyes studied her, and she wasn't sure what he saw.

The man looked the same age as all of them, but she knew it was only because of their wolves. He also had more power in his pinky that she did in her whole body. That thought made her relax. Even though she couldn't feel her wolf, she was connected enough that knowing her Alpha would be there let her feel safe...protected.

"He'll be okay, you know," Edward said quietly, his gaze returning to his son. "He's always been like this. Quiet and steady until something needs done, and then he surprises us all." He held out his hand, as if knowing Lexi needed the comfort.

Lexi took the offered hand and squeezed. "What was he like as a boy?" she asked, needing to think about something else other than the fact that her mate might never wake up, despite Hannah's assurances.

Demon's magic wasn't something to mess with, and, frankly, no one really knew the side effects of it.

"He hasn't changed much, actually. He was quieter than most of his brothers, though not as quiet as Maddox. Being the Omega always took its toll on him, even before he had the powers fully. North, though, was the baby for decades." He cracked a smile. "That is until Cailin came along."

"She's a lot younger than the rest of them, right?"

Edward nodded. "Maddox and North were seventy-three when we had Cailin."

"Wow, I knew there was a gap, but I hadn't realized it was that much for some reason."

"We'd had the boys right after one another because we were growing a family and wanted to keep them similar ages. As wolves, we can have children with our mates for hundreds of years, so the age gaps can be tremendous. Pat and I hadn't wanted that. We were fine with just boys, though I know Pat wanted a little girl, even if she never said it."

"She wouldn't have. She loves what she has. She's just that kind of person."

The Alpha's eyes glinted. "That she is. It wasn't until, ironically, she met Hannah's mother that she wanted to try again for a little girl. Pat had seen Hannah as a newborn, and her baby clock went off again."

Lexi's eyes widened. "Wow. What a small world."

"Indeed," he said with a nod. "Fate works in mysterious ways."

Lexi didn't really want to hear about fate right then, considering it had kicked her over and over again with each passing day.

"North, Maddox, and Cailin always had a special connection. Yes, Kade, Jasper, Adam, and Reed did as well, but I think the twins thought since they were the closest in age, even if it was by seventy-two years, they were the ones who should protect her. Maddox needed her because he needed someone to vent with or just feel. I think he just wanted someone that was different enough from him and knew that Cailin would need that outlet as well. He doesn't think I know, but I do. I know more than they think."

"I know you do," she whispered.

He squeezed her hand. "North...North I think protected her because he didn't know who else to protect. Kade was the Heir and knew his place. Same with Jasper as the Beta and Adam the Enforcer. Reed, I know, felt like he needed to do something since he didn't have a title so went off on his own. North? North needed to protect, even if he didn't have the powers to do so. His wolf has always been closer to the surface, so I think becoming a doctor was good for him...and his wolf."

Lexi's brows rose. "You knew about his wolf?"

"Of course I did. Just because I never talked with him about it doesn't mean I didn't know. I think, if we had sat down and discussed the fact that his wolf is so close, then he would have felt like something was wrong. Though now that I see how much he puts himself out there for those he loves, I don't know if that was the right decision." He met Lexi's eyes, and for the first time, she thought the Alpha looked tired. "I just hope I didn't do wrong by my boy."

Lexi shook her head. "I don't think anything you could have said would have made North feel or think any differently than he always had. He...he tries to do what he thinks is right, even if he hurts himself." She swallowed hard. "I don't like that part. You know? I don't want to lose him because he thinks he's not worth saving. Or that he values other people's lives above his own."

Edward met her gaze. "I think he could say the same about you, my dear."

She froze, hearing the words but not making any sense of them. "What?" she whispered.

"You were ready to sacrifice yourself to us. That's something I'll ignore for now. I'm going to try to imagine that you wouldn't think I'd kill you and your family, *our* family now, without just cause. You were ready to sacrifice yourself because you didn't want to lie to North anymore about who you were and why Joseph had banished you from the Talons. You've always done everything you could to provide a home and safety for your son, even though I know it couldn't

194

have been easy. Lexi, darling, you and North are more alike than you think."

"I don't want to lose him." Her voice broke, and she closed her eyes, done with the tears that seemed to have taken over her recently.

"Then don't. Find a way to fight *together*. That's all we can do. Going in on your own will only get you killed." He looked past her. "Right, son?"

She turned to see her mate staring at her from the bed. "North! How long have you been awake?" She got up and gripped his hands, loving the way he gripped hers right back.

"Long enough to know I love you."

"With that, I'll leave the two of you alone." Edward stood beside her, and she smiled up at him.

"Thanks for sitting with me."

"I'd say anytime, but I'm not in the mood to have any more of my children on their sickbeds." He narrowed his eyes at his son. "Do I make myself clear, boy? You have a mate and child now. You aren't free to play with your life and fate. You can't put yourself at risk anymore, not when you have so much to live for."

"So says the man who took a bullet to protect his mate."

Edward snorted. "You're not supposed to take my actions and make them your own. Find a way to save the world without dying."

North rolled his eyes, and Lexi held back a smile. It was odd to want to smile when the man she loved was in pain, but sometimes she had to take what she could get.

"Don't make it sound so dramatic," North said softly.

Edward growled, and Lexi joined in. "Dramatic?" the Alpha said quietly, too quietly. "You went to the neutral zone with another member of your Pack and almost died because you were outnumbered."

"That wasn't the reason. Caym was the reason. Logan and I would have beaten them all—and had—until Caym showed up."

"Don't defend your actions to me, boy. The demon *did* show up, and you *did* almost die. If you hadn't done it because of a prophecy and to save the Pack, I'd beat you right now...or even call a circle. As it stands, you didn't go against orders and didn't endanger anyone who didn't make their own decision. You're lucky, North. Damn fucking lucky."

With that, Edward strode out of the room, leaving anger in his wake.

"Well crap," North whispered.

"Oh, we're not done yet." She turned to him and placed her hands on her hips.

"I take it by your stance you're not here to nurse me back to health?" North teased.

"Shut up, North Jamenson. You almost died and didn't tell me you were going off gallivanting in the first place."

His face fell, and he reached out for her. "Lexi—"

"No. You don't get to talk yet. I'm so fucking angry you took that chance. If Logan hadn't brought you in when he did, we would have lost you."

His eyes widened. "Crap. Where is Logan? Is he okay?"

Her heart warmed a bit that he worried about her brother, but she put it away. She needed the anger to protect herself, to protect them. "He's fine. Cailin and I patched him up. He's now with your sister, and she's taking care of him." His eyes narrowed. "Stop it. No. You don't get to worry about her virtue or act like the big brother right now. You almost died, meaning you would have left Cailin one less brother in the world.

You lost the right to act overprotective when you acted like an idiot."

"Hey now." His eyes grew gold. "I went out there because Corbin needs to die and because it's my place to do it. I wasn't going to sit back and twiddle my thumbs while we wait for the elders and others to maybe figure out how we're supposed to beat a demon who can't be beaten."

"You didn't tell us you were going!" she yelled, knowing she was more scared than anything.

"I told Maddox," he countered.

"Yeah, and I already yelled at him. You didn't tell *me*. I woke up, and you kissed me, and then you left. You *left* us. Parker and I finally let you into our hearts, and you *left* us." Tears she didn't realize she'd been holding back fell down her cheeks, and her chest lurched. "You left us."

North tried to sit up but winced. He held out his hand, and she went to him, curling into his side, needing him more than she needed to hold on to her anger.

His hands went down her back, and she cried into him. "I needed to do this for us, for our family, for our Pack. I'd do it again, Lexi." She stiffened. "But I should have told you I was going. That was selfish of me."

"Yes, yes it was." He kissed her brow, and she softened.

"How bad is it?" he asked after he'd held her for a few minutes.

"You should be fine according to Hannah. Though we don't really know everything that happened, other than what Logan told us." She paused and licked her lips. "You'll have scars on your back from where your...where your body twisted awkwardly and broke the skin."

She felt North twitch under her. "I remember that part," he said roughly. "At least I'll look more like my twin now."

She smacked his chest softly, knowing he was still healing. "Don't joke about that." Maddox had made a similar joke, forcing Ellie to hit him as well, but Lexi wasn't going to comment on that.

"I'm sorry, Lex."

"You should be, but I'm glad you're okay."

He let out a breath. "I don't know how we're going to beat Caym."

She closed her eyes, not wanting to think about the outside world, if only for a moment. "I don't know either," she whispered.

The war had come and raged, yet she wasn't sure they had the strength and ability to fight what fate and the enemy had laid out for them. The Redwoods were fighting a war they could lose.

And Lexi wasn't sure what she should do.

What she *could* do.

CHAPTER SEVENTEEN

"**M**aybe I should just stay inside this time." Lexi leaned her head against the window, closing her eyes.

North walked up behind and pulled her close, her back against his chest. "You need the moon on your skin, Lex. Everything will work out."

They hoped.

"What if it doesn't work?" she whispered. What if she'd gone through all that pain, all that agony, and she still couldn't connect with her wolf?

He kissed her brow, and she settled closer, needing his touch. "Then we deal."

"Then we deal." She sucked in a breath. "Parker is with Maddox, Ellie, and Charlotte, right?" She hadn't wanted her son there in case something went terribly wrong when she tried to shift.

She already knew something was different this full moon. Her skin felt tight, itchy, like she needed to jump out of it. North had told her that's how all wolves felt on the full moon if they hadn't shifted in a long time. She just hoped that she had a wolf to turn into once she tried to shift.

If not...

Well, that could get messy.

"Parker is with my brother and his family. He'll shift and hunt with them. It's just you and me tonight because that's the way you wanted it."

She turned in his arms. "Is that not okay?"

North shook his head then leaned down to lay a kiss on her nose. "No, it's fine. I thought you'd want to be with others for your first shift, but then I thought better of it. You're afraid something will happen so you don't want to hurt them. I get it."

She swallowed hard. "I know it's selfish, but I want you near me though. I know if something goes wrong, I'd rather you not witness it, but I need you by my side anyway."

He growled softly then cupped her ass. "I wouldn't be any other place tonight."

"Then let's go." Her hands were shaking, and she didn't know if it was because of the stress or whatever was happening to her body. Honestly, it was probably a bit of both.

He took her lips, and she sank into him, knowing they both needed the touch, and then he led her outside to his backyard. Each Jamenson house led into the tree line so it would be easy for any of them to shift and run. While most of the others would meet at the circle tonight to run as Pack, North knew Lexi needed to be apart from them right now. The Pack needed that solidarity after what had happened, what *was* happening. North might have wanted to join them, but he'd stayed away for her.

She would just have to add that to her ever-growing list of things she owed him for.

A slight breeze slid through her hair, and she inhaled, the forest seeming more vivid, alive. She raised her face to the night sky, the moon pulling her even stronger than it had when she'd been fully trapped within her skin.

She took a shaky breath.

At least she hoped her wolf wasn't still trapped within her skin.

She turned at the sound of rustling as North stripped off his shirt. The sight of his washboard abs and filled-out chest never failed to make her pant, and she gave a soft smile.

He grinned back at her as he thumbed the button on his jeans. "No thinking about that now. After the shift, when we're back to being human and our emotions are running high, we can act on any dirty fantasy you have in mind, but stop looking at me like I'm your feast."

She licked her lips, unable to hold herself back. She just wanted to run her hands over his skin, over the dusting of chest hair that marked him, and down to those sexy lines on his hips that went straight to his cock.

"Lexi," he growled, the sensation rumbling over her skin, blending with the moonlight and forcing a shiver down her spine.

"Sorry," she whispered, not sorry in the slightest.

"Get naked, woman. The quicker you do that, the faster we can shift and hunt. Then we can act on whatever sexy thing is going on in your mind."

That fear she'd tried to hold back slithered in like a snake on its own hunt. "But what if..."

Her mate stepped out of his jeans and prowled toward her naked. She blinked and forced her gaze up, her cheeks heating.

He pulled up her shirt, and she raised her hands, letting him take control. He stripped off her pants, and she placed her sweaty palms on his stomach, needing his touch.

He cupped her face and forced her gaze to his. "You will be fine. If you go in thinking of the worst, then you'll just make it hard for your wolf to come out. My wolf can already feel a difference in you. It's like your wolf is closer to the surface, not like mine, but at least there. Before, I had to really search hard for her, but not anymore. She's ready, baby. Trust us."

"I trust you, you know that." It didn't mean she trusted herself...or fate though.

"Then trust your wolf, baby. She's there."

Lexi slid her hands to his back, the new scars there fresh, but healed. North stiffened for a moment then relaxed as she ran her hands up and down the indentations and hard ridges that marred his flesh. Caym might have marked her mate, but he hadn't taken him from her.

She had to remember they were stronger than others thought.

She was stronger than others thought.

"I love you, North."

He brushed her lip with his thumb. "I love you too. Now get on your hands and knees."

Lexi snorted. "I thought you said I had to wait to act on my urges."

North rolled his eyes. "It's how you shift for the first time. Do you want me to shift first to show you what I do? Or do you want me to hold you through it?"

"I've seen people shift before." Hundreds of times. She'd spent hours watching her brother and others shift so she could replicate the movement. Growing up, she'd thought that if she just tried harder than anyone else, she'd be able to find her wolf.

It hadn't worked then, but she hoped to the moon goddess it would work now.

"Okay then, I'll hold you through it, baby." North's words were gentle, as if he was afraid he'd push her too far and she'd break.

She hated that feeling.

Lexi pulled away slightly then knelt on the ground, her fingers digging into the grass and dirt. North got on his knees beside her and ran a soothing hand down her back then up again, the motion calming her even though she hadn't thought the action possible.

"Now call up your wolf, Lexi."

"How?" She'd asked her brother and others countless times, but she'd never been able to feel her.

"You sense that manic energy beneath your skin? Take that and pull it out. Imagine it's a thread that you know is connected to something important. You can't pull too quickly, or you'll break the thread, but you still need to grab on."

She shook her head at his description but did as he was told. She closed her eyes and imagined the aching feeling in her limbs and under her skin was a thread. She pulled on it slightly, a little tug to see if she could do it. The resulting flare of energy made her elbows buckle, and she would have fallen to the ground if not for the strong band around her center.

North held her close, her back arching against his chest as he murmured sweet words that she couldn't decipher over the pain radiating through her body. She pushed against him, not knowing if she needed space or him closer, and he just held on tighter.

"Pull that thread," North repeated.

She nodded, or at least that's what she thought she did. She wasn't quite sure because she felt as though she wasn't inside her body at all, but outside looking in. Lexi tugged on the tread, the energy piercing through her as she closed her eyes even tighter, praying that it would be over soon.

Come on, wolf, come out and play. Please.

It was a soft echo, like a train off in the distance rushing toward her at full speed. She screamed as it crashed into her, the full impact making her body buck against North. His answering yell made her remember she wasn't alone.

Dear goddess, it hurt.

She could feel her bones breaking, the tendons and ligaments stretching and tearing. She could feel her muscles reforming. The bones in her face crushed then shaped into another form. Fur sprouted from beneath her skin, receded, then game back fuller.

She threw her head back against North's shoulder and screamed until she didn't hear herself anymore. Instead, an anguished howl erupted from her throat.

Her throat.

Lexi panted and looked down at her paws and fell to the ground.

Her paws.

"I've been waiting to meet you," a voice said within her mind, and she froze.

Was that her wolf?

"Yes, I'm your wolf. I can't wait to get to know you even more," the soft voice said. *"Go hunt with your mate, and we can talk more soon. Run on four paws, Lexi, feel the ground beneath them and have the moon dance along our fur."*

She could feel her wolf step away, as if the other soul sharing her body knew Lexi needed to get ahold of herself first.

So. Freaking. Cool.

"Lexi?"

Lexi looked up at her mate and tried to smile. As a wolf, though, she wasn't sure how that looked.

North threw his head back and laughed. "Oh, baby, you're smiling in wolf form. I love it. You are so beautiful."

She tried to ask what she looked like and realized she couldn't speak. How on earth did wolves communicate in this form? She tilted her head at her mate, and he grinned.

"Your fur is blonde like your hair and your eyes are the same hazel. It's as if your wolf was so close to you but hidden for so long, that you have the same features. It's pretty cool, actually."

He ran a hand through her fur, and she nuzzled into his palm. Her wolf guided the motion, showing her how to move like the canine rather than the human. She looked down at herself as best she could and saw the blonde fur he was talking about.

She was a wolf.

Finally.

She yipped up at her mate, surprising herself with the sound.

"Okay, okay. We'll go hunting. Let me shift." He stood then and shifted, faster than her by far, faster than most wolves.

Her mate was strong, amazing, and her wolf liked that.

His fur was a mixture of gray and tan, identical to Maddox's. He was also bigger than she was in wolf form, but that wasn't surprising.

He nudged along her neck then circled her body before moving, locking his jaws around her neck. Instinctively, she lowered her head, submitting to him.

This was her mate, her other half. Even without the bond, she would want this man and wolf in the age-old dance of mates and the hunt.

He moved backward, his gaze on hers. She looked down at her paws then up to him and took a step toward him. Or at least tried. She stumbled on four paws and hit the ground. North came to her, nudging and licking along her muzzle.

"Let me take care of the walking and running," her wolf said on a gentle laugh.

That sounded like a better idea. Lexi did what came naturally—something that surprised her—and let her wolf take over. Lexi, the human, was still there, in control, but her wolf led the movements, as if showing her how to walk.

Lexi took a few steps then sped up, running around her mate, who looked as pleased as a wolf could be. She went to his side and burrowed into his body. She felt the happiness of her wolf being able to feel North's wolf, at least in body.

The bond would come once Corbin was gone.

No, she wasn't going to think about that now.

North nuzzled her one more time then tilted his head up before taking off in a run. She yipped and took off behind him, letting her wolf lead the action so she wouldn't fall on her face. Again.

She rushed around the trees as she followed her mate, knowing and trusting that he'd lead the way and keep them safe. That reminded her that she'd have to learn to fight in wolf form now.

Oh my God, I'm a wolf!

She squealed inside like a teenager at a boy band concert and ran after her mate, wanting to play, to hunt, to just...be.

North jumped over a fallen log, and Lexi let her wolf take more control to show her how to jump as well. When she landed on four paws, North stood in front of her, gazing.

She yipped at him, wanting to tell him how much she loved him, loved this moment, but didn't know how to communicate it.

She could have sworn he winked at her, and then his ears perked. Hers did the same a second later.

Padded steps along the soil.

A jump and a hop over a fallen branch.

North tilted his head, as if asking her if this is what she wanted.

Her wolf nudged her, and she sprang, the hunt already in play. She followed the sound of the rabbit, its scent changing to fear of a predator.

She pounced quickly, ensuring its death would be painless. As she ate her reward, North padded toward her, a rabbit of his own dangling from his mouth. They ate together in silence then took off again on another run. Moonlight shone from between the tall trees, bringing her closer to the moon goddess and her Pack.

She sensed the others around her, their hunt almost over as they moved off into pairs and groups to finish hunting...or change back and enjoy the other things that came with the hunt. North stopped then, his ears perked, and then he started to change back to his human form. Lexi pulled on that thread again, this time, allowing her human self to come out.

The change back was just as painful as the first one, but this time, she was a little bit quicker, the transformation becoming something she could get used to, rather than something that would make her scream each time.

In human form, she looked up at her mate and smiled. He growled then pounced on her. Their mouths collided, their tongues fighting for dominance as he pinned her to the ground, his body settled between her legs.

"You're a fucking beautiful wolf, my Lexi, but right now, I want to fuck my human hard."

She licked and nipped along his jaw, the scruff of his beard sending shivers down her spine.

"In me, now."

He grinned a feral grin, positioned himself, and then thrust into her hot channel in one movement. They both gasped at the feeling, but he didn't stop moving. She was already wet just from the adrenaline and fact that she'd wanted him since before they'd changed.

He fucked her hard, and she lifted her hips, meeting him stroke for stroke.

"Rise with me, Lexi. I'm too close," he grunted then moved his hand between them, flicking her clit with his thumb.

She came on his cock, the scream ripping from her throat matching his own growl as he came with her. Their bodies slid against each other, sweat from their exertions only making her want him more.

"I want your ass, my Lexi."

She gasped as his hand reached around, sliding between her cheeks, teasing her hole. "I'm ready for you, but we don't have any lube."

He lowered his face and nipped her lip. "I'm pretty sure between the two of us, we can take care of that." He grinned then kissed her hard.

She moaned as he slid out of her then turned on her stomach so she could get on her hands and knees. This would be an easier position for both of them, plus she liked when he took her this way since he could go deeper.

Over her shoulder, she saw North kneeling behind her, the gold in his eyes flowing from arousal. She wiggled her ass, and he grinned.

"Damn, I love you."

"Back at'cha. Now, are you going to fuck me or what?"

He raised a brow. "I'm pretty sure I just did that. You have a dirty mouth now, my little wolf."

"I've always had one, and you like it."

"True." He slapped her ass hard, and she yelped, the pain and pleasure seeping through her, entwining as one.

She wiggled again then sighed as he prepared her with one finger then two. Soon she was panting, needing to come, but not wanting to without him.

She felt him move behind her and then the head of his cock at her entrance. Her back stiffened, and he ran a hand down her.

"Shh, baby, just relax."

She forced herself to, even though she wanted him in her right then. She felt him enter her slowly, past the tight ring of muscles, and she pushed out against him. The action made him slide in farther, and she felt him gather up her own juices to make it easier for them. He slowly worked his way inside her until she felt his thighs flat against hers.

"You feel so fucking good, Lexi," he grunted, and she moaned, unable to speak.

"Ready for me to move?" he asked, his voice strained.

She nodded quickly, needing something, anything. "Please," she rasped out.

He pulled out partly then thrust back in slowly, doing it over and over again as he picked up the tempo. She lowered her head, the feel of him so freaking good, so full, that she could barely breathe.

He squeezed her hips, and he slammed into her, and she screamed, the sensation a fiery pleasure that she wanted more of.

"Touch your clit, Lexi. Come for me. I'll hold you up."

She nodded then moved so she could rub circles over her clit. The feeling of his cock in her ass and her hand on herself was too much.

She came on a yell and felt North jerk behind her then growl her name. His seed filled her up, and they both fell to the ground, a pile of limbs, sweat, and heat.

"I think you killed me," North grunted.

"Ditto," she whispered, too tired to say more than one thing at a time.

North ran a hand over her hair, his chest to her back, their bodies still connected. "You're a wolf, baby," he said then kissed behind her ear.

She smiled then and felt her wolf settle down for a nap.

Yes, she was a wolf.

Finally.

CHAPTER EIGHTEEN

Something is coming, North thought to himself. *Something bad.*

He ran a hand over his arms, that feeling of something...off... not quite going away.

It had been two weeks since he'd woken up in bed and found his father and Lexi talking beside him. He'd known his father loved him, believed in him, but he hadn't quite known the extent of it.

Apparently, North hadn't been as good at hiding his wolf as he'd thought.

The Alpha had always known and always felt safe with North by his side. North never should have doubted that.

Now, though, now something was off, and he didn't know what.

For a moment, he thought it could be his mate, but he wasn't sure what about her would be wrong. Lexi was flourishing as a wolf and was even, right then, in her wolf form with Logan learning some fighting maneuvers. Parker was also in wolf from, learning a little bit as well.

North would have joined them but had to patch up a couple scrapes from a fight between a couple of adolescent boys. Ever since the circle where Patrick had tried to mutiny, those boys and parents who had acted against North's new family had started to warm.

He wasn't quite sure he was ready to forgive and forget.

Nor was he sure Lexi was.

Parker, however, was as soothing as ever and wanted to be done with it.

That, though, North thought, wasn't the problem either.

His cell buzzed, and he picked it up off the counter.

"Yeah?"

"Get over to the circle," Kade ordered. "Bring the Andersons. The Talons are here, and they said that they are only the first."

The Heir hung up, leaving North with that sickly feeling of dread slashing through him. Shit, if the Talons were here again so quickly, that meant something was up. Kade hadn't told him which Talons were there or *why* they were there, only that North and his new family were needed.

He ran out to the back yard, where Lexi was just pulling on clothes behind a bush. Logan and Parker were doing the same behind the trees.

"What's wrong?" his mate asked as she buttoned up her jeans and walked over to him.

"We need to go to the circle. Now. The Talons are here, and I don't know what else is going on, but we need to go."

"We?" she asked as she put on her shoes.

"Kade said all of us. I think that means Parker too. I'm not sure."

Alarm spread over Lexi's face before she schooled her features. She leaned forward and kissed his jaw. He held still, knowing if he caved and touched her now, he'd either take her and hide her from danger or pull her close enough that he'd never let her go.

Logan came out from behind the trees fully dressed with Parker in tow. The other man looked ready to brawl, and North was glad he was there.

"I have to come too?" Parker asked.

North held out his arm, and Parker went straight to him, holding him around the waist. His heart tightened at the action, and he held back a sigh. He didn't think he'd ever get used to the easy way Parker had fit into his life, but now wasn't the time to focus on it.

"You too," North said. "I want you to stay by Logan's side the whole time though. Okay?" North wanted Lexi by his side, and Logan would be sure to keep Parker out of trouble with whatever was coming.

They made their way to the circle, tension knotting between North's shoulders. He held on to Lexi's hand like a lifeline, needing her, needing her wolf...just needing.

All of the North's brothers, their mates, his parents, and Cailin stood at the side of the circle, their worry and anger reaching him even before he came to their side. Gideon and Mitchell were there also, their faces grave but oddly determined.

"What's going on?" North asked. "Should I have left Parker at home?" He didn't fail to miss that none of the others had brought their children, though Parker was by far older than the others.

His dad turned to him, his face set. "No, Parker needed to be here."

Gideon stepped forward, and Logan took a step as well, a growl escaping from his lips.

"Logan, they came to warn us," Cailin said as she took his hand, pulling him back.

Every pair of male Jamenson eyes went to the movement, but North didn't say anything. There would be time for that later.

At least he hoped.

"Warn us about what?" North asked.

"Caym and Corbin, along with a small Central syndicate, are on their way to you."

North went on alert. "How the fuck did you hear about that?" He turned to his father. "What are we going to do about it?"

An odd look crossed the Alpha's face, and North wasn't sure it meant.

Gideon let out a sigh. "We heard about it because they told us."

"What the fuck?" North exploded.

The Talon Alpha held up a hand. "Corbin doesn't know where we side on things now that I'm Alpha. He will after today. I'm here to stand by the Redwoods' side. And when the time comes for another battle, my wolves, in full, will be by your side."

This didn't make any sense. If there was something coming today, why had only Gideon and Mitchell shown up?

"North, son, Corbin isn't coming here for a full-on battle. He has a...specific purpose in mind." Edward's gaze landed on Lexi, and she let out a choked sob.

"No. He can't come here for me. He can't." Lexi's grip tightened on his hand, but he didn't move to hold her, not when the light in her eyes was of anger, not full-on pain. He didn't want to make her feel weak, but the wolf in him wanted to destroy anyone who came near her.

"Mom?" Parker asked as squeezed in between them and threw his arms around her and North. "What's going on, Dad?"

North froze only for a moment, that connection to the little boy he called his own filling his throat. "I'm not sure yet, Park," he said, his voice sounding rusty. He risked a glance at Lexi, who looked as if she wanted to cry but was holding herself back. He didn't blame her, as he had a feeling why Corbin was coming there.

"He's going to demand a mate claim, isn't he?" North asked, his voice low.

"I'm sorry, son," Edward said, and North threw back his head and howled.

Lexi's fingers tightened around his, her nails digging into the skin.

No, fuck no.

The mate claim allowed a mate to demand that their mate be returned to their side and back into their Pack. The mate claim was invoked when bonded mates were kidnapped and held for ransom. Since that was not the case here, nor had anything similar happened in hundreds of years, the mate claim was no longer used. That did not mean, however, that the law had been repealed or revoked.

North ground his teeth, holding his wolf at bay. Corbin was claiming Lexi in full. North was having none of that.

"She isn't fully mated to him," he whispered, afraid if he spoke any louder he'd scream on a growl. "He can't claim her."

"I won't go," Lexi said beside him. "He can't have me." He looked down at her raised chin but saw the fear in her eyes.

Bonds and mates weren't settled through wars and Alphas but through the magic of the moon goddess. Some things were out of their control...but not this.

"He'll have to go through me," North said.

"He'll have to go through all of us," Cailin put in.

His brothers rumbled in agreement, but Edward put up his hand, silencing them. "North, you know that because of Parker's existence Corbin can lay claim."

"It's not my fault!" Parker screamed, tears running down his face. "I'll run away if I have to."

North growled at his father then moved so he was at eye level with his son. "No, you won't run away. And, no, this isn't your fault. Corbin is a bad man, but he is not your father."

"But he's the one who made me."

North shook his head. "No, Lexi made you. Then Logan helped raise you. And now I, and the rest of my family, will help too. You aren't Corbin's. You're mine. Do you understand that?"

Parker nodded and wiped his face. North turned to his father, but before he could open his mouth, the Alpha knelt before Parker as well.

"I'm sorry, Parker. My words came out wrong. You and I both know that words can be just as vicious a weapon as claws. You're a Jamenson now."

Parker gave a little nod, and the Alpha stood.

"We'll stand by your side, North, but things are tricky."

North looked at his family, his eyes resting on Mel and Kade. "Wait. Shit. Why didn't I think of this before? Since Lexi didn't complete the mating, and we're in the mating dance, there's still time for a circle, right?"

Lexi moved in front of him. "A mating circle? You want to fight hand-to-hand in human form with Corbin for the right to mate with me?"

Kade had fought two mating circles in his life and had won the chance to mate with Melanie through his last one. Kade hadn't completed the bond with either woman before someone had called a mating circle. That was different than a mate claim. The mating circle was where two potential mates fought over who got to keep their mate. Again, it was an archaic rule; however, he'd known women who'd fought as well for the right over potential mates. Even then, no one had to choose. Kade's first potential had wanted the other man so Kade had dropped out, not wanting to fight. For Melanie though, he'd fought and won. The other man hadn't even known Melanie beyond a few conversations. After a time, Melanie had chosen Kade. If she'd been born a wolf, she would have made the choice before the circle had even begun, but because she'd been human, she'd been too scared of everything that had changed to fully understand what was going on.

What was happening with Corbin though, was different. And since dark magic was involved, it might have even been unheard of. In a normal mate claim and fight, the ones who kidnapped the other mate didn't do it because they were potential mates. No, once the bond was set and in place, they couldn't feel any other potentials. They only kidnapped for war or ransom. So when the mate claim happened, it was the mate going into another den and fighting to save their already bonded mate.

A mating circle where the two males—or females—would fight to see who would win the right to mate was something different.

Since Corbin had changed the rules and brought forth dark magic, North was now forced to blend the two. They would have a mating circle to fight the mate claim. All because this fucking prick had used Lexi and stolen her choice.

North would have none of that. He would kill the fucker once and for all.

No matter the cost.

He cupped Lexi's cheeks as Parker moved to the side, giving him room. "I won't let him hurt you."

"What if he hurts *you*?"

"If he doesn't have the demon in the circle with him, then I can beat him. We both know this. I'm the stronger wolf, and I have something worth fighting for. Caym isn't allowed near the circle, and the wards won't let him through. Mating is far stronger magic than anything else we have. This can work, Lexi."

She closed her eyes, and he kissed her cheeks, her eyelids, her mouth. "Don't die on me, North Jamenson."

"I'm going to kill him."

She glared at him. "You better."

Someone cleared their throat, and North turned to Gideon, who stood watching them with interest.

"A mating circle might be the best way to take care of Corbin since the demon can't help. That will be one obstacle."

"But not the last," Edward added.

"Then we'll take one step at a time and keep looking for ways to kill the demon," Logan said.

Edward looked at his family and nodded. "The Talons said that the Centrals will be here within the next two hours. I already have my enforcers working on evacuating the den to the northern part of the enclosure near the elders. I want as many of you to go with them as possible."

"Dad," Kade said, but Edward held up a hand.

"No. As Alpha, I need to be here, as do the Andersons and North."

"I'm not going if they stay," Cailin put in, and North held back a curse. No matter that she and Logan hadn't even started the full mating dance, it was clear that she would be an issue.

"Fine," Edward said. "You will stay with Parker and run with him if needed. He will have to be here because if he isn't, I'm sure Corbin will do something we'll all regret."

North nodded and gripped Lexi's hand.

"I need only one member by my side, as Gideon has Mitchell. My enforcers will be back to watch the circle perimeter, but I need as much of the family as possible with the others. There will have to be leaders there in case something happens here that cannot be undone."

"I agree," Kade said as he stepped up. "I'll stay here."

Edward shook his head. "No, you're the Heir. I need you with your family just in case."

"Then I'll stay," Jasper said, stepping up. He kissed Willow hard and murmured in her ear something North couldn't quite catch.

Their father nodded, and the other Jamensons, after hard hugs goodbye, went off to the rest of the Pack to ensure their safety.

Edward's phone chirped, and he looked down at the screen.

The hairs on the back of North's head rose, and he held Parker and Lexi closer.

"They're here," the Alpha stated. "My enforcers will guide them to the circle. I would rather have them off our land, but with the claim, we need a circle, and I don't want to go to the Centrals' for obvious reasons. North, get ready."

Tension rose around the circle, but North had eyes only for Lexi. "I'll be fine."

"And I'll make sure your back is safe," she stated.

He looked down at Parker, who stood by their side. "I'll be fine," he repeated.

"Just don't die, okay? I don't think we could take that."

Lexi gave a watery laugh and held him to her side. North brought them both close, needing their scents around him. He knew that once Corbin got too close, the other wolf would know that Lexi and Parker were North's and no others, just by their scents.

Fuck what the Central trash thought.

Lexi pulled away first, and North was grateful for it. His wolf was rising closer to the surface, something he needed, but he was trying to wrangle his control so he could explode when the time came.

She kissed her son's cheek then gave him a hug. "Go stand by Logan and Cailin. I need to be with North. Okay?"

"Be safe," Parker whispered before hugging North one last time and going to the other pair's side.

North could practically feel the oily darkness emanating from the horde—really there wasn't another name for the group of enemies coming at them—as they made their way to the circle.

Though he wanted to pull Lexi behind him and shield her from the worst of it, he stayed where he was, leaving his mate by his side with her chin raised. They would show no fear.

He gripped her hand though, needing her just as much as she needed him.

They would show solidarity.

They would win.

They had to.

Corbin and Caym came through the opening in the stone seating, smirks on their faces, and practically strolling as though on a weekend getaway.

They had six other wolves behind them, yet North could scent the stench of rot and decay.

Yes, those Centrals who had chosen to align themselves with dark magic were now dying from within. This, *this*, was the reason the Redwoods were choosing to go the other way.

"I see we're expected," Caym said smoothly, his tone just as dark as it had been before. His gaze darted to Gideon and Mitchell before settling on Edward.

"You're on our land as a courtesy to the rites and customs your Pack has abandoned," Edward said, his voice low.

Corbin raised his chin. "We're here to take my property back where it belongs."

A growl ripped from North's mouth, but he held himself back. Once he was through the circle wards, he'd have his chance. If he acted before, he could risk everything.

"Ah, North, good to see you're on the mend," Caym sneered. "And, Alpha Edward, I see you're healing as well after our Patrick and you had a slight...shall we say mishap?"

Our?

Caym's eyes glittered. "I see you didn't know that Patrick was one of ours. Well, you see, all that nonsense about the greater good really didn't sit well with the bastard wolf. Oh, he might have told you he was fighting for his Pack, but in reality, he was fighting for us. It's a pity he died so quickly...but the weak usually do."

Jasper growled at his side, but North had eyes only for Corbin.

He would kill this wolf.

Soon.

"Now, if you'll hand over Corbin's mate and brat, we'll be on our way and call it a day. No need to shed blood over silly things like this."

North gripped Lexi's hand harder. He wasn't sure if he was holding her back, or she him. Either way, they needed to wait for the right moment. His wolf paced, eager for blood, for redemption.

"No one will be handed over," Edward growled.

Corbin snorted and waved his arm. "That brat is mine, and the bitch is mine too. You can't take away a mate, You've scolded me over that before." He grinned at Jasper, who growled back.

"Are you sure she's your mate?" Gideon asked, his head tilted.

Corbin narrowed his eyes. "You can't fight this."

"No," North stepped in. "But I can."

"You're nothing, you fucking Jamenson," Corbin yelled.

"I call a mating circle," North called over Corbin's voice. "You aren't fully mated, and you mated using force. I'm her potential mate, and I call a mating circle." Corbin's eyes widened, and he snarled. "You can't stop that now, Corbin. Well, you can if you step back and take away your claim."

He'd have to find another way to kill the bastard and break the bond, but North would do that if that's what the other wolf wanted.

Anything to get this bastard off their land and away from Lexi and Parker.

"You can't do that," Corbin objected.

Caym tilted his head, a calculating gleam in his eyes. North didn't know what the demon was up to, but it couldn't be good...for anyone involved.

"Ah, but, my wolf, I do believe this battle must be fought within the circle."

"You're serious? You want me to fight this fucker? I'm the Alpha. I don't *need* to fight."

North risked a glance at Edward and Gideon, who both raised brows at that. Alphas fought alongside their wolves when they could and risked their lives. It's what made them Alphas.

"You will win, my wolf. You know this," Caym crooned, and North fought the urge to shudder at the sickly sweet tone.

There was something wrong with that demon in so many ways it wasn't even funny.

"Fine. Come on, North. Let's get this over with. Once I kill you, I'll take the bitch and brat back to my den."

North growled, crushed his mouth to Lexi's in a heated mark of possession, and then stalked into the circle. He could feel the wards snap around them, locking them in.

There would only be one winner.

No, there didn't necessarily have to be death to win. A yield would suffice.

Today, though, North would kill Corbin.

There would be no other way.

"We fight as humans. Claws okay?" Corbin sneered.

"Done."

North lunged, raking his claws down Corbin's side. The other wolf screamed then pivoted, rolling to the ground before landing on his feet again. Corbin threw his body forward, attacking North, but North was quicker. He knelt and dug his claws into Corbin's knees, and the other wolf pulled away. The action left long gouges in his skin, and blood seeped through the jeans.

He fell to the ground, and North didn't give him any time to take another step. He fisted his hand and punched the bastard in the face. He felt bones shatter and the cartilage of a broken nose under his fist, and he growled.

"Fuck!" Corbin yelled, yet North still didn't relent.

He punched over and over again, the man screaming under him as he tried to fight back. North gripped Corbin by the throat and squeezed like he had before.

"Not...yet..." Corbin gurgled, and North frowned.

Again, like before, something was wrong.

North risked a glance at the demon, who smiled then held out his hands. The resulting shock surprised him.

Mating wards were the strongest of the strong. No one, not even a witch, light or dark, the Alpha, or any other could break through. The moon goddess herself set the wards, not the wolves themselves. He hadn't known demon magic could go through strongest of wards.

Yet he should have.

His head lulled back, and the darkness came.

He'd failed.

CHAPTER NINETEEN

"No!" Lexi screamed and ran to where the demon stood, grinning—though she could tell breaking the wards had cost him. He was weaker. Good.

Pain, unending pain, cascaded through her like sharp blades slicing over and over, but she ran. Her feet pounded into the dirt, her muscles straining as she pushed herself to the limit. She needed to get to him before he noticed her, before she was too late.

She knew Cailin would have her son so she could push that to another part of her mind.

Right now she wanted blood.

Demon's blood.

Her claws pushed from her fingertips, and she sprang, raking them down the side of the demon's face. The feel of his porcelain skin breaking under claws made her wolf howl. She growled, her fangs slicing through her gums, ready to bite, to fight...to do *anything* she could to stop this demon.

Caym wrenched away, blood pouring down his face. He staggered to a stop and put his hand on his cheek. He turned to her, clear surprise in his eyes. "You dare mark me?"

An odd sensation flowed through her limbs. Magic poured into her, the earthy and unearthly taste that she knew was the moon goddess even though she'd never felt it before. Her body grew stronger, her focus sharper. Time almost seemed to stand still and she narrowed her eyes on the demon that would rule them all.

"I don't have much for you, my child. I'm sorry. Use it well."

The moon goddess' voice in her head didn't surprise her. It should have and later she would think about what this meant, but right then, she knew the goddess who took care of the wolves was using her powers to help Lexi—even if it wasn't much.

That the moon goddess would break her silence to the non-elder wolves humbled her.

Using her new found strength, Lexi growled and stepped forward. Caym moved slower, no, Lexi just moved faster. She knew this. The moon goddess had helped her in such a way Caym would at least be hurt. Lexi shouted, then pushed the demon into the wards. The crackle from contact deafened her for only a moment, the bright light of the wards hitting flesh shocking her senses. Yet with the moon goddess running through her veins, she held him there. It might not be enough to kill him, *she* might not be enough to kill him, but she could hurt him.

Caym screamed—the first scream she'd heard from him and she reveled in it. Blood seeped from his nose and mouth as his body shook and scorched within the wards..

"You can break through the wards with a spell, but the wards will break you, you bastard!" she screamed, her heart breaking for what she would have to see once she looked into the circle. The warm sensation of a hand cupping her cheek made her blink and then the moon goddess faded away, as if she was too weak to do any more than she already had. The goddess had broken through to the human realm to save Lexi and her family. It was enough.

It was more than enough.

She would be forever grateful but first she needed to take care of what was hers.

And by doing that, she needed to take care of the demon.

Caym growled then pulled himself up, his face pale and gray. "Take the wolf," he spat. "Corbin's nothing now anyway. He's served his purpose. Or at least he would have. He failed. Like all the others. Bastard."

With that, the demon disappeared. She risked a glance to where he'd been then ran to her mate. She looked up and held back a sigh of relief as Cailin carried Parker away, Logan protecting the both of them. They were leaving the scene without another chasing them thankfully. Parker didn't need to see this. Gods, *she* didn't want to see what was in front of her but she didn't have a choice.

Her baby was safe. Now it was time to protect her mate. Out of the corner of her eye, she saw the other Centrals fighting against the Redwoods and Talons, but she had true focus for only the one who remained in the center of the circle.

"North," she gulped.

He opened his eyes and glanced toward her, and she held back a scream.

His eyes.

Oh goddess, his eyes.

They had once been vivid green with gold rims. Now they were all white with no pupil or iris in sight. Blood dripped like tears as he blinked.

The demon had blinded her mate.

Oh goddess.

Though he hadn't killed him.

"I'm fine, Lexi," North lied, though he wasn't facing her fully when he said it.

They would deal with that in a moment.

"You little fucker!" she screamed and kicked and punched Corbin. The other wolf was cut, bleeding, but not dead.

"You're a fucking bitch, you know that," Corbin spat. "I should have just killed you long ago, but my wolf was too sentimental. I won't be making that mistake again."

"You won't be doing *anything* again," she countered then punched Corbin in the face. His head rocked back, and he struck out, his claws sliding along her arm. She wasn't as good a fighter as North; she *knew* this, but damn it, she had to do better than this.

She kicked and punched, and he countered most moves.

"Lexi, where is he? I can only hear where you are in general." North looked directly at them, but she knew he wasn't seeing anything.

Couldn't see anything.

"We're in front of you, wolf," Corbin called. "Come closer so I can finish what my demon started."

"Your demon?" Lexi asked. "Your demon left you."

Corbin's eyes widened, and he looked over to where Caym had been, and then before she could blink, he had his claws in her belly. She looked down, dazed, at the blood pooling around her then fell to her knees.

She sucked in a breath, an oddly calm feeling washing over her. She knew if she didn't get medical attention soon, she would die, yet all she could do was stare at the wolf who was killing her.

This wolf was nothing.

He wasn't strong.

He was weak.

He used others to gain what he wanted. He killed, raped, stole, and lied to become who he was. The blood in his veins might have been Central royal, but it was nothing. He was just a small little man who listened to a demon who had far different goals than he—even if no one knew what those were.

Yes, his claws were in her belly, yanking and tearing her flesh and organs, but he was *nothing*.

She might die here, but Corbin would never breathe again.

Her family and Pack wouldn't allow it.

Corbin had nothing.

This man, the man who in another lifetime would have been her mate if he hadn't been so corrupt, so evil, was killing her yet she didn't care.

She only cared she wouldn't again see the man she loved.

The man that she deserved.

Lexi was far better than the man who was ending her life and she knew it.

From the glint in Corbin's eyes, he knew it to.

"I pity you," she rasped. The coppery scent of her blood filled her nostrils and she felt the warm trickle of it drip down her chin from her mouth.

"Bitch," he sneered. "I should have killed you then. That bastard you birthed will die by my hand. I won. Can't you understand that? I'm the fucking Alpha and you are *nothing* compared to me. You're dying by my hand. Your fucking precious mate is dying. No wait, he never bonded to you. You're going to die knowing that *I'm* the one bonded to you and you'll never have the eternity you want with the other. How is that for fucking justice?"

"Get your fucking hands off my mate you piece of filth," North said from behind Corbin.

Lexi took a shallow breath, her body fading, but never let her gaze leave North's. He couldn't see her but she knew he *felt* her there.

"She's not your mate, is she? No she's *mine*," Corbin spat.

"No, she's mine," North countered. "She's also her own. She doesn't need you to lay claim you fucking asshole."

Corbin opened his mouth again but North growled, the low sound more dangerous than she'd even heard before. Her true mate reached for Corbin's neck and sank his already bloody claws into the man's flesh.

Corbin gasped as North ripped his head from his shoulders.

Lexi blinked at the now-dead man from her nightmares then up at the man she thought would be her future.

"Lexi? I can smell your blood, baby. Shit." He threw Corbin's head to the ground then fell to his knees the same as she had. She reached out for him, her body weak.

"North, I'm here. I'm here."

He pulled her into his arms, and she held her wounds closed, knowing if she didn't get to a Healer soon, it would be bad.

"I'm sorry," he cried, nuzzling her closer. "I'm sorry I wasn't strong enough."

Tears slid down her cheeks. "You're plenty strong, my mate. You killed Corbin."

"No, *we* did, my love."

She tried to smile but didn't have the energy. "We can bond now."

He cupped her face, but she knew he couldn't see her. "We will."

She closed her eyes, leaning on her mate, praying this wasn't the end but knowing it just might be.

They'd killed the Central Alpha, taken another step toward the end of the war, and wounded the demon.

But it hadn't been enough.

The darkness came, and she was grateful.

****

"Are you sure she doesn't want a fruit basket or anything? It's been four weeks, and I still think we should get her something." Lexi lay next to her naked mate, a smile on her face.

North rolled his eyes, though she knew he still couldn't see from them. "Honey, Hannah is the Healer. If you sent her a fruit basket, she'd only invite you over to share it."

She turned on her side and cupped his face, his beard tickling her skin. "Honey, she saved our lives. We should get her something more than a thank you and a hug."

He moved then, sliding between her legs, his body hovering over her. She knew he couldn't see her, but he could hear her, taste her, *feel* her. "In that case, I'll send her a fruit basket a day. She saved your life, my mate, my heart. I will forever be grateful for that."

She looked into his eyes and sighed. The change in them didn't scare her now as it had when she'd first glanced at them. "I'm sorry she couldn't Heal you."

He lowered his head and nipped at her lip. "She's still trying, and the elders have added this to their ever-growing list of things to find answers for. Caym didn't take my eyes. He took my sight through a curse. There's got to be a way to fix that."

She nodded then winced. All her little non-verbal cues and answers meant nothing to him at the moment. She was getting better at it, but it still hurt to forget. Parker, of all people, was taking this with the most grace. He made sure things in the house didn't have any sharp corners and ensured all pieces of furniture were always in the right place. As a wolf, North's senses were already heightened, but she knew they were even more so now. Parker was making sure that North would feel comfortable with his knew way of life.

"Noah is helping Hannah too, right?"

"Yes," North said, his tone a little sad. "Noah's been great taking over my clinic for me. I can't do what I need to do without my eyes, but since the kid already went through most of medical school, he's a great asset."

"And you're helping him with what he doesn't know. It isn't like you have nothing to do." She was making sure of that.

"You don't have to try and make me feel better, baby. I'm okay with what happened. We're both alive, and Corbin is dead. I don't need anything else right now." He lowered his head and nuzzled her neck. She shuddered beneath him, angling her head so he would have more access. Her wolf ached for her, ached for what they were lacking.

Four weeks had passed, and they *still* hadn't bonded.

She'd been healing all this time, unable to do more than breathe and sleep because the wounds had been that bad. Even though she'd been down for only a couple hours after being bit by two Alphas, that had been different. The near-death was almost always healed quickly because of the change that was occurring within the newly transformed wolf.

Hannah had rushed to her side almost as soon as she'd blacked out. The Healer had used all she could but hadn't been able to Heal her fully. Lexi was fine with that since she'd been alive to feel the pain at least.

She and North agreed that because the moon goddess had put her energy within Lexi's body, it had taken a toll. Yes, they'd hurt the demon, but Lexi knew it also hurt her in the process. She still had no idea why the moon goddess had chosen her at that time and place to help, maybe the goddess hadn't been able to do so until right then. That meant though, that they had no idea if the goddess would be able to help again in the future.

The demon wasn't dead.

Far from it.

Nothing could be done for North though, and it hurt her to think about.

Once the Redwoods and Talons had killed the other Central wolves, they'd cleaned up the bodies, tended their wounded, and tried not to celebrate the death of the wolf that had taken so much from them.

It didn't seem fair to celebrate when so many had died before and when the demon was still alive, ready to fight again.

Yes, the wards and Lexi had hurt Caym, but she knew that hadn't been enough.

Their fight wasn't over, no, far from it.

They'd done all they could with the power they had. Now it was time to find another way...a way Lexi wasn't sure of.

The Talons had left saying they'd be back to help in the war. She had a feeling a bond had been struck, and there would be a future with them...if the Redwoods had a future to begin with. That, though, was another story.

Now she was healed, and her wolf wanted their mate.

She lifted her hips, cradling his cock, and North froze above her.

"Lexi," he rasped out. "I don't want to hurt you."

She tugged on his hair to bring him closer. Her mouth trailed along his temple so he would be able to feel her lips move as she spoke. "You'll only hurt me if we don't complete the bond. Come on, my mate, it's time."

He growled then rose slightly above her. "If you're sure."

She growled back then reached down toward his cock, moving him so he brushed against her entrance. "I'm already wet for you. Make love to me. Mark me. Mate with me. Please, my North."

He filled her slowly, oh, so slowly, and she sighed. She's missed the way he felt inside her, so full, so right. He put both forearms to her sides so that they could tangle their fingers together then pulled out of her. She moaned at the loss of contact, and then he pushed back in, just as slowly.

His gaze met hers. Even if he couldn't see a thing, she could still see the beauty of him and his love for her. He made love to her, soft, sweet, and oh so gentle.

This wasn't about scorching heat and passion—no, that would come later. This was about love, mating, and everything they'd been denied for so long.

Her hips met his with each thrust on a slow roll, and he grinned down at her. They both panted as they rose up, their climaxes almost there. She turned her head to the side, inviting, and then whispered his name.

Taking his cue, he bit down on her shoulder, his fangs sliding in smoothly. It was an exotic pain, sharp, yet erotic as he marked her. He pulled away, blood dripping from his mouth then turned his head so she could do the same to him. He tasted of sweet wine and brandy, a delicious combination that set her off, her body coming around his cock.

His seed filled her, and she felt the snap of the bond settling into place.

She looked at him, at the glow that surrounded them, and felt him through their bond.

"I don't need to see you to know you are beautiful, my Lexi," North rasped out, awe lacing his tone. "I can *feel* you in my heart."

She sniffed, tears running down her cheeks, and lifted her head so she could steal his lips in a kiss.

"This is it, North Jamenson. This is our destiny. Our forever."

He smiled down at her. "You're my forever. You're my everything."

As he was to her.

For eternity.

EPILOGUE

Caym ran a hand down his face, the rigid scars from that wolf-bitch's claws pressing against his palm. She'd surprised him, that wolf. Oh, he'd liked the fire in her eyes when she'd attacked him and then thrown him into the wards.

If he'd cared just a little bit more, he'd have liked to see how long it took to extinguish the fire before he eventually killed her.

Now, though, that didn't fit into his plans. Maybe if he had time when he killed the Redwoods, one by one, he'd play with her a bit.

She seemed like she'd enjoy it as he sliced ribbons into her flesh.

The sounds of Takeo drums filled the air, and he looked at the Pack circle, bored. They were celebrating the rise of a new Alpha as their old one had died so...tragically.

Caym had been smart to blood bond with Corbin—not that he knew how to be anything else but smart. When he'd first come to the Centrals and had found Hector lacking, Caym had decided to make Corbin is prey. They'd blood bonded as a rite of passage and tradition. For Corbin, it had been so he could have demon powers. Or at least that's what Caym had told him. That stupid fool. Corbin had received nothing from the deal but a good orgasm while Caym now had control of the entire Central Pack as Alpha.

Oh no, he'd planned for the eventual fall of both Hector and Corbin and had known that one day he would stand as Alpha for a group of wolves he was slowly killing.

It didn't matter.

They would die, as would the other wolves.

Then he would rule what was left.

The sound of the drums beat faster, and wolves fought against each other in dominance battles, blood spilling over the soil, enriching the battle. He inhaled the coppery scent, letting it linger over him.

He'd planned since the day he'd come all those years ago, and now everything was coming to fruition. Yes, the Redwoods had gotten in some punches, but now they were licking their wounds.

He'd taken limbs, sight, pride, and innocence, and soon he'd take their lives.

The Centrals were prepared for battle, and the Redwoods were scrambling for a resolution that would never come. This is what he savored, what he desired above all else. They stood by their decisions to stay light and pure, and it would kill them. He'd plucked out those who would fall to him and go dark, but the rest stood strong on a path that would eventually lead to the death of what they held most dear.

He would see their blood running in rivers through their precious land, and he'd rejoice. He was a demon, not something to be trifled with. Corbin's loss meant nothing to him but the end of a dalliance that had done nothing but bore him. The Central wolves were so far gone in their downfall they didn't care that a blood-bonded demon and not a wolf now stood in the position of their Alpha. They didn't care that the goddess hadn't seen fit to reveal the Beta and the Heir. They didn't have the other positions and that meant the goddess was giving up on the Centrals. At least that's what Caym thought anyway. The lack of real connection to the goddess was good though, which meant Caym didn't have another in competition for the loyalty of the Pack.

It didn't matter, as the Centrals would soon die and Caym would remain strong.

He was Alpha.

He was a god.

He was the savior.

He was eternity.

He would not fail.

Coming Next in the Redwood Pack world:

Jasper and Willow find their peace in a novella that visits them one last time: A Beta's Haven, coming Feb 14th, 2014.

Then the Redwood Pack Princess and the wolf that just might save them all get their story in the final installment of the Redwood Pack: Fighting Fate, coming June 2014

A Note from Carrie Ann

Thank you so much for reading **HIDDEN DESTINY**! It seems like forever ago that I started the Redwood Pack book and now we're at book 6 in the series. North and Lexi were a blast to write even when it pained me to put them through what I did. I do hope if you liked this story, that you would please leave a review. Not only does a review spread the word to other readers, they let us authors know if you'd like to see more stories like this from us. I love hearing from readers and talking to them when I can. If you want to make sure you know what's coming next from me, you can sign up for my newsletter at www.CarrieAnnRyan.com; follow me on twitter at @CarrieAnnRyan, or like my Facebook page. I also have a Facebook Fan Club where we have trivia, chats, and other goodies. You guys are the reason I get to do what I do and I thank you.

Make sure you're signed up for my MAILING LIST so you can know when the next releases are available as well as find giveaways and FREE READS.

What's next in my Redwood Pack world? Next month (Feb 2014), I'm releasing my next after the HEA novella called *A Beta's Haven*. In it we get to see a glimpse into Jasper and Willow's life since we saw them fall in love in *A Taste for a Mate*. Not everything is sunshine and roses once an author says The End in a book and I'm so excited for you guys to see a little more about Jasper and Willow. The next—and last— full length book in the Redwood Pack series is *Fighting Fate*. While it does come out in June, I am just now starting to write it. I can already tell you that Cailin and Logan's story is the hardest I've had to write. It doesn't help that I don't want to say goodbye to these characters.

You don't have to worry though because this year I also have 2 more Redwood Pack novellas, and then in 2015, we will see the start of a brand new series, The Talon Pack. We're going 30 years into the future and not letting go of the Redwoods. You'll see them again, only this time, you get to meet a whole new batch of Alpha wolves.

Redwood Pack Series:
Book 1: An Alpha's Path
Book 2: A Taste for a Mate
Book 3: Trinity Bound
Book 3.5: A Night Away
Book 4: Enforcer's Redemption
Book 4.5: Blurred Expectations
Book 4.7: Forgiveness
Book 5: Shattered Emotions
Book 6: Hidden Destiny
Book 6.5: A Beta's Haven
Book 7: Fighting Fate
Book 7.5 Loving the Omega
Book 7.7: The Hunted Heart
Book 8: Wicked Wolf

Want to keep up to date with the next Carrie Ann Ryan Release? Receive Text Alerts easily!
Text CARRIE to 24587

About Carrie Ann and her Books

New York Times and USA Today Bestselling Author Carrie Ann Ryan never thought she'd be a writer. Not really. No, she loved math and science and even went on to graduate school in chemistry. Yes, she read as a kid and devoured teen fiction and Harry Potter, but it wasn't until someone handed her a romance book in her late teens that she realized that there was something out there just for her. When another author suggested she use the voices in her head for good and not evil, The Redwood Pack and all her other stories were born.

Carrie Ann is a bestselling author of over twenty novels and novellas and has so much more on her mind (and on her spreadsheets *grins*) that she isn't planning on giving up her dream anytime soon.

www.CarrieAnnRyan.com

Redwood Pack Series:
Book 1: An Alpha's Path
Book 2: A Taste for a Mate
Book 3: Trinity Bound
Book 3.5: A Night Away
Book 4: Enforcer's Redemption
Book 4.5: Blurred Expectations
Book 4.7: Forgiveness
Book 5: Shattered Emotions
Book 6: Hidden Destiny
Book 6.5: A Beta's Haven
Book 7: Fighting Fate
Book 7.5 Loving the Omega
Book 7.7: The Hunted Heart

Book 8: Wicked Wolf

The Talon Pack (Following the Redwood Pack Series):
Book 1: Tattered Loyalties
Book 2: An Alpha's Choice
Book 3: Mated in Mist (Coming in 2016)

The Redwood Pack Volumes:
Redwood Pack Vol 1
Redwood Pack Vol 2
Redwood Pack Vol 3
Redwood Pack Vol 4
Redwood Pack Vol 5
Redwood Pack Vol 6

Montgomery Ink:
Book 0.5: Ink Inspired
Book 0.6: Ink Reunited
Book 1: Delicate Ink
Book 1.5 Forever Ink
Book 2: Tempting Boundaries
Book 3: Harder than Words
Book 4: Written in Ink

The Branded Pack Series:
(Written with Alexandra Ivy)
Books 1 & 2: Stolen and Forgiven
Books 3 & 4: Abandoned and Unseen

Dante's Circle Series:
Book 1: Dust of My Wings
Book 2: Her Warriors' Three Wishes
Book 3: An Unlucky Moon
The Dante's Circle Box Set (Contains Books 1-3)
Book 3.5: His Choice

Book 4: Tangled Innocence
Book 5: Fierce Enchantment
Book 6: An Immortal's Song (Coming in 2016)

Holiday, Montana Series:
Book 1: Charmed Spirits
Book 2: Santa's Executive
Book 3: Finding Abigail
The Holiday Montana Box Set (Contains Books 1-3)
Book 4: Her Lucky Love
Book 5: Dreams of Ivory

Tempting Signs Series:
Finally Found You

Excerpt: Fighting Fate

From the next book in New York Times Bestselling Author Carrie Ann Ryan's Redwood Pack Series

The couple looked so in love, so at peace, that Cailin Jamenson thought she might break out in hives or a cold shiver at the thought of them. Her palms itched, and a line of sweat trailed down her back. She licked her lips, trying to keep her mind off of the rabbit hole of heartache her thoughts would eventually find. It wasn't that she was upset her brother North had finally found his mate, Lexi. Just like it wasn't that she was sad that the rest of her brothers had found their mates as well.

No, it was something much worse.

She was jealous.

Like angry-green-monster, wolf-howling-rage jealous.

Jealous and refusing to do anything about it because once she did...well, once she did, everything she'd fought so hard for would have been for naught. It had taken years, but she finally felt like she was worth something more than the title—at least in her mind. Going down the path where her wolf begged to be led wouldn't accomplish anything but pain and rapid denial.

The wind picked up, knocking a strand of hair out of place and she tucked it back behind her ear. She could hear the sounds of her Pack, her wolves, sniffing, murmuring, and paying attention to the ceremony. The noise mixed with the sounds of nature, the birds chirping and the leaves rustling in the breeze. None of that centered her though. No, she only knew of one way to do that. One way she wasn't ready to face.

Her wolf might crave the dark wolf with rough edges who haunted her dreams, but that didn't mean the woman inside would succumb.

She was stronger than that.

She was Cailin Jamenson.

Redwood Pack princess.

Lone daughter of the Jamenson clan.

Younger sister to six over-protective yet loving brothers.

Aunt to countless nieces and nephews.

The Beta's assistant.

And lost.

So *fucking* lost.

She knew what the others saw when they looked at her, the raven-black hair, the light green eyes. So many others had told her she was one of the most beautiful people they'd ever seen. What a load of crap. Even if they weren't just saying that because of who she was, she wouldn't take it at face value. She'd seen true beauty in the selfless acts of her sisters and friends. They were the beautiful ones. Cailin usually responded to those who spoke only of her looks that they hadn't seen that many people. Most didn't see beyond the surface, beyond the blood in her veins.

Someone murmured something behind her, and she blinked, forcing her attention to what was going on in front of her rather than wallowing in the shames she should have buried. Shames that weren't really shames at all, not in the grand scheme of things. She'd always tried to be so strong for others, and in turn, hadn't treated those she now loved with the respect they deserved. She'd tried to fix that over time, but she wasn't sure she was worth it. Others worried so much for her and her safety, she knew they weren't taking care of themselves like they should. She needed to stop acting so self-centered, so hurt and broken when it was her own doing.

When her father, the Alpha of the Redwood Pack, put his hand on North's shoulder then did the same to Lexi's, solidifying their bond and mating in front of the Pack, Cailin sucked in a breath and pasted on a smile.

She was happy for them, she really was.

She hated herself for wanting what they had and what they were just beginning.

North cupped Lexi's face, kissing her so softly it looked as if it was barely a whisper. Their gazes never left each other, though Cailin knew North couldn't see Lexi. He'd been blinded in their last battle with the Centrals, but that didn't stop him from living his life to the fullest. Cailin swallowed hard, burying her own pain. Her brother looked so in love, so *whole* after being alone for decades, hiding his own darkness until Lexi came along and found what Cailin and her family had missed.

North had needed his mate, his Lexi.

Had needed her more than anything in the world.

He needed their son, Parker, and the bonds that came with mating and fatherhood. Those grounded him and kept his wolf calm.

Cailin would never allow the love and connections to settle her.

She vowed she wouldn't. At least, that's what she'd told herself over and over, what she said to herself the moment she'd laid eyes on Lexi's brother.

Her gaze met that of the other man at Lexi's side, and she raised her chin. She wouldn't have him.

Couldn't have him. She just needed to remind her wolf that.

Remind everyone who thought so much of her of that fact.

He gave her a small nod, and her wolf brushed against her skin, a soft caress. A plea for submission, dominance, mating, and everything in between.

Logan. Lexi's brother.

Cailin's potential mate.

No, she wouldn't be mating with him. She'd lived her life with seven dominant men—not even counting the others in the Pack who'd watched her grow up—telling her what to do, how to act, how to behave. She'd vowed to herself long ago she wouldn't be following the same routine for eternity tied to a man she felt was even stronger than her brothers.

Even darker than her brothers.

The wolf wouldn't be able to stop himself from dominating her, and that wasn't what she craved, what she *needed* in order to survive whole.

Logan narrowed his eyes, but Cailin didn't miss the promise in his gaze. Promise of something far greater than the anticipation and trepidation she'd been burying deep inside since she'd met him. Damn it, she'd run out of time. She'd been dancing on the fine line of temptation and playing hide and seek for far too long when it came to the wolf standing across the aisle. The wolf wouldn't wait for Cailin's cue anymore. No, he'd take what he thought was his. What he thought the Pack and she herself wanted.

Cailin's wolf, though she panted as well, sneered. Well, he'd just have to wait an eternity for that, wouldn't he?

Cailin wasn't some weak-kneed little girl. She'd fight for her freedom—just like she'd always done.

"Stop growling, little sister. You're scaring the children."

Cailin winced at her brother Maddox's words and tried to smile again. It came out more like a grimace, but at least it was something. "Sorry," she whispered. She'd let her emotions get the best of her and let others know what was going on inside her mind when she hadn't wanted them to know too much. Not the best way to observe a mating ceremony while trying to remain stoic and happy at the same time.

Maddox put his arm around her shoulders and pulled her close. Her wolf calmed down from the storm Cailin wasn't even aware was brewing. She didn't sigh or relax, even if her wolf was ready to bare her belly for her brother who seemed to know just how to make her feel loved and cared for. This was why wolves were such tactile creatures. The barest touch and her wolf felt cemented, loved.

Her brother bushed his lips over her temple. "The ceremony is over, Cai. You can go stand in a corner and hide from the big bad wolf if you'd like. No one would fault you." Though his words were teasing, the meaning behind them held the hints of truth she wasn't ready to face. And having her brother call her meekness out filled her with a rage she knew wasn't fully on his shoulders.

He would bear the brunt of it anyway.

Cailin turned and faced him, her claws scraping along the insides of her fingertips at the taunt. She lifted her lip and bared a fang. Maddox only laughed, the scar on his face tightening as he did so. Her heart tugged at the sight. She despised that damn scar and all it represented. The now-dead Central Alpha, Corbin, had carved him up years go. The bastard had tortured her brother because of a prophecy that hadn't even been about Maddox to begin with.

No, it had been about North.

The same North that had killed Corbin anyway.

The prophecy had been correct, and Corbin had scarred the wrong brother.

The fact that she couldn't kill Corbin again enraged her and she had to push that familiar feeling back. No good would come from what-ifs.

Her brother bopped her on the nose, that smile on his face infectious. God, she loved this Maddox—the Maddox that smiled, laughed, and looked *happy*. His mate, Ellie, had done that, and Cailin would always be grateful.

Taking a deep breath, she forced her hands to relax. Instead of beating her annoyingly astute brother up, she patted the scarred side of his cheek, something she hadn't done in the past because of her fear of hurting him. She'd been an idiot, and the lack of touch had only pulled him deeper into himself, away from his family and those that loved him. Now she tried to make sure he knew that she loved him, scars and all.

"Thank you, big brother, but I will not cower." She refused to. There would be no hiding from the wolf that haunted her dreams...and now her days. She might not want to deal with it, but she wouldn't run away with her tail tucked between her legs. That wasn't who she'd been her entire life, and she wouldn't resort to becoming that person now.

Maddox raised a dark blond brow. "If you won't let me beat Logan up, or at least maim him a bit, then you'll have to do something about him."

Cailin rolled her eyes. "Stay out of it, Mad."

Maddox traced a line down her cheek, and she sighed. Her wolf brushed along the inside of her skin, settling under her brother's touch. "I don't know that I can, Cai. Your wolf isn't happy, I can feel it. The woman isn't that happy either."

Her wolf rumbled, agreeing with the man. No, she wasn't happy. She wouldn't be without a certain dark wolf.

Damn them both.

Her brother was the Omega of the Redwood Pack, meaning he could feel the emotions of every Pack member other than his twin, North. He had once been unable to feel his mate, Ellie, before they'd bonded, but now their mating bond was stronger than most. His role was to ensure the emotional needs of the Pack were met and they were healthy from the inside out. It also meant he took in each pain, hurt, and overabundance of happiness right into his soul. Cailin just thanked the moon goddess he had Ellie now to share that burden.

His role as Omega, though, didn't mean Cailin liked having her brother intrude on her feelings. It wasn't that he was reaching inside her through that fragile bond that connected him with the Pack on the emotional level. No, when she was this angst-filled, she was apparently blasting her emotions clear and far. She was usually much better at hiding everything having to do with that and erecting a shield from his nosy wolf.

"I'm fine. Butt out, Maddox."

Maddox growled a bit but put his hands up. "Deal with it, Cailin. You're on edge, and this isn't the time to have your wolf weak because she's not getting what she needs. We're Pack animals, Cai. We need touch. We need that connection."

She ignored the last part of his statement, concentrating on the part that dug deep. Cailin lifted her chin. "I'm not weak. Despite the fact that I don't have a penis, which you Jamenson boys think one must have in order to be strong, I can and *will* fight for my Pack."

Maddox lifted a lip, his eyes glowing a soft gold. "First, don't say penis. You're my baby sister. You're innocent and pure."

Cailin snorted. Her brothers kept saying that. If they only knew...

No, she didn't want to give them all heart attacks. Or go attack her ex, Noah...or hurt Logan for playing some key parts in her dirtiest fantasies.

And it was time to get her mind off that particular track.

"Second, what the hell do you mean about women being weak? Have you seen our mates? Do you really think any of the six of us consider our mates weak? If that's what you believe, you aren't looking close enough, and it's fucking insulting. Get your head out of your ass, Cailin, and fix this. Find a way to deal with Logan. Either mate with him or let him down. Running away and hiding behind your need to find another way to live isn't helping anyone. We're at war. And even if we weren't, you deserve to be happy."

Chastened, she took a step back, her heels digging into the ground underneath her. "I'm sorry. I didn't mean that the way it came out." Oh, she did, but only when it came to the way they thought of her, but that was another matter. "I'm going to go get some air." Maddox raised a brow, and she shook her head. "I know we're outside, but I need different air. Jamenson-free air."

Maddox pulled her into a hug then kissed the top of her head. "I love you, little sister. I'm sorry for pushing, but you're so bottled up I'm scared for you. Something's coming, something darker than we've ever faced before, and I want to make sure you're as ready as you can be for it."

She had the same oppressive feeling as Maddox and the rest of her family. There wasn't any way to tell what the darkness was or what danger it might bring, but she knew it was coming.

They all did.

Cailin cupped Maddox's face and leaned forward. He was a full half foot taller than her, but in heels she could rest her forehead on his scarred cheek. "I love you, Maddox. I'm sorry. You won't have to worry about me. I promise. I won't let you down."

Maddox squeezed her. "You could never let me down."

She pulled away with a small smile at his lie, then turned toward the line of trees, needing space. Maddox might have said she could never let him down, but she knew that wasn't true. She'd been letting everyone down around her for years. Her brothers were all around seventy years older than she was and had practically helped raised her along with their parents. Kade, Jasper, Adam, Reed, North, and Maddox didn't know how *not* to be overbearing and protective.

It was just their way.

They, however, all had roles within the Pack, whether it be powers blessed from the moon goddess herself or roles they'd created for themselves so they were worth something.

Cailin had always been a step behind.

She hated it.

What worried her more than all of that, though, was the fact that her brothers didn't trust her to take care of herself. No matter how grown up she thought she was, she'd always be their baby sister, too weak, too frail to fight in the war with the Centrals.

They'd been at war for almost four years.

Four. Years.

Those years didn't even include the tension and pain they'd experienced for decades before the Central Pack summoned and teamed up with a demon named Caym. The other Pack had sacrificed their own princess, Ellie's twin sister, and brought forth hell into their world. One by one, year by year, Cailin had watched her brothers not only fall in love but fight for their lives against the cruelty that was the Centrals.

Now, though, the war was coming to an end.

At least that's how it felt to Cailin.

The Centrals had lost two Alphas in those four years, Hector and his son, Corbin. Now Caym ruled them with an iron fist. His own dose of dark magic prevented the Redwoods from being on the offense, forever on the defense and trying to scramble the protection needed to survive.

Oh, she'd fought by her family's side when they let her, when there was no other way to hide her behind closed doors. God, she hated sounding so ungrateful for her family's worry and care, but the smothering had to stop.

And mating with Logan would only intensify that feeling. She was sure of it.

She took long strides toward the tree line, nodding at other Pack members who stared at her as if they knew what her innermost thoughts were. Her innermost fear and insecurity. Knowing the way she couldn't seem to hide anything today, she wouldn't be surprised if that was actually true. No one called out to her, telling her to come to their side and join them in the celebration.

She was alone.

Just like she'd always thought she'd be.

Just like she'd forced herself to be.

"What are you doing out here all alone?"

The deep timbre went straight to her core, her body shaking at just those words alone. Words that didn't mean anything beyond the fact they were spoken by the one wolf she'd truly tried to hide from.

Cailin stopped moving, her hand pressed against a tree as she prayed for composure. It wouldn't do well to bite and snap at him or, worse, press her body up against him and rub her scent all over him. She turned to face Logan and tried not to swallow her tongue. No matter how hard she fought her attraction to him, her wolf ached for the man in front of her.

The woman wanted him as well but tried to hide it.

Damn it.

Those hazel eyes bore into her, the dominance held within them not begging for her wolf's submission—only the woman's. Within those eyes she could see the man and the wolf, two halves of a whole. Two distinct ideas and desires. One wanted her submission, the other wanted her by his side. That was the difference between him and the other wolves who might have laid claim to her.

The difference she wasn't ready to accept.

The difference she wasn't sure she understood.

Her hands ached to run through his dark hair that he'd recently shorn so it lay close to his scalp. At five-five, she wasn't the shortest of women, but next to Logan's size, she always felt small, fragile.

And that's why she would never mate with him.

She needed to be strong, not weak—not how she felt around him. How she feared he'd make her be once she gave into the yearning both she and her wolf craved.

"Following me now like a lost puppy?" she sneered.

Logan pinched her chin, forcing her gaze to his. She narrowed her eyes, but her damn inner wolf wouldn't let her move back. No, the annoying canine wanted to rub up all along the man and make sure all those women eyeing him at the ceremony kept their paws off of him.

Not that she'd been paying attention to them.

No, but she had felt their gazes digging into her back and on the tall drink of water in front of her.

If her mind had been making any sense at all, she should have been happy other women wanted to lay claim—if only for an evening. Instead, she battled within herself so much her head ached.

"You should be with your family," he said, his voice low, *tempting*. "It's a day of light rather than the darkness you've been fighting for far too long."

"You say that as if you aren't a Redwood." She held back a wince. Damn it, she did not want to get into a conversation with this man. Not when she needed to breathe, to feel like she had a choice in the matter.

Logan rubbed her chin with his thumb before pulling back. Cailin immediately wanted his touch back, the loss almost overwhelming.

Her wolf whimpered.

Freaking whimpered.

"I might have the bond with the Alpha, but we both know that finding your place within a Pack is more than a bond and a promise."

She blinked up at him, surprised at his insight. That sliver of connection to the man in front of her she'd tried to ignore thickened just enough that she had to hold back a gasp. Her wolf wanted that bond, badly.

They stared at each other for a few more moments, though it felt like longer before she shook her head, clearing thoughts of forever and a promise she'd never intend to keep.

"I should get back. They'll be wondering where I am." And wondering how to fix her because everyone knew something was off, that the broken parts within her were fragmenting even more.

"I'll walk with you," Logan said, his voice low, enticing.

Stop wanting him, Cailin. Don't give in.

"I don't need a chaperone, Logan. I'm a big girl."

His gaze raked over her body, and she fought the urge to wrap her arms around him and never let him go.

"I know who you are, Cailin. I never forget that."

She glared. "You know nothing. Don't follow me."

She stormed off, knowing the wolf prowled right on her heels. Damn him. Damn fate. Damn everything.

Someone stepped on a fallen branch in front of her. A deliberate action alerting her to his presence. Her wolf stood at attention, ready to run toward the sound. Toward the comfort.

"Cailin, come here, baby girl."

Her head shot up at her father's words, and she went to his side, wrapping her arms around his waist and burrowing into him. Her wolf immediately calmed, their Alpha soothing hurts she hadn't known she'd had—or maybe known all along but ignored for far too long. The daughter, though, needed her father, and the feeling grated. She was an adult, yet she wanted her father's hold to make it all better.

Maybe her brothers were right and Cailin wasn't ready to grow up.

The doubt ate at her, but she ignored it, inhaling her father's crisp scent of forest and home, letting it wash over her so she could breathe again.

People milled around them and she could feel their looks, but ignored them. Apparently when she'd run from Logan—or rather, walked quickly away—she'd made it back to the celebration in the field without even realizing it.

"Feel better?" her father asked, his voice so low she knew that his words were just for her and no one else.

She pulled back so she could look up at him but kept her arms around his waist. "Yes, thank you, Dad. I didn't know I needed a hug so much."

Her father cupped her face, and she leaned into him. She was a daddy's girl at heart, and everyone knew it. "You crave touch, darling girl. And not the touch an Alpha provides. Your wolf is restless."

She knew her father was treading the line on the subject of Logan, but she couldn't speak about it. Not then. Maybe not ever.

"I'll try to hang out with the pups more often."

Her father raised a brow. "As much as we all love how much you care for your nephews and nieces, we both know that won't be enough. That's not the type of touch you need."

She blushed hard at her father's words. "I'm so not talking about this with you."

"I really don't want to talk to you about this either. I'd rather your mother handle it, but I'm here and I care. If you won't do anything about Logan, then what about that wolf you were secretly seeing, Noah?"

Cailin closed her eyes, wishing there was a hole to swallow her up and take her away from this conversation. "Noah and I are just friends now. And if it was a secret, why does everyone seem to know about it?"

Her father patted her back. "We're a Pack, darling."

Meaning there were no real secrets. Not anymore. Not that there ever were. "I'll figure it out," she said after a few moments of silence.

He cupped her cheek and smiled. "I know you will, baby girl. I know I don't say this enough, but I'm so proud of the woman you've become. You're so strong, Cailin. I know between me and your brothers you sometimes feel like you can't breathe, but it's only because we love you. I love you, Cailin. Never forget that."

Tears filled her eyes, and she hugged her father hard. He knew the exact words to say to make her feel better. She didn't know what she'd do without him.

"I love you too, Dad."

A chill washed over her, and she pulled away, her hand on her father's arm, not wanting to lose his touch. The trees seemed to freeze in the wind, their leaves rustling no more. The birds had stopped chirping, their song of silence a warning of what was to come. The hairs on the back of her neck stood on end and she inhaled the scents around her, trying to discern what was wrong, what had changed.

Her wolf bucked, rubbing along her skin, ready to break free and find the danger that had arisen out of nowhere.

"What is it?" she whispered.

"Something's coming." Her father didn't sound like the warm man who had just comforted her then. No, he was the Alpha.

Everyone around them quieted, their wolves going on alert. Cailin straightened, her senses going out, trying to feel what was out of place.

Her father stiffened then looked over his shoulder at his Pack. "Grab the children and run!" He turned to her, his eyes gold, Alpha. "The Centrals are right outside the wards."

The others didn't waste time, grabbing their pups and moving at their Alpha's command. Cailin focused on the clearing in front of them, her wolf ready to howl. She wouldn't run with the others, she would stand and face what was coming. The maternal wolves and submissives would take the pups and do what they were born to do—to protect what was theirs.

Cailin would do what *she* was born to do—to *fight* for what was hers.

Then a sharp pain slammed into her, her knees going weak. The connection she had with her den snapped and bile rose in her throat. Her father gripped her elbow, keeping her steady.

"The wards," she whispered.

"I know, they're gone. The Centrals have come to us. Fight well, baby girl. Fight hard."

She met her father's gaze and nodded, pride filling her, warring with the fear. She looked out into the clearing again and swallowed hard.

Dozens of Central wolves in wolf form prowled into the clearing, ready to kill, to fight. That wasn't what scared her.

No, the demon who led them brought forth the fear to end all fears.

The demon with dark hair and chiseled features gazed in her direction and smiled. The chill shooting down her spine made her want to retch. She pulled her gaze away, instinctively searching for the one person she had to be sure was okay.

Logan stood by her mother, his fists clenched. He met her gaze and nodded.

Immediately, a small trigger relaxed within her and she lifted a lip, baring fang as she turned toward the demon. She was ready. Caym gave her one more slow smile, then nodded.

With Caym's nod, the Centrals attacked, teeth and claws bared.

The battle had begun.

The war had come to the Redwoods.

It was time.

Dust of My Wings

**From New York Times Bestselling Author
Carrie Ann Ryan's Dante's Circle Series**

*Humans aren't as alone as they choose to believe.
Every human possesses a trait of supernatural that
lays dormant within their genetic make-up.
Centuries of diluting and breeding have allowed
humans to think they are alone and untouched by
magic. But what happens when something changes?*

Neat freak lab tech, Lily Banner lives her life as
any ordinary human. She's dedicated to her work and
loves to hang out with her friends at Dante's Circle,
their local bar. When she discovers a strange blue dust
at work she meets a handsome stranger holding
secrets – and maybe her heart. But after a close call
with a thunderstorm, she may not be as ordinary as
she thinks.

Shade Griffin is a warrior angel sent to Earth to
protect the supernaturals' secrets. One problem, he
can't stop leaving dust in odd places around town.
Now he has to find every ounce of his dust and keep
the presence of the supernatural a secret. But after a
close encounter with a sexy lab tech and a lightning
quick connection, his millennia old loyalties may shift
and he could lose more than just his wings in the
chaos.

Warning: Contains a sexy angel with a choice to
make and a green-eyed lab tech who dreams of a dark-
winged stranger. Oh yeah, and a shocking spark that's
sure to leave them begging for more.

Ink Inspired

From New York Times Bestselling Author Carrie Ann Ryan's Montgomery Ink Series

Shepard Montgomery loves the feel of a needle in his hands, the ink that he lays on another, and the thrill he gets when his art is finished, appreciated, and loved. At least that's the way it used to be. Now he's struggling to figure out why he's a tattoo artist at all as he wades through the college frat boys and tourists who just want a thrill, not a permanent reminder of their trip. Once he sees the Ice Princess walk through Midnight Ink's doors though, he knows he might just have found the inspiration he needs.

Shea Little has spent her life listening to her family's desires. She went to the best schools, participated in the most proper of social events, and almost married the man her family wanted for her. When she ran from that and found a job she actually likes, she thought she'd rebelled enough. Now though, she wants one more thing—only Shepard stands in the way. She'll not only have to let him learn more about her in order to get inked, but find out what it means to be truly free.

Made in the USA
Lexington, KY
21 April 2016